He slid in while Christopher nodded off

watching a game show on television and made note of the man's thoughts of falling into such a weird dream. A low tenor voice laughed that some dead guy, some zombie-like creature, was trying to take over his life. Slowly, the man's thoughts became Nathan's.

He woke, rose from the couch, walked into the bedroom and changed into a pair of jeans, pulled on a pair of suede cowboy boots, and slung a light jacket over his shoulder. Chuckling to himself, Nathan kept the t-shirt. "How appropriate. I'm dead, and I'm very grateful right now."

Taking Christopher's wallet, Nathan peeled off a five and three ones, slipped them back in, returned the wallet to the top of the dresser, and pocketed the rest of the cash. He left the keys and cell phone on the kitchen counter where they'd been tossed. With the light and television still on, Nathan walked out into the night with few worries; plenty of people simply walked away from their lives.

It didn't take as long to make his way back to the truck, since Nathan got plenty of rides by sticking out his thumb and plastering a broad, friendly smile on his newly acquired face.

Nathan's Clan of Deadheads

by

Paul Atreides

World of Deadheads Series

Nathan's Clan of Deadheads

Cover Art by *Debbie Taylor*

The Wild Rose Press, Inc.
PO Box 708
Adams Basin, NY 14410-0708
Visit us at www.thewildrosepress.com

Publishing History
First Mainstream Paranormal Edition, 2018
Print ISBN 978-1-5092-1894-3
Digital ISBN 978-1-5092-1895-0

World of Deadheads Series
Published in the United States of America

Dedication

To my "wild child" niece, Heidi Howard,
who gave her life to save a little boy from abuse.
~*~
With thanks to the folks in the
Tuesday and Wednesday critique groups:
Roger Storkamp,
Bill Walles,
Gregory Kompes,
Tonya Todd,
Doug May,
Laurey Ray,
Kristen Halliday,
and Regina Estrada.
Your guidance has brought a new depth
and richness to my writing.

Chapter 1

He believed younger would be stronger, and last longer. But after ten short years, signs of wear began to show on the body he'd taken over, and Nathan noticed the odd expressions sent in his direction from both the living and the dead.

He had already searched for over a month, figuring it should've been easier with so many more live people in the world to choose from. Heck, the entire U.S. population stood somewhere around twelve million in 1827, the year of his birth. He scanned the crowds, and it appeared a lot more dead occupied the world now, too. There but not there, slightly transparent, ghostly folks, deadheads as they'd come to be called, mingled among the living in almost any direction one cared to look, if one could see them like he did. Though the dead never hustled about as much as the living who scurried around to wherever their hectic lives led. Yet, now, Nathan himself needed to hurry things up a tad. His daddy had told him often enough, "Get a move-on, boy! The sun ain't about to hang suspended waitin' on you to figure things out."

A pleasant looking, middle-aged man in a business suit walked by and nodded with a half-smile painted on his face. Nathan returned the greeting and then watched as the guy rounded the corner. After glancing nervously in each direction Nathan followed, quickening his pace.

Keeping an eye peeled, he sat on a bench and slipped out of the body he occupied. After so many years, and the encroaching decay, there would be no chance the kid could suddenly regain real-world cognizance. Positive he could trust the shell of a body to still be there when he got back, he ran to catch this fine candidate. The man stopped at the corner to wait for the WALK sign, and Nathan got as far as slipping his right side into the guy's left before the commotion began.

To the after-lunch crowd of living passersby the man must have looked as if he was some homeless schizophrenic who suddenly lost his mind. Some people laughed, cell phones held aloft taking pictures and videos, no doubt for the amusement of friends and family on Facebook, Instagram or YouTube. The man's right hand slapped at his left arm, and his left leg kicked, shaking the foot in a wild dance. He yelled at no one a live person could see, "What the hell do you think you're doing? Get out of me, you fool."

Nathan pulled out and backed away. "Sorry, sorry."

"What the heck you want with a body this old, anyway? If you're looking to buy booze, walk into the store and take it. Who's going to know?" This guy looked right at—not through—Nathan, as if he could actually see him.

"No, that's—Sorry." Stung by the rude reminder that some live folks could see, hear, and feel the dead, Nathan scurried back to the bench and slipped in to the kid.

He moved his ever-present toothpick to the other corner of his mouth and then stuffed his hands into pockets to hide the blackness creeping from the fingernails and spreading down along the fingers. It was a good thing he had on work boots, otherwise people might be able to see the same thing happening to his toes. There was little he could do to hide the ears, save putting on a hat of the sort he could pull down over them.

The asphalt on the roads emitted the smell of hot tar and offered up a quivering landscape. As a deadhead, warmth may have been welcome but the heat and humidity in late August created rivers of sweat Nathan wasn't sure he could afford to swipe at, not at this point anyway.

Though the borrowed body—he didn't like to think of them as 'stolen'—showed no outward signs of distress from the skirmish, Nathan's mental state was flummoxed. He knew it happened sometimes, a live person being so aware of the dead. But, how did such a phenomenon happen? What made a person so adept at sensing the dead; actually able to see and even communicate with them? It took a good thirty minutes for him to recover from the episode and feel ready to continue his search.

Nathan had heard of the big to-do about to take place in the Caribbean, the same as most all deadheads had; the one being extolled as the Wedding of the Millennium. It seemed word managed to spread through the dead world like a greased hog; as if they all carried cell phones and communicated through social media like live folks. But finding a new body was much too important to worry over such things.

He chewed on his toothpick and scanned the crowd. His eyes grew wide when he freed his left hand from the pocket of his jeans to check the time. The blackness had progressed another quarter-inch. For a fraction of a second, the idea actually crossed his mind to consider a woman. But only for a second. Imagine going through any amount of time as a girl, having to deal with menstruation and... He shivered in disgust and pushed the image from his mind.

A tall, blond guy, perhaps in his late-twenties, sauntered along the sidewalk on the opposite side of the street. Nathan stood, checked traffic in both directions (because it just would not do to get the current body run over, maybe killed, before he'd found a replacement), and darted across the street.

Approaching the man from behind, Nathan leapt from the boy and left him standing limp-limbed on the sidewalk, and breezed right through his target. An incredible buzz rattled through Nathan's brain. He shook his head to clear it and found himself face to face with a middle-aged deadhead who'd tumbled out.

"Oh, no you don't. Get back where you belong."

"Up yours, old man," Nathan retorted.

The two glared at one another for a split moment, turned, and raced toward the blond guy who walked along unaware of the fight taking place over his body.

"What are you doing?" the old guy shouted as Nathan took the lead. "Will you stop? That's my son-in-law and I need to stop him from...well, from doing what he's planning to do."

Nathan came to a sudden halt. "What's he fixing to get himself into?"

"A hot redhead who isn't my daughter! Now, would you scram?"

"Sorry," Nathan said, hoping he wouldn't come to regret the choice. He couldn't bring himself to be downright mean or callous. Family and children were important. His mama had taught him proper, more genteel country-like manners. Despondent, he watched the old guy move into his son-in-law.

A strong, heightened vibration burned through Nathan as someone walked through him. He dared a glance back to find the kid standing where he'd left him in the middle of the sidewalk, limp and unaware of anything. And then Nathan turned his attention to this new possibility.

From behind, this body seemed in fit shape; narrow waist, broad shoulders, back straight, and a confidence in the gait. When the man hesitated at the next intersection, Nathan rushed over and pushed his way in. A few pedestrians cursed as they bumped into a statue of a man who'd halted mid-stride.

Nathan wanted to grab permanent hold of the guy immediately (well, as permanent as taking a body could be). But over the course of his stolen lifetimes, he'd learned better, easier ways to accomplish the task. Looking back at the boy, he realized the kid was too far gone, too used to simply leave there on the sidewalk. A casual inspection rendered him just another brain-addled druggie. Nathan needed to find a good spot to shed the kid's body and come back for the new self.

He burrowed around in the brain of his prospect (the man was pondering his upcoming fortieth birthday) until he found the information he wanted: home and work addresses. Then he slid out.

Nathan's chosen new body awakened with a quick shake of the head as if coming out of a daydream, and headed across a parking lot toward a large office building, apparently unaware of what had happened, unless you count the quick shiver which might be attributed to a blast of air conditioning from the store he walked past.

Chapter 2

Leaving his old F-150 pick-up alongside the rural road with an "Out of Gas" note on the dashboard, Nathan hiked a few miles north. He walked into the thick brush, and stepped out of the body which kind of slumped to the ground in a heap. Leaning down to check the breathing, he tore a bit of fabric from his shirt and tied it to the base of a nearby wild blackberry bush, then rushed away. It just wouldn't do to have this kid die while he stood there, requiring Nathan to answer all manner of questions.

It took him almost two days and nights to hike back into Roanoke. Once he hit a main thoroughfare, Nathan supposed he could've hitched rides with lots of unsuspecting folks, but he found himself rather enjoying the landscape and antics of the living as they bustled about, and wondered if that's what he looked like to others. The time spent as a full-on deadhead had been nice for a short change, but he looked forward to returning to the land of the living. Well, living, sort of. He chuckled and mused aloud, "Or should that be sort of living?"

Sort of living did not suit his tastes. Not at all. He couldn't stand the thought of it. It made him jumpy inside, much like jonesing for a shot from the still as witnessed in some of the miners his family had employed. Proof of that was in the number of different bodies he'd inhabited over the years.

Sitting on the curb in the parking lot of a well-maintained apartment complex, he recognized the man he'd selected, and followed him into the building. To have this guy suddenly change direction might draw the attention and questions of the other residents, questions Nathan wouldn't be able to answer. Plus, he had learned easier ways to take over the living.

The man stopped at a bank of mailboxes in the lobby and pulled out a pile of mail, shuffled through it and dumped the entire stack into a trash can. Then he headed up the stairs. Nathan grabbed a few of the discarded envelopes, just to double-check himself. Resident. Resident. Valued Customer or Current Resident. Ah, there. His name was Christopher Allen and he did indeed live in Apt. 2E.

Nathan sauntered up and sat in a chair. He watched and studied his target for almost three hours, while the guy changed out of a business suit into sweatpants and an old, vintage Grateful Dead t-shirt (no worse for the wear), went through a one-hour routine in the complex exercise room, then returned to nuke and eat a frozen dinner. After the sun faded and Christopher Allen closed his drapes and turned on a light, Nathan made his move.

He slid in while Christopher nodded off watching a game show on television and made note of the man's thoughts of falling into such a weird dream. A low tenor voice laughed that some dead guy, some zombie-like creature, was trying to take over his life. Slowly, the man's thoughts became Nathan's.

He woke, rose from the couch, walked into the bedroom and changed into a pair of jeans, pulled on a pair of suede cowboy boots, and slung a light jacket over his shoulder. Chuckling to himself, Nathan kept the t-shirt. "How appropriate. I'm dead, and I'm very grateful right now."

Taking Christopher's wallet, Nathan peeled off a five and three ones, slipped them back in, returned the wallet to the top of the dresser, and pocketed the rest of the cash. He left the keys and cell phone on the kitchen counter where they'd been tossed. With the light and television still on, Nathan walked out into the night with few worries; plenty of people simply walked away from their lives.

It didn't take as long to make his way back to the truck, since Nathan got plenty of rides by sticking out his thumb and plastering a broad, friendly smile on his newly acquired face.

Chapter 3

In the time it took him to return to the spot, the strip of fabric he'd left as a marker must have moved in the wind or something, because Nathan had trouble finding it. After hours of searching, driving the same five-mile stretch, he at last caught a glimpse of familiar material and slammed the old truck to a shuddering stop alongside the road, opened the door and scrambled out. He ran to the brush and bramble lacing the edge of the woods which stretched on for miles. Popping sounds mixed with the tread of his steps; buttons yanking against the thick material of his jeans. His head thrown back, an audible exhale lasted almost as long as the great arc of his stream accompanying it. The chirp of crickets and swarms of early evening insects accosted his ears. His free hand swatted at mosquitoes while a hint of decomposition crept into his nose. He glanced down to note the splashing against a boot and swiveled at the hips to adjust his aim, but never took his eyes off the pair of scuffed and worn work boots with the frayed denim bunched at their tops.

Nathan thanked God the kid was nowhere in sight. Heck, he'd been so close to death Nathan almost met him as he shed the body. And then he would've had some bit of explaining to do—like how he managed to be right there, hip-high in weeds and thickets at the time of death. He certainly did not want to have to stand

and bald-faced lie to a new deadhead, if indeed he could lie. What if a borrowed body had some recollection of him? Nathan had never stuck around to find out. Now that he'd managed to locate the boy's body and the young man himself was nowhere to be seen by the living or the dead no sense of worry, concern, or immediacy entered Nathan's mind.

But Nathan needed to return; he wasn't soulless. He wanted the family to have closure and doing this ensured they would. He heard tell this kind of thing happened all the time: a kid ran away and the body would be found dumped at the edge of a road, half buried in thicket.

The pressure in his abdomen lessened. He cleared, shook, and stuffed his now more than ample parts back into his pants. Walking to the truck he buttoned up, adjusted for comfort, got in, adjusted again, thinking that task would take some getting used to, and drove away. Three miles farther down the country road he rolled over the black hose next to one of the two ancient gas pumps at the Phillips 66 to ring the attendant bell, cranked down the window, and waited.

A man, looking to Nathan to be about in his mid-forties, ambled out from the door of the building. "Lucky you caught me. 'Bout closin' as you can see," he said, hooking a thumb over a shoulder toward the closed door of the service bay. "What can I get ya?"

"Directing me to the sheriff's office would probably suffice."

"There a problem I might could help with?" the man asked, sincerity written in his voice and expression.

"Doubt it, 'less you can deal with a body laying in

the weeds up yonder about three miles."

The attendant's jaw dropped an inch and surprise bugged his eyes open wide. "You ain't serious."

Nathan nodded, his lips held in a grim line for effect. "I am."

"Well, huntin' season ain't started yet, but there's always some knucklehead flickin' his nose at the rules. S'pose it could be accidental and the nitwit who done it was too afraid to say nothing to nobody?"

"Mmm, well, I'd doubt that. Not from the cursory look I got, anyway."

"Ain't that somethin'." The man removed his grimy, threadbare baseball cap, wiped his brow with the back of his grease-laden forearm, and returned the hat to his balding head. Wisps of his brown hair poked out in an odd array. "There ain't been a killin' in these parts in…well, I can't remember when. Not unless you count the kid old man Kesterson shot a few years back, but that was pure mishap. Sheriff said so hisself. Ruled it strickly accidental manslaughter on account of the kids was tormentin' the poor old geezer somethin' fierce, and all he tried to do was scare 'em off. I heard tell one of 'em just got a might too close to the pattern of buckshot."

"Sheriff ever call in anyone else about that?" Nathan asked, putting real effort into phrasing and tone so it came off as an innocent question and not rouse suspicion. The answer could turn his decision toward home rather than law enforcement.

"Nah, he didn't see much need. Clear cut case."

Nathan allowed a slight smile to cross his lips as he moved the toothpick from one side of his mouth to the other. "Well, then, I guess he knows what he's doing.

He is the sheriff, after all."

The attendant bobbed his head in agreement. "That he is, that he is."

They fell silent for a minute. Then the station's grease-jockey straightened up and slapped the rim of the door window he'd been hanging over. "Well, now, I'm hopin' the sheriff ain't too far out of your way. I'd offer to report it for you myself, but if I don't get on home Mary Rose is likely to give me a tongue lashing to last me three weeks."

"I got a sister in Pittsburgh I'm headed up to see, but there's no rush."

"That's right along your way then." The man nodded in the general direction. "Sheriff Stanton is likely to be gone home hisself by the time you get there. You'll see one of the deputies. More'n likely Deputy Baylor; Big Bill everyone calls him."

Nathan flashed a white-toothed grin, hoping sheer friendliness showed in tiny wrinkles around the cobalt blue eyes. "I'll tell him hey for you."

"Now, that'd be most kind. Ain't many kind folks around anymore. Now, you head on up that-a-way, about five-six miles," a finger pointed the way Nathan had been going and continued to emphasize directions. "Go on past Route 33 into Elkins. That's a city, but mind you they got no jurisdiction out here. You'll find the Randolph County—that's where you are, you know—you'll find the county sheriff's office on your right-hand side about a mile-and-a-half in, just past High Street. Now, if you get to Gay Street, you gone too far."

"I sure appreciate it." Nathan tipped his non-existent hat at the edge of the shaggy and slightly wavy light brown hair hanging across his forehead.

"You're mighty welcome. And maybe you'll stop in for a fill-up on your way back. You drive safe now, hear?"

The man slapped the door again as Nathan rolled away from the pumps, the service bell stuttering its sound as the wheels of his truck ran over the hoses. He watched through the rearview mirror as the guy shuffled back into the store. Nathan turned on the headlights and pulled out onto the road.

On the trip into Elkins the dash panel began to cast a reflection on the cab windows and Nathan gave a studied nod of approval to this new self he'd acquired. It had been a shame to shed the kid, he'd accomplished a lot of necessary chores through the use of that mind and body. But, a bit on the older side fit better. Much better.

The very first new person he'd become had happened 'strickly accidental,' as the guy at the gas station had turned the phrase. Yet over the ensuing years he'd been many different ages in many different bodies. Almost as many as there were dead bugs now splattered across the windshield.

He'd spent damn little time in the world of the dead after dying in an explosion in 1858 at one of the coal mines his family owned. The blast threw him with such ferocity he was pushed right into another man whose heart still beat and lungs drew breath. He awoke in the makeshift medical facility near the mine entrance, a place gladly supplied by the family who, unlike their competitors, believed the lives and well-being of miners were more important than the amount of coal they could haul out. He knew right away he wasn't himself; too many thoughts and memories which didn't belong to him swam up from a fog-filled brain. Nathan sat up, swung his feet over the side of the bed, and called out to the nurse. He got no response. She carried on with her work changing the dressings of a nearby wounded patient. He turned around to see a broken, bandaged body lying next to him on the bed.

He walked around, listening to the moans of injured men, thankful he wasn't among them. But the knowledge he'd "…died. I died," did not sit well. At thirty-one years old he hadn't nearly lived. The transparency of his limbs frightened him. He tentatively reached out to touch a bed. The feel, the sensation of it registered, but in an odd way. Because, with added pressure, his finger didn't make a dent in the padded material, it pushed through. Telling himself there wasn't a dang thing he could do about it, he walked to the bed and stared down at the person lying there, yearning.

The longer he stayed, the stronger the urge struck to return. After all, the body and head were bandaged so thoroughly and their frames so similar, no one could tell it wasn't really him. And, he'd slipped right out. But the question remained, and he murmured it aloud, "Can I get back in?"

He sat on the edge of the mattress and pushed his way on top of the man. Each new portion of Nathan's body that made full contact resulted in a buzz, a tingling of sorts, and dissipated after a few minutes. Fully in, he winced from the pain of the injuries. But he smiled, too. The pain meant he was alive again.

The man everyone thought was under the bandages, including Nathan's own family, shocked staff and relatives alike when he asked for Nathan's kinfolk. They all stood stunned for several moments. Then the whole place went into a tizzy. Though they'd been sure they had buried Nathan, he gave so many details and facts about family and business that even after the bandages came off nobody bothered with further questions; they eagerly attributed such a different appearance to injuries.

Though the body stayed in the Crockett cemetery, the other man's family was left to change out the headstone, and grieve.

When that man died some forty-odd years later, within hours Nathan longed to be alive once again. Life was too good. Things amongst the dead felt diminished to him. Items solid to the touch (including a body), the sweetness of the air after a rain, true sensations—rather than what felt like phantom to him—thirst or hunger, heat and cold, these were the things which signaled life for Nathan. He looked for and found another body to inhabit. Not entirely sure it would work a second time, he cautiously slipped in while the person slept amidst a strange fitful dream.

Mostly a change was forced. Nathan knew time was near when vision started to fail, with darkness around the edges as if struck by disease, but when extremities began to turn a bit on the gray side he knew it had reached the point where he needed to rush things along.

He almost missed the driveway into the parking lot of the sheriff's office. The glaring lights on the US flag, and those splashed across the front of the building, caught his attention. Still, the driver's side wheels bumped over the curb, jostling him in his seat. He eased the truck in to one of the angled spaces and sat for a moment to think about what to say. No, he had it straight: He'd pulled to the side of the road due to an enormous need to piss, and there it was under the splashing stream; the body that was too young, too used, though he wouldn't make mention of that last part.

He introduced himself as Nate and led Big Bill through the story a couple times, and then a third as he filled out the report. It took some doing in the dark to find the exact spot again, but Nate showed him to the place he'd left the young man.

Big Bill's face screwed up. "He's a might ripe, ain't he?" he asked, his rail thin torso leaning over the kid but with his head turned and shining the beam of his flashlight in Nathan's face. "And you say this is exactly as you discovered him? You didn't disturb a thing at all?"

"Well, except for the bit of piss on his boots. And I'm rightly sorry about that, Deputy. I mean, I wouldn't have done that if I'd been aware; that's just downright...well, you know what I'm sayin'."

Big Bill straightened up, all five-foot two-inches of him, and sighed. "I guess I better call the coroner. He won't be none too happy being pulled away from the T.V., but there's nothing else for it."

"Is it okay if I head on out, then? I'll stay if you think you need someone with you though," Nathan offered, gazing around the deep shadows of the moonlit area. "But, the way things stand I'd hate to put my sister through more unnecessary worry than I already have with as late as I'll be."

"Well, gosh darn it, I should've let you call from

the station house. That was downright un-neighborly of me."

"That's all right, Deputy, I can see how it slipped your mind. Long's there's a tower nearby, I can use my cell phone if the need strikes."

Big Bill started toward his squad car. "Well, son, I've got your information on the report you filled out. I know where to find you. You tell your sister hey for us when you get there."

Standing in the beams of headlights, Nathan shook a hand that felt tiny in his own. "I'll do that. And I'm right sorry again for dragging you out like this."

"That's just quite all right. It sure weren't your fault." Big Bill hollered, "You drive safe now, hear?" at the retreating tailgate after Nate had circled around.

Nathan lifted a wave out the window and gave two quick toots on the horn. He drove as far as Route 33, where he turned east and circled around to head to a cabin deep in a West Virginia hollow. Not far from where the West Virginia, Virginia, and Kentucky state lines merged, the simple one-room building, surrounded by a cluster of smaller ones, had been his home for decades except in winter when, with a new body, he would lose himself somewhere among city crowds.

Chapter 4

Nathan pulled from the highway onto a gravel road not easily detected, bouncing in his seat as the truck jumped ruts and holes and thumped over tree roots. Up hills and down gullies, a little more than two miles into the hollow, he found a spot among the various other vehicles and parked. He got out, tapped down on the lock button, and slammed the door.

Three-quarters of a mile along a path which included trekking over a crudely made footbridge above a steep-banked stream, Nathan finally caught sight of home. Though it may not have been the grand, stately manor of his (living) youth, the rustic building of one large room stood off to the right of a small meadow. From his vantage point on foot, eight smaller cabins were tucked under the spreading boughs of trees so thick the encampment wouldn't be detectable from the air, even after the leaves blazed in variegated hues of red and gold, and dropped to the fertile ground.

"Hey, Zach." Nathan walked toward the tiny glow of red as the cigarette moved from hip to mouth. "Everything good?"

"Hey, Nate," a quiet voice called out of the early morning dark. "Everything's good. Nice new timbre to the voice. Does the body match it?" A soft chuckle rolled over the expanse between them.

"Well, I'd say you'll have to judge that for yourself

in the daylight." Nathan shook the proffered hand. "Damn shame to lose the use of the kid, though. The exchange was a might tough this time. I'm seriously beat."

Zachariah thumped a hand to Nathan's shoulder. "Hang in there, buddy."

"Oh, you know I will." Nathan scanned the night sky, and took a quick glance around at what he could see by moonlight. Satisfied all was well, he nodded to himself. He'd been grateful to his grandpappy for acquiring so much property so many years ago; thousands of acres of pristine West Virginia hills far from prying eyes. He loved the land, and loved the solitude as much as he appreciated the ability it afforded him to live so many lifetimes without rousing suspicion. Of course, the kid had made it a lot easier with his boundless knowledge of computers.

The facts were not lost on Nathan any more than they were lost on those he'd invited to join him here over the years. Each new self of all the inhabitants brought some useful skill to the place. Improvements had been made to the hundred and fifty-year old original structure Nathan had built as a young man. A different self had provided the know-how to get a gravity waterline to Nathan's place, something he thought should be expanded soon to the other cabins; maybe the following summer. Another developed the portable solar system they wheeled out to the clearing for short spurts to provide ample electricity for small things like recharging cell phones, and the equipment the kid Nathan recently shed brought in to help them with their changing identities.

"I think I'll turn in. You wake me if you need to,

hear?" Nathan ditched the chewed-up toothpick and headed for the door of his cabin.

"Will do. You can sleep tight with me on watch."

The night watch had been in place for so long even Nathan couldn't remember anymore when it had been started, or why. Even without weapons of any kind on hand, it gave him a sense of security, especially right after he'd slid into a new body. With each exchange, the fear of having been detected and followed gnawed at the back of his mind like a hound worried after a fox hiding in its den. Even in death his sense of moral code knew using the living, as his clan did, would not be exactly ethical. But, he couldn't let life go. He didn't want to let it go. None of them did.

He went inside and stripped off his clothes, tossing his pants across the bottom of the bed for easy reach if an emergency cropped up. He slipped under the blanket to stave off the chill that stole through the air in the hills much sooner than in low-lying cities full of concrete and asphalt. Nathan dropped into sleep with the sounds of crickets and night birds in his ears.

The next morning, the sun blazed through a small window casting a beam of brightness into his face. Nathan woke and rolled out of his bunk. The vision held strong, the fingers and toes looked pink and healthy as he examined himself. The body wasn't exactly muscular but certainly more fit than the previous one. In the small mirror, hung by a strand of wire over his cold-water sink, he smiled at the new image. Tiny wrinkles formed at the corners of his eyes. He liked it even better now that he could see it in natural daylight.

Hoping the bank of truck batteries still held enough

of a charge from the small solar system, he plugged in his little coffee pot. When the sound of the water heating and pumping in tiny spurts reached his ears, he grabbed a fresh toothpick and strode out the front door and crossed the covered porch.

Nathan stretched in the sun and, taking his morning leak over the edge of the wooden planks, returned a greeting with a slight wave and squeaked out, "Hey, Sarah," to one of the two current female residents. The compound's inhabitants shared three outhouses, but the men never used them to pee. A strange pang hit the pit of his stomach at her seeing him naked; something he'd never experienced with any woman before.

"Will you *look* at you! My, oh my, Nate, you're gonna have hearts goin' pit-pat over that." Sarah fanned her face with a laugh.

"Hey, I should be so lucky. 'Less, of course, you'd care to come in for a spell," he joked to hide his odd embarrassment.

"Well, now, you know I would," Sarah teased, "but I got a feelin' Steve might object to that some."

"Damn stingy bastard, ain't he? 'Course, he's free to join us." Nathan laughed nervously and winked, even as he wondered where that idea had come from.

Sarah let loose with a fun-natured giggle. "Nice to see you back in good condition, Nate. And, I'll allow it's mighty well distributed."

"Gonna take a bit of getting used to, but it feels right. I'll see you later." Nathan tipped his non-existent hat and went inside to begin his chores.

Taking his coffee to the laptop he shared with the rest of his clan, Nathan sat and flipped the pages of the notebook until he found the proper instructions. He thought retraining a new self would be tough; it generally was. But it appeared the knowledge of gadgets he'd never dreamed of as a kid, came as second nature to most these days. With the slightest of glances at the notes, his hand took control of the mouse and his fingers began tapping the keys. Between sips of coffee, in rather short order he had a new picture stored on the desktop and inserted it into the graphic. He entered a birth date, and changed other pertinent information; Eyes: BLU, Hair: LT BRN, Hgt: 6', Wgt: 190, (mighty well distributed)—though he'd guessed at those last two—and soon his new West Virginia driver's license was spitting out of the printer. He inspected it, nodded, then shut down the computer equipment to save power and leaned over to switch on the laminator.

He grabbed one of the official sheets of plastic a member of the compound had pilfered from the state's Division of Motor Vehicles and once again marveled at having the best of both worlds at their disposal. On the dead side, he could go anywhere and take anything sight unseen—well, unseen by live people, anyway. On the other, he lived as he always had, if you didn't count people reacting to an unusually cool touch. Body temperature dropped almost three full degrees and he found reactions to that amusing upon seeing the odd expression when shaking hands with a new acquaintance, or whenever he needed to see a doctor. Sure, it was easy enough to pilfer a new body, but why discard a perfectly sound one over a minor illness or a little needed routine maintenance?

While Nathan waited for the machine to heat, he went about his morning routine and dressed. With the machine ready, he laminated his new identification, turned off the electronics, and went out to introduce the rest of the clan to his new look, along with requests to remind him to stay out of Roanoke for the foreseeable future. It was a given he couldn't remove himself from this body, at least for a while.

After all these years, Nathan knew it took months for all sense of the host body's ego to be pushed down into unreachable depths of consciousness. That also meant trips to town for necessities would fall on the others, just in case someone from Roanoke had reason to wander to another town. He sure didn't want to have to deny an identity, or spend time trying to convince anyone that they were mighty mistaken; that he didn't know them.

It sure wasn't horse and buggy days like in his youth. Heck, even trains had lost ground to cars and trucks. Until recently, the Concorde jet plane could have a person from New York City all the way to Paris in less than two hours. Yes, sir, these days it seemed masses of folks moved around faster than a newt scrambled under a rock.

Chapter 5

Jenna turned from the bow of the schooner, loaned for their honeymoon cruise from the small island where their wedding had been held, and went to the chaise where Marvin was stretched out. "Can't this thing move any faster, Marvin?"

"What's your hurry, kiddo?"

"There are things I need to attend to."

"Aren't you having a nice time? The wedding was spectacular. Davy did a bang-up job, everybody who was anybody on that island said so. "Didn't you enjoy it?"

Jenna had enjoyed everything; the incredible wedding and reception, and the honeymoon cruise. Though, if pressed, she would have to admit she'd been antsy through it all to get home, which might explain why she didn't waste time after the ceremony to pull the veil from her head and remove the train. "Now, what am I going to do with these? It's not like I can put them in a box for my own posterity. What would be the point?"

"Ah, but they should be kept, no?" Gianni Versace, who had designed her unique gown, held out a hand to take them from her.

"Where? If I put it in the closet at the hotel, it'll just end up in the lost and found when some maid comes to 'scatter the dust' as Mike Hamilton puts it."

"I shall take it back to Milan, *mia bella*. There it will be put in a place of honor—where my sister will discover it and wonder who it was for. It will be great fun for me to say, 'Ah, Donatella, my silly little sister, this is from the only wedding gown the great House of Versace has ever done. Made for one of the greatest beauties of the world.' " He kissed the back of Jenna's hand, then smiled as he drew his gaze slowly up her frame.

"The gown is gorgeous. Greatest beauty? Now that could easily be argued."

"What could be argued?" Marvin approached Jenna and leaned down to plant a small kiss on her bare shoulder.

Jenna shrugged. "Nothing. Where did you come from? Why aren't you down in the thick of things with the others?"

Word of the event rapidly spread through their plane of existence, and the reception for the Wedding of the Millennium—perhaps ever among deadheads—was in full swing on the small Caribbean isle. Royalty from as far back as the 12th Century drank and laughed, mingling among the more recently departed blue bloods. No one, not even Jason or Teresa, could recall an event quite like it, and they both traced their origins to days soon after *homo heildelbergensis*.

Marvin moved to Jenna's side and hooked an arm through hers. "I want to dance with my wife." He smiled at Versace. "Wife. Damn, I like the sound of that. Maybe we should borrow the schooner that brought us here." Marvin waggled his brows.

Jenna poked an elbow into his side. "Down, boy. We've got an island full of guests to consider."

"Ah, who can blame him for being eager? But, if you must decline his invitation for that, surely you must accept his offer to dance with his bride."

"I suppose. But, then the skirt has to come off as well."

As Jenna took hold of the gathered material at her waist, Marvin stopped her. "What are you doing? You can't—"

"Hush, Marvin." Jenna pushed his hands away. She grasped the top layer of the gown, which the designer had so brilliantly done and, from knees in front to the cascaded ground-length folds at her heels, it slid to the sand to reveal a matching skirt that ended just above the knees.

She stepped away and Versace retrieved it. "You see, Marvin? Gianni would never embarrass such a creature as your Mrs. Broudstein."

"Wow. And, look, still as beautiful," Marvin stated. "Gianni, you are as clever as you are talented."

"Now, you must go. Go and enjoy the party." Versace waved a hand through the air.

Jenna planted air kisses on each of his cheeks, then hooked an arm through one of Marvin's and they walked down from the crest, weaving their way through the hundreds of tables to a dance floor set in front of a large bandstand on the northern beach. To sounds and comments of delighted wonder at her transformed dress, and deafening applause (if one were a deadhead), Marvin held Jenna's hand and, in a wide circular motion, brought her into his arms. Still holding hands, they separated and bowed to a throng of people, both famous and infamous. Some they knew, most they didn't, still others they'd only heard about. The orchestra played "Begin the Beguine" as if Cole Porter himself conducted from his original sheet music. Jenna's bare feet glided along, following Marvin's every lead.

At the end, they bowed once more to applause. Jenna called out to the crowd, waving them onto the floor. "Well, don't just sit there."

When the vibrations of too many deadheads bumping into them got to be intolerable, Jenna led Marvin off to find longtime neighbors Colleen and Patrick. Jenna plopped down into a chair.

"Don't you two just make a pair," Colleen exclaimed, passing a glass of wine into Jenna's reaching hand.

"Who knew the big oaf could be so graceful?" Jenna winked at Marvin.

"Hey, watch it, there, kiddo. You don't graduate from Harvard without some of the social graces."

"And why aren't you and Patrick out there? I'll bet you haven't been dancing in years. Come on, this is a party."

"Oh, for goodness sake, Jenna, I'd stumble all over the place. I'm afraid I'd embarrass poor Patrick to death. Besides, we're too old for that. This is for you young people."

Marvin drained the water from the crystal goblet in front of him. "Who says you're old? You two are spry as teenagers. And, I've seen the glint in his eyes."

"Oh, go on with you." Colleen gave a wave of her hand that accompanied a big grin.

Almost an hour later, Davy, who'd organized the event down to the last silver dessert spoon, approached their table in a rush of flapping hands and gasping breath. "Oh, my, God. Oh, my, God! This is too perfect. You are just too perfect."

Jenna scowled at Marvin's eye roll, then smiled up at Davy. "It's all perfect. Every candelabra, every morsel of food, every light on every tree."

"You certainly outdid yourself, I'll give you that," Marvin said.

"Oh, but I'm not done. Guess who just offered up their yacht for you to use when this shindig is over?"

"Who would do such a thing? We've got our chartered ship."

"You're never going to guess." A hand placed to his chest and his brow creased, Davy stood holding his breath and waited as if he'd burst. "Oh, my, God. Dodi and Di! I mean, could you just..." He commenced flapping his hands again.

"That's sweet but, really, Davy. The one we—"

"Oh, no. No, no, no. We'll need that cargo hold for stowing things after this has all been torn down, remember?" He turned to Marvin. "And that's not all. Don't think I forgot about you. Is there a special surprise in store for you! Are you ready for it?"

Marvin sat speechless. Jenna watched him cringe behind a hand when Davy stood on an adjoining chair. A single wave of his hand stopped the music. Jenna, Marvin, Patrick, and Colleen all turned to learn what had brought it to a halt. After a moment of silence as two men exchanged places, four thumps of the bass drum echoed up the distance, a beam of light pooled over the musician, and an unmatchable solo performance brought Marvin to his feet.

"Are you kidding me? You got Gene Kruppa to play at our wedding?" Marvin pulled Davy into a bear hug. "Are you—You little schmuck, I could kiss you. In fact, I think I will." He grabbed the man's shoulders and planted a kiss on his forehead.

After Marvin ran onto the stage to thank the band, thank Davy, thank the entire dead world for such a dazzling display, Jenna pulled him down off the platform. "We should be going, Marvin."

"Why? Aren't you having a good time?"

"Yes, but that's not the point. Davy said we have the use of the schooner for a limited time. We should say our goodbyes and go."

On the way through the crowd, Jenna stopped to remove the sapphire and diamond necklace. She handed it to Diane, who had become her second-in-command of the new sect of Keepers. "And make sure you return it. I don't want that poor jeweler to suffer any more anxiety." In response to the scowl Diane presented, Jenna pointed a finger at her. "You promised me it would go back."

It took Jenna and Marvin another two hours to get on board. After two yanks on the ship's bell as the signal to leave, the engines fired up and the captain maneuvered America II, with its black hull and gold lettering gleaming in the moonlight, through the mass of yachts, schooners, and small ships that packed the bay.

Now two days into their honeymoon cruise back to Key West, where the schooner moored, Jenna's nerves jangled. She couldn't sit or stand in one place for more than a few minutes. "The sect needs my help. I can't just leave them on their own."

In a surprise twist, rather than the World Council of Keepers punishing Jenna for infractions against the living, they made her the head of a new sect. One sect, Teresa's, welcomed the departed to rest, another, Jason's, held evil at bay, and Jenna's had been granted watch over the living, helping victims escape abuse and violence.

From his reclined position on the chaise lounge on the fore deck, Marvin shaded his eyes from the midday sun. "Come on, Jen, this is beginning to sound like every old excuse when you were alive and working for that law firm that sucked the life out of you. Can't this wait?"

Jenna shook her head, her scowl deepened. "No. I have to get back."

"I thought you had a whole contingent of helpers in your…police force, or whatever you call it. You've got deputi—"

"Something's off; wrong."

Marvin shook his head. "Something's off all right."

"No, Marv. I can feel it."

Chapter 6

The number of Jumpers, a title they'd given themselves after someone described Nathan's longevity as jumping from body to body, living at the compound fluctuated. Three of the cabins currently stood empty; one when Steve and Sarah grew tired of sneaking into one another's places. Of course, by then, the rest of the clan had long since figured things out. In fact, it was Nathan who laughed when he finally told them, "You two may as well be shacked-up in the same shack."

Once, an older woman who'd come to their encampment had stayed until the body she'd taken over withered. As that self slid toward death she said, "This is like dying a second time. I don't think I can do this again. It was hard enough and painful enough the first time. This feels no different. When it's over, I think I'm just gonna wander off."

"You can go now, if you like. We'll keep a watch," Sarah offered.

"No, I wouldn't feel right about that. I'm the one who used her, I should be here."

To her credit, she slipped from the body and waited. Then she welcomed the new deadhead and they walked away together. No one was surprised when, moments later, a pure white glow appeared from the path leading away from the compound. Arrayed fingers of light reached toward the sky between the leaves and branches. They expanded, grew brighter, and then flickered out. The two women had made the choice to go with the Sanctuarians of Teresa's sect. Every deadhead had seen it happen before. In fact, the offer was always made to the very young, the chronically infirm, and those who expressed a weariness of the world upon their first death. All but Nathan that is. Having been thrown into the miner's body with such sudden force he neither received the offer, nor witnessed it for the other miners, though he'd observed it plenty over the ensuing years.

Nathan and the rest of the group gave the body she left behind a proper burial. Steve even said a few reverent words. The grave site went unmarked except for initials carved into the trunk of a nearby tree.

As years passed and chain stores came into existence, life became easier. The group alternated between two major big box warehouse stores, though one of them required a much longer trip all the way into Harrisonburg, Virginia. Nathan always footed the bill, fed from his initial inheritance which had grown to enormous sums in investment accounts over the years; it paid to have come from a wealthy Tennessee family and he never minded. Of course, finding an attorney who managed to connive the system into creating a fund available to Nathan in perpetuity made the real difference, and ensured money would always be plentiful.

"We lead simple lives," Nathan explained to an interested deadhead while on one such run into Charleston for supplies. The guy had recognized them for what they were and followed them out to Nathan's truck. "We take turns with the chores around the place, we look after one another's welfare."

They helped the middle-aged man pick out a physical self and waited for him to make the transition. The guy stayed at the compound about six months before he declared inhabiting someone turned out to be more trouble than he cared for. "Shit, Nathan, I forgot how hard it can be. Well, sir, no offense, but ya'll can keep it. Not needing no money, walking in and taking what I want, sight unseen, doing what pleases me, when I please…that's livin'."

"No offense taken. I'll allow it ain't for everyone." Nathan's tone turned stern. "But, I'll also allow you best wait until we get near a town to shed this body. And we'll thank you to keep your mouth shut. We don't need no trouble up here. Agreed?"

The man nodded. "Agreed."

Obviously, Nathan didn't agree about the quality of living as a deadhead.

Over the years, whenever he missed some of the finer things life could offer, like central heat and a hot shower in winter, he would leave the enclave and spend time in a city. He searched out good food, museums, libraries where he read voraciously and, of course, women. Another weakness also drew him: movies. From the first Nickelodeon he witnessed in New York City during the winter of 1905 he became hooked.

So, one early morning in mid-October, when he woke and walked out to see the first light blanket of snow covering the meadow, Nathan sought out Zach, who he'd become strangely close to over the past weeks. "It's about time for me to head out 'til Spring."

"Where ya gonna go this year, Nate?" Zach came out of his cabin, zipping his coat.

Nathan pulled the toothpick from his mouth and shrugged. "Not sure. I just know it won't be Roanoke!" When they both stopped laughing, he added, "You can stay in my place if you've got a hankerin' to." The knowledge of the man living in his cabin made the thought of leaving for six months somehow easier to bear. As if family were there awaiting his return.

"That's kind of you. I appreciate it." Zach clapped a hand on Nathan's shoulder. "You know you can rest easy that it'll be spic and span when you get back."

"I know. I'll trust you to keep an eye on things while I'm gone, too."

"'Course. You need anything special done while you're away?"

"Not that I can think of," Nathan said, replacing the toothpick. "Unless ya'll get the druthers to extend that gravity water line to the other cabins before the ground freezes. Check for an email from me now and then." He slapped Zachariah on the back, then pulled him into a hug with a heartfelt squeeze. "Ya'll take care now, hear?" He headed for his truck wondering why he'd done that. In fact, as Nathan looked back on his time in this new body, there had been many instances of behavior he found odd.

He'd always spent more time with the men, but only because they did most of the hard-labor chores around the compound; thinning out nearby dead trees and brush as a fire deterrent, then splitting the logs for wood stoves, or planning and making repairs to structures. Yet, even outside of those tasks he found an increasing amount of enjoyment in being around them; especially with Zach. For some reason neither of them could quite fathom, it was as if Nathan couldn't do a thing without having the man nearby. Nathan realized he would find excuses to spend time with his friend and took any opportunity to keep the man in sight, stealing looks when he was in any stage of undress. If the man was totally naked, as often happened around the site—particularly when they went to swim or bathe in the stream—something Nathan didn't understand compelled him to be there.

The question nagged at him during the almost one-mile walk to his truck. What caused this sudden unusual attraction? It seemed a lot of strange things had come over Nathan since he'd taken on this new self. The only explanation could be the assertion of Chris' personality but, from Nathan's perspective, it was more deeply rooted than id alone. He found respite from the debate as he stopped to inspect the repairs they'd completed on the footbridge. As he continued onward, the issue resurfaced.

He stopped at the edge of the parking area to relieve himself before heading out on such a long trip. He stuffed things back in and buttoned up, adjusting for comfort. Crawling into the cab of the truck, he adjusted again. Though it had become second nature by now, the need to do so still confounded him. Yet he felt an ego boost in the task; particularly within plain sight of the men of the compound, which he found stranger yet.

In a snap decision, he shrugged it all off; there would be time enough to sort those things out when he arrived in Cincinnati to see the Great American Ballpark stadium that housed the Baseball Hall of Fame. He might even pay a visit to the National Underground Railroad Freedom Center. Right now he needed to concentrate on getting there. He double-checked the wad of cash in the pocket of his jacket, moved the toothpick to the other side of his mouth, pushed the sunglasses up the bridge of his nose, and drove off.

Chapter 7

Nathan's drive to Cincinnati took longer than he'd expected. Traffic snarled to a halt on the I-64 a ways outside of Lexington, Kentucky. Inching toward an exit, he about made up his mind to get off and spend the entire winter. Surfing through the offerings of the city on his cell phone changed his mind about that in a hurry; there just wouldn't be enough happening for him. Plus, the remainder of the trip would only take another ninety minutes or so once traffic cleared. A car horn blared from behind, and he looked ahead to see things had begun to move again. He bit down on his toothpick, dropped the phone onto the bench seat, and hit the gas.

As he did that, his vision glanced to the rearview mirror and he lifted a hand of thanks to acknowledge the car behind him. That's when he saw them; a fairly transparent couple in the bed of his pick-up, shifting to put their backs against the cab to avoid the draft of wind as the truck gained speed.

Rapping his knuckles on the glass behind the seat, Nathan motioned them to join him up front. "You may as well be comfortable," he said when the man began to crawl in.

"I'll be damned. Ya'll really could see us." The man turned and pushed his face through the back again. "Come on up, Nadeen."

Nathan grinned. "Who else would I be talking to?"

"And you can hear, too. Well, now, I wasn't quite sure, you know. You got to allow it's rare."

"I will. Name's Nathan. Where're ya'll headed?"

"I'm Wayne. This here's Nadeen." He jutted a thumb toward her as she settled into a spot between the men. "Not going nowheres special. Just out for a spin, really. It's something we like to do from time to time to break the monotony."

Peripheral vision enabled Nathan to catch Nadeen staring at him and he turned a broad smile toward her. "It's okay darlin', I won't bite."

Wayne let out a guffaw. "Wouldn't get much if ya did!"

Nadeen shifted closer to her friend. "So, how is it you're able to…you know…"

"Just can, I guess," Nathan lied. "Could for years." He flipped his blinker light on and changed lanes where the highway merged to I-75 and headed north.

"You from around these parts?" Wayne asked.

"West Virginia. Got a place out in the boondocks. Guess that's why I invited you two up to ride with me. Get's kinda lonely traveling alone, you know?"

"You're a ways away from home, ain't ya?"

"That I am, Nadeen. For the same reason, I guess. Every once in a while a man's gotta find some excitement." Nathan flipped the blinker to the opposite direction to merge with the oncoming traffic.

"How come you ain't got any luggage, or nothin'?" Nadeen asked.

Nathan glanced at her and shrugged. "Don't need any. I can get what I need when I reach the city."

"Exactly how far are you goin', if you don't mind

my askin', that is?"

"Well, Wayne, when I headed out this morning, I wasn't quite sure. Then, as I plopped my butt down on the seat here, pretty sudden-like, Cincinnati popped into my mind."

"Never been that far north. Maybe we should go all the way with you. What you say, Nadeen? You game?"

Nathan turned to Nadeen to find her still staring. He shifted the toothpick in his mouth and returned his attention to the road ahead. No sense in mangling a perfectly good body.

"I think it'd be a bit of a hoot," Wayne said. Nadeen didn't answer. He waved a hand in front of her face. "Hello? Are you with me?"

Her voice trembled when she answered. "I think we should get out up ahead."

"Now why's that?" Nathan asked.

"Just do."

"Aw, come on, Nadeen. Let's do like he says and find some excitement for a change. Sure as hell ain't nothin' ever happening around here. Come, on, what could it hurt?" Wayne insisted.

Nathan noticed her slide even farther away. If she got any closer, she'd be right in the guy. "I swear to you, I ain't dangerous. Besides, let's be honest here, darlin', you're already dead." Nathan chuckled. "Shouldn't I be the one shakin' in his boots?"

Nadine leaned forward, studying Nathan's face. "Not so sure about that."

"What's that supposed to mean? Here he's nice enough to invite us in outta the cold wind, you ought not to be givin' Nathan a hard time." Wayne gave her a few seconds to respond. "Now, are we goin' or not?"

"There's somethin' not quite right about you, mister."

The dead rarely recognized him for what he was and, though it did happen, none had ever expressed fear. There was something unnerving about the quaver in her voice, a veiled tone of threat, as if she meant to expose him to an authority somewhere. Nathan lifted his boot off the gas pedal and pulled to the side right at the exit to Newtown Pike. Self-confidence be damned, he didn't dare take a chance of being caught overstaying his time in a borrowed body. Without turning his face toward them, he said, "I wouldn't want to cause the lady any undue distress. It's been mighty nice talkin' to you, though. You stay safe, hear?"

"Well, we thank you for the ride, don't we?"

The tone of Wayne's voice as he slid from the truck told Nathan all he needed to know. He lifted a hand in a slight wave of goodbye and pulled back into traffic. In the passenger side-view mirror, he witnessed Wayne's wild arm gestures as the man tromped down the exit ramp after Nadeen, most likely giving her what-for.

Nathan shook his head even while he sighed with relief. The manner in which the woman had been eyeballing him meant she was trouble and he felt a twinge of sorrow for Wayne. What good could there be in being dead if you didn't take advantage of it, and have some fun once in a while?

Sixty-five minutes later the lights of Cincinnati beckoned him. He peered at signs looking for a nice hotel. One of the higher end chains would do. One with a nice steakhouse nearby. Then, after dinner, back to the hotel for a hot shower and a heavenly night's sleep in a comfy bed with a really good mattress; things he'd dream about over the months on the compound.

Not seeing anything to strike his fancy, he pulled to the break-down lane right before the freeway interchange south of the city. He picked up his cell phone, swiped to the internet app and searched. There. A five-star hotel, and within a block to the north a tavern and pub, where he bet his life—well, if he had an actual life to bet, anyway—he'd be able to get a damned good steak smothered in onions and mushrooms, a baked potato drenched in butter and sour cream; maybe he'd treat himself to a nice dessert. He patted his waistline and nodded, though in doing so he reckoned he best find a gym to keep this body in shape. According to the map, to the south was a contemporary art center he could wander through in the morning. It looked to be a good winter.

Chapter 8

When the clerk asked if he needed assistance with luggage, he flashed his brightest smile hoping the small dimples would show in the soft lighting of the hotel lobby. "No, ma'am. I'll get it on my way back in." He leaned forward on the counter to get a better look at her. "What can you recommend about the pub up the way?"

"Well, that would depend on what you've got a taste for," she answered, handing him a card key in its paper holder.

"A really good steak, made to order, and grilled to perfection."

"Then I'd suggest you stay right here in the hotel for that."

"Well, thank you kindly," Nathan said, and took three steps in the direction she'd pointed before turning around. As he heard Pa say every time he'd found some new venture to invest in, "No risk, no gain." Nathan removed the ever-present toothpick, and peered at the nametag on her jacket. "Victoria, is it? I bet it would taste a lot better if I had someone to accompany me."

She laughed in a light, pleasing sound before she politely turned him down.

"Well, all right then. Can't say I didn't try. Though, I might come back down for a drink when your shift ends." With the smile still firmly in place, Nathan tipped his non-existent hat and strolled off amid the sound of her soft laughter echoing through the lobby.

The restaurant maître d' met him with a frown of distaste but, after Nathan flashed his room key, he pulled a menu from beneath the podium. "Right this way then, sir."

"I do apologize for my state of dress," Nathan said, following behind, "but it seems I arrived before my luggage."

Pulling a plush leather padded chair partially away from a table on the far side of the wainscoted oak-walled dining room separated from other diners, the man sniffed. "Understandable, sir. Will this seat meet with approval?"

"Anywhere is fine," Nathan replied, sat, accepted the proffered menu and, without looking at the man, added, "Send out a bottle of your finest Bordeaux, if you would be so kind."

"Yes, sir. Right away, sir." The host rendered a slight bow with a smile and left.

Not that Nathan liked doing it, he much preferred issuing gentle southern charm, but he'd learned long ago to deal with attitudes. Let them know the wallet is fat enough and noses would pert' near scrape the floor, snobbery dissolving into sudden flattery. It irked him, but his manners remained firmly intact; an automatic reflex akin to the bible study prayers he'd learned as a child.

He never opened the leather-bound menu. Without thought for any allergies this new body might have, he issued instructions to the waitress even as he nodded to the sommelier's offer of the label for inspection. "I want a Porterhouse steak, one inch thick, medium.

Onions and mushrooms grilled in butter—real butter, not clarified. Baked potato; butter and sour cream, no chives. Keep the vegetables." He lifted his glass, swirling the dark red liquid, held it up to the light to see how it clung to the sides, then brought the glass to his nose and inhaled. He took a small sip and nodded.

Nathan took his time, his every sense brought into play: the aroma wafting from the plate, the sizzle and crackle of the fat on the metal insert as the meal was presented, the steam rising from the potato; the texture of each bite, relishing each morsel of the meat, its juices flooding the taste buds of this borrowed body; the blending of butter and sour cream melting into the potato; all brought a smile of satisfaction.

He pushed back a few inches from the table, dabbed his face with the linen napkin, and sighed with contentment. It brought to mind the image of a bobcat of his beloved West Virginia hills taking time to purr and lick its paws after consuming a fresh kill. The waitress rushed over to clear the dishes, and the sommelier refreshed his wine glass.

If there could be one thing Nathan missed about his life, being in his own body, it would be in times like this when memories flooded his mind; recollections of retiring with the men-folk to the parlor after a meal, to sip on Cognac and smoke cigars, and discuss important matters of the day.

The more empty the bottle of wine, the fewer thoughts of a rendezvous with the desk clerk filled his mind. He signaled for his check, charged it to his hotel room leaving a hefty tip, drained the last sip of the liquid from his glass, and left for his room.

Up in the third floor suite, he dropped his clothes

on a chair, and spent almost an hour sitting on the floor of the shower, the hot water creating a steam room effect, and dozed. After drying himself, he snuggled down under the thick blankets of the bed and slept.

Nathan woke the next morning and stretched. He called for room service and went about his morning ablutions. The knock at his door came sooner than expected, and he pulled on the plush robe that hung on a hook in the bathroom.

"There's a message for you as well, Mr. Crockett," the waiter said, transferring the order to the small table near a large window at the far end of the living room.

"Really?" Nathan wondered aloud and reached out to accept it, "I can't imagine," and then he laughed as he accepted the handwritten note on hotel stationary. 'Some Don Juan you turned out to be. Here I imagined a tryst with a brazen Lothario and I find you retired to your room without me.—Vicky.' "Well, then, we'll have to see about making this right."

The waiter stood ready to push his service cart out, hovering for a tip. Nathan went to the chair and retrieved his wallet from his jeans, peeled two twenty-dollar bills from the stack, handed them over, let the man out and lingered to watch him strut down the empty hallway to the elevator. He perused the internet on his cell phone while scarfing down the breakfast, then dressed and headed out to buy a few clothes. It wouldn't do to wear the same thing when he met his date. And he fully intended to meet her. Despite the strange attraction and fantasies about Zakariah it had been a long, dry summer.

Chapter 9

Nathan approached the front desk, sans the typical toothpick, dressed in a black sports jacket, white shirt, and tight black jeans that accentuated his waist—not to mention what was packed in below it. The boots added another inch to his stature.

Vicky's face lit up. "Don't you clean up nice."

"Well, now, I suppose for an old country boy it'll have to do. It's about as dressy as it gets for me." Nathan glanced up at the clock on the wall behind her. "What's the chance of skipping out a few minutes early?"

Vicky turned toward an archway to a back room. "Sharon, are you ready to take over? My date's here." Then she smiled, winking a brown eye at Nathan. "I sure wouldn't want this one to get away."

Sharon came into view and immediately halted in her tracks. "I should say not. Girl, how is it you're always getting the good ones?" She waved her hands at Vicky, shooing her from behind the counter. "Go, go. Don't be letting such prime beef stand idle, he's liable to take off for better pastures."

"Why, thank you kindly, ma'am," Nathan let loose with his dimpled smile and tipped his non-existent hat. This self looked to be exactly what he needed to get exactly what he was looking for. "Ya'll are much too kind." He turned his attention to his date. "Now, where shall we go? Drinks, dinner, or both?"

Vicky snuggled in tight to his side as he placed a hand to the small of her back. "Let's just go for a drink and see where it leads us."

"As you wish, pretty lady."

The walk to the pub two blocks away took less than ten minutes, and they found they had the place pretty much to themselves, if you didn't count the people she couldn't see but Nathan could. He chose a table nearest the bar and signaled to the bartender who stood behind the mahogany poised to take their order. "What would you like?"

"I think a vodka with a splash of cranberry."

Nathan repeated her choice and added, "What do you have in the way of top shelf whiskey?"

"Jack Daniel's Black Label is about the best you'll do here."

Nathan nodded. "That'll do. A double. Neat."

Though Vicky regaled him with small talk through two drinks, Nathan's concern wandered to the conversation he overheard from two tables away, positioned conveniently behind his date so it appeared he paid her rapt attention. He responded with nods and a verbal "Oh, uh-huh," often enough to avoid detection.

"Look closer. I'm telling you, that there is not a normal guy."

"So what? Let him have his fun."

"Let him have his fun. He looks much too comfy to just be having fun. I'm telling you, he's been in there for a while. I think we should say something."

"Like he'll answer? Even if it is a deadhead in there, he can hardly talk to thin air, it'd freak her the hell out," his friend said with an indicating nod at

Vicky.

"Wouldn't you like a warning about this new gang of watchers or keepers or whatever the hell we're supposed to call them? If they catch up with him, he's a dead man."

"Don't be ridiculous. He's a dead man anyway."

The suggested warning made Nathan's ears perk up. He didn't think if he slid out of the body that Chris would go anywhere. Nathan was pretty sure of that. But chances were he'd sit like a deaf-mute and that wouldn't do either. He drained his glass and tapped it to the tabletop. Excusing himself, he pointed toward the men's room as he walked past the two deadheads.

He didn't waste time on niceties. "I know about the Keepers you two talked about, but who are these watchers?"

"Well, it's nice to meet you, too."

"Name's Nate." Nathan stretched out a hand.

"Jack. That there's Danny."

The image over the two sinks in the men's room of a man talking to himself made Nathan feel a bit foolish. He leaned over to check under the stall door, thinking he should've done that as soon as he entered the room rather than being found babbling to himself after the fact, when the answer came to his ears.

"It's a group of women—" Jack began.

Danny interjected with a poke to Jack's shoulder. "I heard there are some men, too."

"Who cares? The point is, this gang goes around looking for folks like you. If they find anyone messing with live people, doing them harm, well, it's total curtains, baby."

Nathan scowled at the ghostly image before him.

"And what makes you think I'm doing harm? I'm living. That's all I'm doing."

Jack leaned in to peer right into Nathan's eyes, then he backed off an inch or two and took a large sniff. Nathan tried to shove him away, but of course his hand swiped through the air.

A snort of a laugh burst from Jack. "And how long do you 'live' in one of these before it... I don't mean no disrespect, man, but doesn't it go bad after a while?"

"Don't be ridiculous. No, it doesn't 'go bad.' " Nathan found it interesting that Jack, who'd scoffed at the suggestion of a warning, was now the one doing all the talking. He turned his focus on Danny. "But, let me ask you, how did ya'll know? What gives it away?"

Danny hoisted himself up onto the counter between the two sinks. "That was easy. When you move, there's a," he paused for a moment and shrugged with the word he chose, "stutter I guess you'd call it."

"A stutter how?"

"It's like the real guy is a split second behind." Danny's face lit up in a smile. "Hey, can we talk to him? It'd be cool if we could ask him what it's like."

With his concentration on watching his arm move up and down and around in a large swinging circle, it took Nathan a moment to respond. He shook his head. "I don't rightly know, but I don't think he'd respond. After a month or so, maybe longer dependin' on their personalities, they just kind of fade off into the background."

"How do you mean?" Jack asked, joining in again.

"Watch." Nathan stepped out of the body and Chris stood there, staring at his own reflection, with no discernible reaction.

"Ah, that explains the blue blur I noticed when you walked in," Jack stated, pointing to Nathan's denim pants. "I thought you might be naked in there."

"Now why in the name of Jesus would he be naked?" Danny asked, his voice so full of ridicule that Jack threw a punch that breezed right along as if it hadn't connected with anything, though Danny did utter a soft, "Ow, what the hell was that for?"

He couldn't be sure Jack and Danny didn't notice the tilt of his head and slight knit to the brow of the borrowed body, as if the person inside noticed his odd surroundings and wondered how or why he'd gotten to be there. Taking no chances, Nathan easily pushed his way back in and leaned against the stall door. "Could we might get back to the issue here, boys? I do have a date waiting."

"Sorry, man."

Not sure who Jack had responded to, Danny's question or his own, Nathan asked, "This gang goes around looking for offenders. What happens if they find one?"

Danny's hands popped out from his body, fingers splayed. "Poof! They swallow them up."

The news rattled Nathan to the core, his brow creased in concern. He swiped a hand across it, and paced inside the small room. He stopped, leaned against the exit door as if blocking it closed would prevent this new breed of watchers from getting to him, and gazed hard at the two men. "Ya'll ain't pulling my plow, are you?"

"Serious as a barn mouser after a rat," Danny swore, his right hand raised in the air.

"Shit," Nathan said, putting more weight against

the door. The two deadheads remained in place and watched until Nathan stated in a quiet voice, "Well, what does that change? Nothin'."

"Well, I just thought you'd want to know, so you could be a bit more careful. Come on, Jack. My beer's getting warm." Danny waved Jack in the direction of the hallway to the bar proper.

A shivering buzz ran along Nathan's borrowed body as the two walked through him the way any collisions between deadheads would feel. He turned on the cold water and scrubbed his face while contemplating if he should try to contact Zach with the information. Everyone at the compound expressed the opinion that what they did in using bodies for so long might not be accepted practice. They all felt a bit like guilty children dipping a hand into the cookie jar, but none had ever heard it might be some type of capital offense. Deciding to give it more thought later, he returned to the barroom, signaled for another round of drinks, and conjured his brightest smile.

Vicky smoothed the material of a sleeve. "Is everything okay?"

"Just as sweet as can be with such a beautiful lady sittin' across the table." Nathan pointed to her half-full drink. "Ready for another?"

She laid a hand on his as he toyed with his empty glass. A momentary flicker of confusion clouded her expression. "I think this will be sufficient. I sure wouldn't want to be tipsy enough to miss it when you flirt with me and invite me to your room."

The smile on his face broadened. "Now, would a proper country boy do such a thing like proposition a pretty little lady such as yourself?"

Vicky withdrew her hand and placed it over her mouth. Her brows raised and her eyes grew wide with shock, and laughed. "Oh, my…I sure hope so."

Nathan went to the bar, picked up his double shot, downed it in two gulps, laid a one-hundred-dollar bill on the bar under the empty glass and turned to Vicky. He held out a crooked arm and nodded toward the door. "Then what do you say we two-step it right on outta here?"

In his suite, Vicky ran her hands along the naked torso now under Nathan's control. "You feeling okay, Nate?"

He knew the concern exactly and kissed her forehead. "I always seem to run a few degrees cooler than usual. Nothin' to be alarmed about, I promise."

An hour later, watching Vicky sleep nestled into him, Nathan hoped the clumsiness he'd felt hadn't translated to her. The last question he wanted to hear was why he hadn't appeared to enjoy himself. Because, even after lying awake through the night he had no answer. It certainly couldn't be the three double shots of whiskey, he'd consumed more than that before and still functioned. The sense of it escaped him as easily as piglets in a sty.

With moonlight streaming through the windows, he shook her awake so she could slip out of the hotel before the morning staff began to arrive. "It's four, darlin'."

She rolled to her back and stretched. "Thanks."

"A gentleman, particularly a Southern gentleman, keeps his promise." Even though she'd whispered, "go back to sleep," Nathan watched as she rolled out of bed, dressed, and threw a kiss as the door to the suite's bedroom closed behind her. After so many selves, as fleeting thoughts of the bartender crept into the mix, he struggled to understand what was different this time. He tucked his hand behind his head and stared out the window to the cityscape until sleep overtook his brain.

Chapter 10

Jenna walked along the dark, empty streets of Dayton without purpose. Her stride and the heaviness of her footsteps caused nearby deadheads to clear a path around her. Since arriving home from the wedding she and Marvin argued a large part of the time. The more he pushed, the more she pushed back. Maybe he was right; maybe she did take her new position with the World Council of Keepers too seriously. She had never considered any job as inconsequential. Not the paying one with the law firm and not the volunteer one with the women's shelter.

The walk, meant to calm her, did nothing to accomplish the goal. The farther she went, the more aggravated she became, the darker her mood. Overseeing a vast network of deadheads who looked after the living victims of abuse could be time-consuming and overwhelming. She just did not have time for Marvin's interferences and constant complaints. No, not complaints. She may as well call it like it was, whining. Tedious whining.

Jenna rounded the corner and noticed a couple standing in the road ahead, arguing. With anger in his muffled words, the man grabbed the woman's arm and yanked her into an alley between two stores. Jenna quickened her pace, stopped at the entrance, and peered into the shadows.

"You'll do it if I tell you to."

"I said I'd earn my keep, but I ain't doing that no more."

The guy took a fast glance toward each end of the alley and a sudden backhand landed high across her cheekbone. "Keep your voice down."

"Screw you, asshole." The woman lunged away from a swinging fist and headed toward Jenna.

"You come back here. Kate." His voice turned apologetic. "Come on, wait up."

"What?" Kate halted and turned.

He grabbed her wrist, and pulled it tight behind her back. "You owe me money and if I tell you to get in a car you'll do it."

The woman looked familiar. Now that the man used her name Jenna was positive. A huff of air escaped her lungs. "I don't believe this. What, the last guy wasn't bad enough? A busted arm didn't convince you, his waving a gun around in a drunken stupor didn't wake you up?" Why would this woman, one Jenna almost killed for, take up with yet another man like the one she'd barely escaped from with her life. Granted, three weeks later in that inebriated state, the idiot shot himself in the head and died right in front of Jason, who gobbled him up and shoved him into a darkness he'd never escape. A long sigh broke from Jenna's throat. "Now you take up with one pimping you out?"

"Bullshit, Robbie. I'm not a whore for nobody. I don't like it." Kate struggled against the restraint but got nowhere. "Now let go of me."

"You listen to me, bitch—"

The word developed into a high-pitched scream as Jenna, taking a page out of one of her lieutenant's books, strode to the man, shoved a fist around his privates and squeezed. He released his victim and grabbed at his groin.

Kate placed a hand on Robbie's arm. "What? What's wrong?"

"I don't know, I don't know. Jesus Christ! Get away from me." He shook her hand away as he pawed at his genitals. "What the fuck?"

Jenna tightened her grip and he let out a yell. She turned to Kate with a scowl. "Would you wake the hell up and leave? Go!" Kate stood motionless. "It looks like we'll have to do this the hard way." Jenna clamped down hard one more time, eliciting another curdling holler from Robbie, released him, then slid in and took control of Kate's body.

Through swift sucking of breath between his teeth, he growled, "Where the fuck do you think you're going?"

"You told her to get away from you. That's exactly what she's doing," Jenna replied with Kate's altered voice, and sprinted away.

No buses ran that late at night. The walk to the shelter took more than an hour, taking her farther away from home. Using Kate's fist, Jenna pounded until a light inside cast through the small window at the top of the locked door. "Help. I need help. Please let me in."

The deadbolt turned, and the sound of a secondary lock reached her ears before the door cracked open enough for Jenna to stick fingers through. "Please. You have to let me in." Though Robbie hadn't followed, she swiveled a frightened gaze left to right in hopes the sentry inside gave in. "Please. He's after me. He'll kill me if he finds me."

The door flew open and Jenna stumbled into a small lobby. The woman who let her in slammed the entrance closed and threw the locks into place before turning to help Jenna to a chair beside a tiny laminate reception desk. "Are you all right? Are you bleeding anywhere?"

"No, just…mostly shaken up." Jenna rubbed softly at the injured wrist and moved up the arm with short, gentle squeezes. "And a wrenched arm."

"Let me get you something to drink." Her slippers scuffed along as she disappeared down a narrow hallway of splotched commercial tile that reminded Jenna of several childhood foster homes. Designers intended it to be a warm, homey feel that never quite worked in her opinion. A moment later cold bottled tea pushed into Jenna's hand before the woman sat at the office chair, pulled out forms and a pen, and slid them across the desktop. "We're full, but I think we can put you up for tonight. You'll have to sleep on the couch in the day room. That all right?"

A tiny sound of relief, then, "Yes."

"Fill out the paperwork. We'll call around in the morning for any openings." The woman yawned and ran a forearm across her mouth. "What's your name, sweetie?"

"Katherine. Kate." The pen moved from line to line.

Middle-aged eyes peered at her, then dyed blonde hair bobbed as she nodded. "I thought I recognized you. You've been here before. Same man?"

A pause to contemplate an answer on the paperwork, then, "No."

"Well, that's something at least."

Jenna slipped free. Kate shook her head as if she couldn't believe what her brain registered. The older woman led Kate down the hall, and Jenna went through the door and headed for home. Her thoughts returned to the troubles with Marvin and she shook her head. "Marital bliss. My God, what would it have been like if we weren't dead and able to escape through a wall?" She wished once again for the counsel of her old friend Colleen, the one who'd tumbled down the condo stairs with her. They landed at the bottom in a tangle of limbs to the death of them both.

Jenna had to admit that sometimes this position of power took its toll. Looking after the safety of others grew wearisome, but saving lives made it worth her effort. Marvin would have to accept it or there would be a lot more arguments to come. If he didn't, well…as they liked to tease one another with the circumstances of their deaths, he could go step in front of a bus. Only she wouldn't be joking.

Chapter 11

After his night with Vicky, Nathan woke mid-morning, showered and dressed in jeans and the shirt he wore the previous evening. As he'd promised himself, he walked to the art gallery found during his cell-phone internet search on the way into the city. On the short hike the few deadheads he passed gave him no more than a typical glance; only enough to avoid walking through a live person. Perhaps it helped to have put thought into each, slightly slower than normal, deliberate movement of limb or turn of head, to ensure complete synchronization.

Satisfied with the progress on that score and bored with the exhibit, at 2:00 pm he went back to the pub to grab some lunch. Maybe he'd run into the guys from the night before and pump them for more information. Pushing through the door, he stopped until his sight adjusted to the dimness of the room and then made his way to the bar.

The bartender greeted him, scanning Nathan from head to toe and back to his midsection where his gaze stayed locked, a sly smile on his lips. "Afternoon. What can I do for you?"

The innuendo wasn't lost on Nathan. His temperature rose, and a hot blush invaded his cheeks. He lowered his gaze even as he returned the smile, a sensation Nathan hadn't experienced since he'd been fourteen-years old and the prettiest girl in town brushed against him. Three years older and obviously amused by his condition, she remarked, "Nathaniel Ray Crockett, I do believe you like what you see," and let loose with a teasing laugh.

Nathan sat on a stool and ordered a bottle of beer and burger.

He took his drink to a table, though—for reasons he didn't understand—he couldn't take his eyes off the bartender. Now, part of him hoped Danny and Jack wouldn't show up so he could continue with the introspection of the struggle apparently happening with this new self. He'd been in possession of it for close to three months yet, unlike previous identities, something kept bubbling to the surface. He imagined it akin to watching oil in the cook's pots boil up and consume the battered chicken she'd delicately lowered in; the pieces pushed their way upward in a fight to the top while his eight-year old stomach rumbled with hunger, eager to be filled.

The strange attraction to men, and the foreign changes in speech patterns which left more and more of his southern roots behind, concerned Nathan. Not from a guilt standpoint, or was it? Regardless, the struggle to continue his experience of life might be leaving space in the handcuffs, enough for the man inside to keep wriggling out.

Yet, Nathan wanted the two to show up again in the bar so he could learn more about this new breed of Keepers, these Watchers as Danny and Jack had called them.

News traveled through the dead world. Even to remote places like his compound, where things of

61

interest learned during trips for supplies would be brought back and shared over drinks or dinner. So, he'd heard something of them, just as he heard about the big wedding which recently took place in the Caribbean; the wedding of the millennium it had been called, or something like that. In fact, it had been rumored the bride headed up this new sect. Of course, he'd been too occupied with a deteriorating body to give those things much consideration at the time.

Nathan turned his attention to several deadheads enjoying drinks together. They sounded happy, content. But he knew he never would be satisfied on that plane of existence.

The moment he'd thought of approaching them to see if they might be able to "shine a light on the stash from the still," as his Pa used to say while searching for a lost item, three deadheads burst through the wall of the building, their stature growing enormous; a woman slightly in front of her female and lone male companions.

The leader spoke in a loud, stern voice as her glowering countenance hovered over the customers. "We've heard about you. We know you've broken the rules of the dead by interfering with the living. This will not be tolerated and your punishment is absolute."

The group seated at the table backed away, the chairs screeching across the tiled floor. The fear written on their faces didn't keep them from defending themselves. "What are you talking about? We been sitting here minding our own business. We haven't broken any rules."

"We'll decide if rules have been broken," the male of the group pushed a finger into his own puffed-out chest.

"What exactly is it you think we've done?"

"You've inhabited the living," their leader stated. "This is unacceptable. Only members of our sect have been given permission to—"

"We ain't done no such thing."

"Do you believe the balls on this guy? Do you know who you're mouthing off to?"

A flurry of accusations and denials clouded the air. The argument grew focused and more intense. Confusion and chaos erupted among the two groups. Nathan took a risk and slipped free. He ran through the closest wall, and found himself standing chest high among cases of beer and soda. A tiny crack in the boards separating the storeroom from the main bar provided a means of watching the fracas unfold. In the end, it took less than fifteen seconds for the three intruders to engulf the other deadheads. Only the sound of clinking glass drifted through the room, as the barkeep restocked clean mugs on the shelf of a clear-fronted refrigerator, not able to see the bottles now littering the table and floor.

The male walked over to peer down at the body Nathan had jumped from. Like some type of automatronic movement, the body that was Chris lifted the drink to his lips, took a long drought of the beverage, and lowered it back to the table never once taking notice of the towering ghost beside him. The study went on for such a long time, Nathan feared his new self would begin to regain awareness.

Nathan reflected on his experience thus far: Most larger cities teemed with deadheads. Dead folks should be haunting damn near every nook and cranny of this one. The low numbers he'd seen over the past two days surprised him, right up until moments ago. That was all the light on the still he required. He needed to get out of this city as soon as possible.

A sigh of relief escaped Nathan's throat when the three intruders shrank down to normal size and departed. He slipped back into Chris' body and headed toward the door.

"Hey! What about your burger?"

"You eat it," Nathan shot the remark over his shoulder.

The man hollered as the door began to close on Nathan's retreating backside. "What about paying for the beer?"

"Shit. Sorry." Nathan scurried over, pulling cash from his wallet. He slapped it down on the bar, turned and ran. He didn't care if other deadheads could see a delay in the motion or not.

He would've left Chris sitting there, but he needed to check out of the hotel. Otherwise his trust accounts would take quite a hit until he figured out how to stop the charges from racking up. Plus, he couldn't very well get in the truck and drive it away without a body. No, the only open option was to check out and drive out of town. Fast.

Breathing hard, he approached the front desk of the hotel and presented his room key. "I need to checkout. And quickly, please."

"Yes, sir. I hope there isn't anything too serious that has shortened your stay with us," the clerk stated.

"Some sudden business I need to attend to on a very tight deadline, I'm afraid." Nathan's hands shook as he pulled a credit card from his wallet and slid it across the desk. Keeping a watch on the lobby as best he could, yet still remain aware of the transaction, he wondered if he should leave a short note for Vicky. He decided he didn't have time for regrets over what turned out to be an unsatisfying one-night stand, though he did allow for a twinge of remorse at having to leave the Grateful Dead T-shirt behind; his private joke, or what he'd thought of as private until moments ago. It wasn't only his own well-being he needed to be concerned about: the fate of the entire clan could be at stake if things went downhill.

The toe of his boot tapped reflexively against the floor. The hotel desk clerk slid the bill over for a signature. Nathan scratched his name across the line, dropped the pen, gave a quick tip of his non-existent hat with a curt "Thank you, ma'am," and headed for his truck.

Chapter 12

Nathan didn't bother about travel direction. Planting his foot to the floorboard, the truck gained speed to enter the freeway on the first ramp that caught his attention. He drove for almost half an hour with constant checks of the surroundings, no matter how quick things blurred into the past through the windows, before his heart rate slowed to normal.

He found himself oddly hoping Vicky wouldn't be upset over his quick departure. Granted, the relationship hadn't blossomed as he'd wished, but something in his gut told him the explanation lay buried, deep within the psyche of his host. The strangeness of the summer gave him pause, but then again, maybe Vicky just wasn't his type.

Recovering from the short reverie, he realized he'd been traveling on the beltway around the outskirts of the city. He noticed an increase in the number of deadheads hitching rides when he caught sight of an overhead sign announcing Exit 43B to Dayton. He flipped the turn indicator, merged, and headed north. Granted, it took him farther into cold weather, but escaping it had never been the point of his winter excursions. If it had, he would've gone south like he'd done in one of his earlier incarnations. It seemed snow-birding didn't cease simply because one had died. No, Nathan wanted the things he missed during summers with the clan; movies, concerts, plays, books, art galleries, and museums.

An hour later, as he passed the interchange with Route 35, the dryness of his mouth and the deep hole in his empty stomach reminded him he left his lunch to the barkeep in his rush to find safer ground. He pulled to the shoulder to search Google Maps with his phone for a place he might quench both. Near Sinclair College several establishments popped up. One described as a sleek cocktail bar serving gourmet bites, and a bit up from that a wine gallery. Both piqued his interest. Another spot caught his attention, but on the west side of the river dividing the populace: the Dayton Art Institute. He panned the map and discovered the Air Force Museum, a place he'd vowed to visit one day, to the northeast of the city just south of Wright-Patterson Air Force Base. He shrugged.

It may have been only a bit more than an hour's drive north of the danger he just left, but with the current rush of activity by the living and dead it seemed far enough. At least for the time being.

He dropped the phone on the seat, stuck a fresh toothpick in his mouth, and eased back into traffic. After taking the nearest exit, multiple signs crept into his awareness as he drove along city streets in a search of the restaurant he'd decided on. He passed a library, several small art galleries, two theatres, and a museum, all only blocks from one another in what seemed to be a one- to two-mile area.

He shifted the toothpick and gave a smile and tipped his 'hat' to a woman moving along the sidewalk at a leisurely pace. He pulled to the curb, put the gear into park, and rolled down the passenger window.

"Excuse me, ma'am. Could ya'll point me in the right direction. I seem to be a bit lost."

She turned toward him as he got out of the truck, brushed a lock of dark shoulder length hair aside, and looked slowly from his boots to his head. "Oh, honey, allow me to save you."

"I'd be rightly appreciative."

"What can I help you with?" she asked. Then added in a soft voice Nathan barely heard, "Oh, let me count the ways."

Nathan pointed to the West Virginia license plate on the back of the truck and turned to face her again, ensuring his dimples blazed. He pushed the southern charm. "As you might could tell, I'm not from around here. I'm a bit parched, and I feel the need to fill the tank some, too," he said, patting his stomach. "You think you could suggest something?"

"Oh, have I got suggestions." She lifted one manicured hand to the turtleneck collar of her white sweater. An adjacent store window reflected light of late afternoon sun and glinted off glittery-red nail polish. Gold bangle bracelets clattered as she held out the other hand. "I'm Stacey. And," she continued, her eyes' focus lowering for a millisecond, "besides built, you are?"

His cheeks burned hot with embarrassment, much as they'd done the first time Sarah had commented on this new self of his. Nathan took her hand and a tiny waft of wind brought an enticing fragrance of perfume to his nostrils. "Nathaniel Ray Crockett, ma'am; Nathan. Though some folks call me Nate."

"Modest beyond reason." Stacey smiled, her lips parting to reveal teeth whiter than the sweater. "And polite, too. Well, Nate, it is certainly a pleasure to be stopped by the likes of you."

Nathan smiled, going for full-on country charm. "Why, thank you, ma'am. Now, if it's not too bold of me to ask, it'd be a true pleasure if you'd allow a stranger to buy you dinner. I always prefer company when I dine. It makes everything taste better, and so much more enjoyable."

She withdrew her hand from his. "You country boys sure know how to turn a girl's head, don't you?"

"We like to try, yes, ma'am." Nathan gave her a wink.

"If you'll close and lock the door to your truck, I believe there's a quiet place right around the corner," Stacey said, pointing. She followed him and waited on the sidewalk next to the truck, then held out her arm to be hooked through his as he approached. "It's nothing fancy, but…"

"As long the food's tolerable and the drink is fit to wash it down, I believe it'll do just fine." He stood between her and the road, as a gentleman should, and tucked her arm around his. A hint of cologne registered in his mind and he brushed it off as perhaps residual of his own still on the shirt he wore. Hoping for a better outcome than he'd experienced with Vicky he said, "I'll follow your lead, wherever it takes us."

Seated on a vinyl-clad bench across the Formica-topped table along the far wall away from the window, her voice low with a lusty timbre, she laughed at all his jokes and demurred in all the right places. The meal of an overcooked pasta dish with little flavor at least filled the cavern for him and took his mind off his stomach. The second bottle of dry white wine of some nondistinct label and questionable vintage took his mind off anything but his growing anticipation. When one of her shoeless feet found its way up between his thighs and lingered there, the toes making tiny circles, his excitement mounted. And, apparent to him, his fears of another failure were unfounded.

He signaled the waitress for the check and reached for his wallet. "Now, I wonder if you could top off such a wonderful time by telling me where I might find a decent place to lay my head tonight."

"Well, if you wouldn't think it…distasteful, or think less of me—" Stacey removed her foot from his lap.

"Now, why would I think that?" Nathan tried his best to shield the adjustment before he stood to help her from her seat. Perhaps the issues he'd experienced with Vicky were off base. Way off base.

Stacey winked and placed a hand to her throat. "Well, a lady has to be sure, uphold a proper reputation. But, if you're, well, willing, I can think of no more decent a place than mine."

"I put myself into your proper and capable hands." Nathan said as he handed cash to the waitress, who accepted it and, with an odd smirk, nodded to Stacey.

"And they are extremely capable, I promise you." She nudged her forearm against him as he helped her from the bench seat.

"Maintain your grip, little darlin', and I'll believe my safety to be well guaranteed." He gestured toward the exit. "Ma'am?"

Nathan followed her out the door fairly hypnotized; she the charmer, he the coiled snake rising and swaying side to side in rhythm to the hips beneath her coat. In the truck, Stacey cuddled in as close as possible and wasted no time in showing Nathan just how capable her hands could be. It made concentration on driving difficult, but he managed to follow directions to her apartment, which included a bit of finger pointing, without any mishap.

In her darkened apartment, Stacey took his hand and led him to the bedroom. She undressed him, pushed him down onto the bed, and with slow, steady skill drove Nathan's senses to the point of not caring when he made the eventual, unavoidable discovery.

Chapter 13

A new and different experience, though not expected, Nathan couldn't say he didn't find it satisfying. Or pleasurable. Which may explain the so-far inexplicable. Not that there was anything wrong with it. He'd changed with the times, adjusted easily, especially when it came to people having more freedom in the area of sex without the harsh judgment that used to accompany such behavior.

Waking with the dim streetlamp light filtering through the curtains, Nathan located his jeans on the floor next to the bed. He retrieved his cell phone and crept out to the living room of the small apartment, thinking to look through Chris' Facebook page to confirm the suspicion. Before completing the search field, it occurred to Nathan: why not get the knowledge the same way he'd found Chris' address when first deciding on him; burrow around some in his brain.

It sure clarified a lot. It became obvious that part of the psyche couldn't be controlled, or pushed into a new direction. Nathan was okay with the realization. He just knew it wasn't right for him, not a constant diet of it anyway; though the occasional tryst might be welcome. The time to find yet another new, more consistently compatible self was in order. He'd have to let Chris go. But not before another good meal and securing a safe place to stash the truck while he looked. He intended to take an appropriate spell of time to get it right.

He crept through the bedroom to the small bathroom. After a fast shower, he dressed, and then shook Stacey awake. After all, Nathan didn't want to leave two people wondering what had gone wrong; he had been raised a proper gentleman with proper manners, not to be rude or unkind. "Sorry to wake you, but I do have to leave, now. I surely thank you for your hospitality."

Stacey never opened her eyes. "Mmm. You're welcome. Maybe I'll see you around again."

Nathan glanced at a row of large posters adorning the bedroom wall above a shelf containing a variety of wigs. "Mmm, not likely, but I guess you never know."

"Whatever," Stacey mumbled and rolled, wrapping the blankets around his body to stave off the chill air. The wig, which had disengaged during the height of the encounter, tumbled off the side of the bed.

Nathan let himself out and drove the city streets as a means of exploration. A couple hours later, dim shades of gray relinquished themselves as sunlight infused full color onto the palette of the world. On the west side of the river and south of where he'd spent the night, he noticed a string of people outside a delicatessen. With his stomach again rumbling requests, he pulled into the only parking space available around the corner. He paused to peer through the front window as he sought out the end of the line, and noticed one waitress dashing around taking orders, dropping menus, clearing dishes, doing her best to keep up with the crowds. He also saw plenty of deadheads pilfering; more coffee than anything else, but still…it told him all he needed to know. The food would be stellar.

At the back of the procession, Nathan engaged in conversation and did his best to avoid eye contact with any of the numerous transparent beings who passed by. "It sure looks to be the place for breakfast," he said to a woman who moved in behind him, and gestured to the twelve or so in front.

"It is. Don't worry about the line, though. I don't know how she does it, but Tina gets them in and out pretty fast."

Leaning forward to watch through the window, Nathan could've told her. Two men she wouldn't have been able to see, one with long, wild blond hair and the other with short, dark hair, hustled about keeping fresh coffee brewing and cleared dishes from the bus tub at the wait station. Anything they picked up winked out of sight of the living. If any of the live folks noticed, they gave no indication. What's more, as long as cups stayed full and food arrived hot, they probably didn't care.

Indeed, in less than thirty minutes Nathan found himself seated. The aroma of frying bacon and grilling sausage permeated the air of the packed diner. The clatter of dishes and flatware scraping plates, and loud conversations brought a smile to his face. A tad guilty about occupying a table for two, he motioned to the woman who stood behind him during the wait. "Ma'am? Care to come on over and sit a spell. I promise I don't bite."

She returned his smile, shifted her weight to the opposite foot, and checked her watch. "Thanks, I'm just here to grab a coffee and bagel." She turned her attention to the bakery case and a moment later moved to the counter to place her order.

A menu dropped in front of him, and a female

voice asked, "Coffee?" He responded in the affirmative. She filled the cup in front of him and swiveled on her feet as she said, "Be right back to take your order," and scurried off to other customers.

Moments later, "What can I get for you?"

Nathan glanced at the name tag over her left breast. *TINA* in bold print and under that in smaller lettering, *I'll be your server today*, she stood poised with pad and pen in hand. "Yes, ma'am. I believe I'll try the corned beef hash, two eggs, scrambled, and some wheat toast. And a side of that bacon I smell?"

Tina scribbled the order and said, "You got it," without once actually looking at him.

Nathan's "Thank you kindly, ma'am," received a grin before she spun away.

He'd been right. A superb meal; the corned beef not too salty, the bacon crisp but not burned, the eggs scrambled to perfection in butter just like his Big Mama did when the cook took ill. After a deep breath, he let loose with a satisfied sigh. He leaned back to enjoy the coffee and realized a calm sanity had been restored; a few tables now sat empty. The two men who helped the waitress poured themselves coffee, filled a plate with four bagels, and joined a young couple already seated in a booth along the window.

Nathan turned his attention to them, hoping to learn something more about this new sect of Keepers or Watchers or whatever they called themselves, though he shifted his gaze out the window to avoid seeming as if he could actually see and hear them.

"Hey, where's the *schmear*? You know I can't have a bagel without cream cheese."

"Oh, for cryin' out loud, Brody." The man with the

dark hair rose, went behind the counter, and returned with a small metal container but stopped short of taking his seat. "Tommy, what are you staring at?"

"That guy over there," the guy with the wild blond hair replied, pointing at Nathan.

"Well stop it, it's not polite," the woman said, accepting the bowl and passing it down with, "here, Marvin, are you happy now?"

Her partner, Marvin or Brody, Nathan couldn't be sure which name the man used, leaned forward to see who Tommy indicated. "Eh, what difference does it make? It's not like the guy knows he's being watched."

"Dudes, I'm telling you, there's somebody in there." Tommy expressed his curiosity by peering toward Nathan.

"All the more reason. Now stop it," the woman chided.

"Why would someone want to do that? Sheesh, it gave me the creeps and I didn't even do it on purpose." The man shivered in dramatic fashion.

"A lot of us do it for amusement. Making the living do weird things can be quite entertaining sometimes. As long as we don't hurt them, or do any permanent damage, I don't see the harm in it." The woman lifted her bagel to take a bite, and stopped to look at it. "Maybe he just wants to experience real taste again."

Nathan allowed a smile at that remark.

Tommy looked across the table and started to laugh. "Oh, man, Marvin, I remember when that happened. It was hysterical, dude. Very entertaining. You looked like some nerdy guy at a nightclub trying to dance. You were all," his arms flailed around, bumping through the guy next to him, and his laughter turned to giggles.

"Okay, okay, hippie, we get the point," Marvin snarled, and slathered cream cheese across one half of his bagel.

"Oh, lighten up, Marv. Is it his fault if it strikes him funny?" his female companion asked.

"Yeah, Brody," the man next to Tommy agreed. "You've been surly all morning."

"It'll strike him funny all right." Marvin shook a balled-up fist in the air.

"Oh, does someone need a hug? Do you need your Uncle Tommy to give you a hug this morning?" Still laughing, he rose to push his way through the table.

Marvin laughed. "Hey, you can both eat my shorts."

"Marvin, is that any way to talk?" the woman asked, shoulder length auburn hair glistening as it shifted with the sudden turn of her head.

The man next to Tommy lifted his coffee cup toward her. "He missed the Harvard class on manners, Jenna."

"I keep trying remedial lessons. They don't seem to stick, Mike," she replied.

Tommy still stood with the table surrounding his translucent body, turned toward Nathan and started walking.

"Where're you going?" Mike asked.

"Over there to talk to him," Tommy said. "I want to ask him something." He sat in a chair directly opposite Nathan and smiled. "How's it going, dude?"

Careful not to make eye contact, or provide any indication he saw or heard anything beyond the living norm, Nathan took a sip of his coffee and turned to watch Tina sort through her morning order tickets. He even made it a point to stare directly past Tommy as if he wasn't visible at all.

"Hello?" Tommy waved a hand in front of Nathan's face.

A loud crash erupted as silverware clattered to the floor amongst the shattering of plates and glasses, and Nathan flinched.

"Oh, come on, dude, I know you're in there." Tommy waited another moment, then made his way back to the group. "Huh, guess he's not the social type, but there is definitely someone in that guy."

"Or maybe you're just imagining things, hippie," Marvin taunted.

"No, I swear, dudes. I saw a blur when Tina dropped the bus tub. Watch when he moves. You can see the hesitation. The real thing is just a tad behind."

"I think you're a tad behind." Marvin took another bite of the bagel he held in one hand.

Moving with deliberate purpose, Nathan pulled his wallet out, peeled off a twenty and a ten, dropped them on the table, and walked out. After the skirmish in Cincinnati, it wouldn't be good to have anyone, particularly a dead anyone, recognize him after he slipped out of Chris. That was a risk he couldn't take.

Chapter 14

Upon quick consultation of Google Maps, Nathan decided the best place to shed this body and stash the truck for safekeeping would be a small park between some railroad tracks and what was labeled as the Mad River. Fairly close by, it would make walking an easy chore. Not that walking around caused the dead to tire. Well, not that he was aware of in his limited experience of negotiating the realm of the deceased outside of a host body.

He drove across the nearest bridge, made his way to the park, and pulled the nose of the truck as far into shrubbery as possible. It wouldn't be the first time he'd left the vehicle like this, but it still caused jitters. His previous switches had all been done near enough to West Virginia where folks didn't worry about an old pick-up truck left at the side of the road. Heck, one could sit and rust completely away in some parts of the county, weeds and bramble overtaking the whole entire thing. What if someone here called it in as abandoned? He'd be stuck trying to sneak the damn thing out of an impound lot in the dead of night. Well, he couldn't think of an alternative.

Near the riverbank, yet hidden from any possible boaters and the open park, he retrieved wallet, keys, and cell phone from the various pockets he'd stashed them in, and stuffed them into his jeans. He slipped out of

Chris' body and gave a wide berth to the truck as he retraced his steps back into the city.

Chapter 15

After spending several days testing the lay of the land near the Wright-Patterson Air Force Base, where he figured his best chances might be for a new self, he stopped at a small bar outside the main gate. With the bartender otherwise engaged, Nathan poured himself a mug of beer from the tap. He perched on a stool nursing the drink, watching the local news on a muted television. Two uniformed Airmen from the base tossed darts at a well-worn board, a foursome hovered around a pool table, and two more argued over the rules of the shuffleboard game along the far wall.

Nathan sat alone; not another dearly departed soul inhabited the entire place.

The beer tasted okay to him, but it didn't have the vibrancy he craved. It lacked intensity on the tongue without a live body. A sigh built in his chest and cut short when the news anchor shared the screen with a photo of Chris. The image swapped to a film clip of the man wandering aimlessly, courtesy of a Mindy Dawson according to the text on the screen, with a vacant stare in his eyes. Nathan scoured the bar top, located the remote stashed next to the register, reached over and turned the sound on. The news feed cut back to the studio and the anchorman.

"The man emerged from Eastwood Park asking people who and where he was. When police questioned him, he had no form of identification, and no recollection of how he'd gotten there or where he belonged. If you have any knowledge of this man's identity, you're asked to please call the number for Missing and Exploited Persons, listed on your screen."

The bartender looked around the room with a confused expression, and muted the set. "No messing with the TV, guys. If you want the sound on, ask." No one responded. Ignoring the No Smoking sign, he went back to his cigarette, and sipped from his own bottle of brew.

The report continued as a street reporter stood outside a medical center interviewing Dr. Haj Hassan, or so said the printed information below his image. Nathan thought he picked out the word "fine" from the doctor's lips that accompanied a nodding head.

"Well, at least I know he's okay," Nathan mumbled, "but thank God he doesn't remember anything." He shrugged, swigged the last of his beer, and put down the empty mug. The barman stared, mouth agape, and then shook himself as if trying to wake up. "Sorry," Nathan said, more out of habit because the man couldn't hear him anyway, and faded through the front door to continue his search.

After a fast check on the truck, Nathan took his time and wandered to many different corners of the city over the next week, determined to get this one right. But sitting at the bar in Mr. C's restaurant, rumored to be a popular steakhouse due to the food and top-shelf liquor they stocked, he decided to forego any meal until it could be savored via a breathing, tasting person.

Though meals of squirrel, rabbit, wild hog, and the occasional duck or goose served up at the compound at home were supplemented by steaks (sometimes purchased along with the necessary dry goods) nothing compared to a top-notch chef creating magic. From the aroma wafting from the kitchen, this place firmly hit the top ten on Nathan's list of places to try.

The second segment of the noon news telecast opened with a wide shot of the anchor and Stacey in make-up, a wig coiffed to perfection. "In a follow-up to one of last week's stories on the plight of an apparent amnesia patient, we have an exclusive interview with Stacey Grimes." The anchorwoman swiveled her chair. "You say you met this man several days ago and he introduced himself with the name Nathaniel?"

"Oh, yes. Nathaniel Ray Crockett. Nathan. He said some folks call him Nate."

"Oh, shit!" Nathan choked on a sip of beer, and looked around to see if anyone noticed the reaction.

"And he seemed perfectly fine at the time?"

"My, yes. Isn't it just awful, him found wandering around like that? I can't imagine what might've happened. He was so kind, so polite—called me ma'am and everything. He took me to dinner and then we…" Stacey visibly blushed with a demure expression, and changed tracks mid-station. "Well, that would be a bit TMI, wouldn't it?"

The newswoman didn't skip a beat. "Can you supply any other information about him. Did he tell you where he was from?"

"No, not that I can remember. Only, he spoke with a bit of an accent."

"Foreign?" the newswoman interjected.

"No, no. Southern."

The camera changed view to zoom in on the news

anchor. "Anyone having additional information that might assist Mr. Crockett should call the number at the bottom of the screen." She turned and the camera shot widened to include her guest. "Stacey, thank you for your help. I know his friends and relatives will be relieved."

"Oh, I sure hope so. You're very welcome."

The report made Nathan consider upping the ante on the timeline, but also gave him pause. It brought a situation to light Nathan had never considered. His name was out there and connected to someone. How soon could he introduce an entirely different face with the same name? Maybe he needed to lie low for another few days. It didn't mean he couldn't look, and perhaps even decide on someone. The other issue that sprang to mind: the truck plates could be traced to that name. As he considered how to handle the situation, like remove the plates and bury them under a rock or next to a tree, familiar-sounding voices behind him jumped into a conversation.

"Did you see that?" Tommy asked.

Mike followed a finger pointing to the television. "See what?"

"The guy on that report?"

"What about it?"

"Dude, that was the guy in Epstein's. I'm sure of it," Tommy insisted.

"So?"

"Come on, Mike, that means the deadhead is somewhere out in the city."

"Good for him. Now, finish your soda so we can—"

"But, that means he was in there a long time.

That's more than messing with people. You think we should tell Jenna, or maybe Nancy?" Tommy's voice carried a serious tone.

Nathan considered asking what this Tommy meant about the two women, but fear of possible discovery kept him from turning around. The southern dialect may have diminished while he inhabited Chris, but in phantom form it bellowed like a cow giving birth. Maybe that wouldn't be enough to arouse suspicion, but if they tried to ask for a name, well, sir, that could be a might tricky. Maybe he could use Zakariah's name. But maybe…

"I think we should get to the theater before we miss the beginning of the movie."

"Aw, Marvin, you do look out for your Uncle Tommy, don't you. I think someone deserves a hug for that."

"I'll give you a hug, hippie." Marvin said in mock threat.

Thankfully, the voices receded and saved Nathan any further immediate angst.

Chapter 16

Jenna escaped the tedium of Marvin's attitude, and spent the bulk of the day following her need to rescue victims of violence. Not more than two miles from Epstein's, right after leaving the "boys," as she liked to refer to them, a young girl struggled to keep from being pushed into a van.

She slid into the teen, pulled the knapsack from the girl's back and swung in a roundhouse. It knocked her assailant off balance and she ran. Several blocks away, she slowed to a walk, digging into the girl's memory to figure out where she belonged. Not home. She'd left there months ago. She lived in an encampment under the bridge, next to Eastwood Park, with a contingent of homeless youths. Jenna contemplated taking her back to her parents, but knew that rarely worked. The majority of children simply returned to the streets.

The increase in domestic violence stunned her. How much of an impact did the poor economy play into the situation? Couples, young and middle-aged trapped, mired in mountains of debt, barely holding on; older ones falling into the too old to hire, too young to retire gap; the elderly who rose to the dead plane from a suicide pact saying, "We wanted to leave the children something besides a pile of debt."

Her mind turned to the youngest of victims, the children too young to be left to their own devices, to fight for a place of survival in the world. The weight of it made her ache, like struggling to get from under the whole of Mt. Everest. They were the toughest to deal with; where to take them, what to do with them. Certainly not to any Child Protective Services, where they'd end up in foster care. That was a life she knew all too well. Not that all foster families treated their charges like personal servants. But her own experience turned her against that option.

Finding no signs of drugs in the young girl, Jenna walked to the encampment, sat on a rock at the water's edge, and slipped out. She watched the girl for a while, her mind seeking a way to help these children who ran from abuse, molestation, and neglect, or all three. Kids who listened to their parents argue and fret, because one less mouth to feed might be of help, kids who thought the streets their only refuge.

Jenna's ears picked up on piercing screams of pain and fright. They were close. Where? Anger pushed her stature above the trees as she scoured her surroundings. She moved to the south end of the park. The sounds emanated from an interior glade hidden in the trees, the one she knew Jason had used to regain his strength after a particularly difficult take.

A gaggle of teenagers surrounded a young man. His face bloodied, pants torn to reveal scraped knees, jacket covered in dirt and leaves, his chest heaved to breathe. He managed to get up and, wearily but steadily, turning in a tight circle, faced his attackers.

"Come on, faggot. Show us what you got."

"Yeah, come on, cocksucker."

"What do you want from me?" Tears spilled down his face.

"We're gonna teach you a lesson. We don't like queers in our park."

"I didn't—"

Three of the gang lunged at him. They shoved him in a sadistic round robin. He hit the ground face first, and the cartilage in his nose crunched. Two grabbed his pants and yanked them down to his ankles. The young man tried to stand and stumbled to the ground. Kicks to his torso and groin landed, and landed again as hateful epithets of disgust flew about the clearing. Chants of encouragement and suggestions of torture from the surrounding tormentors increased.

For the first time in her dead life Jenna stood helpless. Her mind whirled until she gave up on a plan and dove into the fracas. Her punches swung through the attackers. She needed to slow them, check them. An "oof" expelled from one of the boys, and she spread a grim, determined smile across her lips. Her kicks landed in groins, fists grabbed at them and squeezed. Their screams of pain increased her determination. When those three scrambled out of her reach and ran for the parking lot, she turned to face the rest of the group.

They stood with confused expressions. "What the fuck?"

"Hey! Where're you going?"

"I'll finish this fucker off." One volunteered and took a step.

Jenna launched herself to protect the young man lying on the ground. "You aren't finishing anything, you little shithead." She raised her fist and swung. It raked through an arm. The surprised yelp halted further punches. Astonished, she leaned in for a closer look. "A girl?" Is this really what being a kid had become?

The girl's eyes grew wide as a hand rose to her face. "A rock? Did you just throw a rock at me?" She looked down at the boy on the ground with hatred.

For as much as she didn't want to, Jenna's balled-up fist pounded into her stomach as the girl dove at the still figure on the ground. The girl's left knee slammed into a jagged rock and she screamed out. The remaining kids turned and ran.

"Want some more? Come on, I'll play your game. You little assholes think you can go around bullying." Jenna threw a kick into her side. "Come on, bully me."

Jenna stood over her waiting for even the slightest move toward the victim. Instead, the girl stood and limped off to follow her friends to the parking lot. A soft groan drew Jenna's attention. With arms encircling his chest, the boy pulled knees to stomach, and silent sobs wracked his torso. Leaves crunched beneath his rocking motion, and gave up the aroma of their death.

Putting herself into a prone position behind him, Jenna slid in. As she tried to move to stand up, the boy cried out in pain. She searched for injuries. Moving him would increase the damage, the internal bleeding might kill him. Slipping back out of his bludgeoned body, she couldn't leave. "Phone. Where's your cell phone?"

She found it at the edge of the clearing and brought it to life. "Dammit. Now what?"

She crawled back into him until she recovered the password, punched in the numbers and dialed.

"Nine-one-one, what is your emergency?"

"Help me," was all she said.

"Nine-one-one. What is your emergency?"

"Help," she repeated. Removing herself to stand

over him, she hoped the phone's GPS system would lead them to the boy. She moved to the base of a tree and leaned against the sturdy trunk to wait with him.

Aware of more violence not far from where she sat, Jenna let out an exasperated sigh. Somewhere there would be an answer, there had to be an answer.

Chapter 17

In a spur of the moment decision, Nathan followed Marvin, Tommy, and Mike out of Mr. C's, but kept a safe distance behind. He wanted to ease into things, approach them on his own terms.

His Big Mama always told him, "there's two nickels in every dime." If he managed to become friends, instead of taking the word of the two deadheads in that pub he might be able to lick the gravy right off the plate, so to speak, and know exactly what this new sect was all about. In fact, now that he thought about it, it sounded like a good plan. The right plan. The awful inquisition he'd witnessed in Cincinnati scared the bejesus out of him, and the rapid ingesting didn't sit right.

At the Cineplex, Nathan lost sight of them in the crowds of the living who stood in the concession line, milled around talking to friends, or rushed about so as not to miss the start of their chosen film. And the number of deadheads jostling for position behind the counter to snatch popcorn, or nachos, or hot dogs numbed his mind. In his estimation that was not food, it was fused chemicals. As a result, he had to stick his head into each screening room until he found the three men sitting through commercials and previews. Climbing up to the back of the theater, he found a seat as close to them as possible, and waited for the right moment to open a dialogue.

Marvin dropped his head back, looking at the ceiling, and moaned. "Holy mother of Mary. It's not enough we get all these same ads on television, we have to sit through them here, too?"

"Oh, come on, Brody. Give it a rest, will you? You make the same comment every time we come to see something," Mike said, leaning forward to talk around Tommy, who sat between them.

"I hear ya. I'm dead tired of them, too," Tommy deadpanned and tossed a handful of popcorn he pilfered from the concessions stand into his mouth. "But, speaking of being dead, dudes, I'm telling you. There was a deadhead in that guy at the deli. I'd bet my life on it."

Reaching behind Tommy, Marvin tapped Mike's shoulder. "Now who needs to give it a rest?"

"Dudes, I'm just saying, I think we should ask Jenna or Nancy if it's against the rules."

Nathan opened his mouth to ask about the women, but Mike reached into the bag and grabbed a handful of popcorn and beat him to the punch. "How can it be against any rules when you did it yourself for an entire week? Did either Jenna or Nancy even threaten to swallow you up?"

"Oh, come on, dude, that was different."

"How was that different, hippie? You pushed your way into a guy and manned the grill for seven days until Moe recovered from his heart attack."

"That's what made it different, Marvin. I was helping, not stealing someone's life." Tommy held the bag out to him.

"That stuff sticks in my teeth." Marvin waved it

away. "Yeah, well, tell that to the homeless man you used."

"Hey," Mike interjected, "the guy had nothing to complain about. He got new clothes, new shoes, three meals a day, and a shower every night. And he was no worse for the wear at the end of the week."

"Besides," Marvin continued, "you're the first to start with the pranks, when did you turn all vigilante about deadhead behavior?"

"Excuse me," Nathan leaned forward and butted in. "But, could ya'll explain somethin' for me?"

Tommy turned to him. "Sure thing, dude."

"You seem to know a lot about this new sect I heard tell about. These two women you mentioned, are they part of it?"

Marvin nudged Tommy's arm. "What's it to you?"

"Well, now, it might could be important, might not. But, do ya'll know if they've been in Cincinnati recently?"

"They haven't left Dayton in months," Marvin replied without swiveling around to talk directly to the man.

"Are you sure?"

"Marvin here," Tommy said, pointing to him, "should know. He's married to Jenna. But, you know, dude—"

"What's this about?" Marvin asked, twisting his body in to the conversation.

"Well, sir, I just come up from that way. Folks are scramblin' and a-flutterin' like a fox snuck into the henhouse, on account of them," Nathan explained. A vision of the deadheads he'd seen hitching rides out of Cincinnati leapt into his mind, furrowing his brow.

A concerned expression spread across Marvin's face. "Well that makes no sense. Jenna and Nancy are the first to give people the benefit of the doubt."

Mike pushed an elbow into Tommy's side. "Movie's starting."

"This doesn't sound right at all, dude. Can you hang out when this is over?" Tommy asked.

"I guess. There's no deadline nipping at my butt."

"Far out, man." Tommy smiled, and turned to watch the film.

Nathan's concentration wavered each time the theme of the movie moved to question the life of the main character; was it better as the star of films, or better proving his worth and skill as an actor on Broadway reviving an old script. The end left Nathan hanging when the character leapt from the rooftop, not knowing if he hit the pavement with a loud splat, or he really could soar like Birdman, the superhero he'd portrayed. Nathan's opinion leaned toward the former and would've counseled him to keep on tasting the keen flavors of life's offerings.

"The buzz that dude is getting for an Oscar is totally right on," Tommy stated and rose from his chair when the credits ended and house lights brightened.

"Do tell, Mr. Ebert," Marvin said.

"Oh, dude, you tease, but I'm telling you. That was one very cool performance. You wait and see, he is knocking on Oscar's door."

Nathan stood and stretched. "It sure leaves a body to ponder, doesn't it?"

"What's that?" Mike asked, making his way toward the exit aisle behind Tommy and Marvin.

"The movie. It makes you think about the quality

of your life, don't you think?"

"Right now, the only thing I'm 'pondering' is my stomach," Marvin offered. "Anyone else hungry again?"

"Good lord, Brody, it's been less than four hours." Mike turned to Nathan. "Don't mind him, he's not really much for analyzing anything."

"About all I'm hungry for right now is finding out why these new-fangled Keepers, or whatever, seem to be delivering some pretty tough sentences." Nathan followed them down the stairs of the theater. "Any knowledge ya'll might bring to the schoolhouse would surely be welcome."

"Maybe you should get your answers straight from the source," Tommy said over his shoulder.

The meaning wasn't lost on Nathan. He knew all about Jason's version of Keeper. Nightmares aside, if he'd done anything to deserve that certain demise, it's right likely it would've happened already. The thought of meeting one of this new breed face to face made him wonder if this might be a bit like poking a bear just coming out of hibernation. He bit down on his toothpick, breaking it in half.

"What do you think, dudes, would Jenna mind if we brought a friend home?"

"Friend? We don't even know the guy's name," Marvin said, rounding the dividing wall at the base of the steps and looking directly at Nathan.

"Well, sir, where I come from everyone's a friend," Nathan said from the back of the line.

Tommy poked Marvin. "Dude, did I know your name before I took you under my wing?"

"As a matter of fact, you did."

"Oh, right. Hey," Tommy called over his shoulder, "what's your name?"

"Nate," spit out of his mouth before he could stop it and he cringed.

Tommy halted and before he could stop himself, Mike marched right through him. He turned to face Nathan and broke into a smile. "That's the same name of the guy they found. Hey, you're not him, are you?"

"No. No, sir. Purely coincidental, I assure you."

"But, Nate is short for Nathan, or even Nathaniel, right?"

"Uh, I suppose it could be." Nathan fought to stay focused, to avoid appearing guilty. "But, that's a pretty common name, don't you think. I mean, it's right out of the Good Book."

Tommy stared at him for a long moment, frowned, and then shrugged it off. "I guess. So, then, anyway, this is Mike."

Nathan exchanged a handshake, and nodded. "It's a pleasure, sir."

"And," Tommy continued, winking, "the hungry, surly one is Marvin."

"I'll give you surly, hippie." Marvin scrubbed his knuckles across Tommy's skull.

"Dude," Tommy said through laughter, and moved away, "the coif, man. But, see Marvin? Now we know his name."

"And I suppose you think that means he's a friend." Marvin accepted the offered hand.

"It's a pleasure, sir."

"We won't be friends long if you don't stop with the sir bullshit."

Nathan smiled in agreement. "Consider it done."

He discarded the mangled toothpick in a nearby trash can and pulled a fresh one from a pocket as he followed them out of the building.

Chapter 18

Nathan walked close behind Marvin when he pushed through the door of the hotel suite. Tommy and Mike, claiming in the elevator ride up to be tired but too interested in hearing what Jenna might have to say to return to their own room, were right behind them.

Marvin called out to the empty living area. "Jenn, hon, I'd—"

Jenna came in from the balcony and put her wine glass on the counter that separated the kitchen from the living room. "Not now, Marvin. I have some things I need to attend to."

"It'll only take a few minutes."

Jenna scowled as she breezed past them. "I said, not now."

"Can't it wait? I mean, this guy is here to—" Marvin said to her retreating back, his words trailing off when Jenna melted through the door and out into the hallway.

Tommy turned to him. "Well, dude, I guess that answers that."

"Jesus H. I hate when she does that. What would it take to stay long enough for an introduction, would that be so terrible?" Marvin started toward the door to go after her.

Mike grabbed the back of Marvin's shirt. "Brody!"

Though Mike's hand breezed right through the

98

shirt because of the opposing forces, Marvin stopped. "What?"

"I'm guessing Nate did not come here to listen to one of your rants. Why don't we just sit with a glass of that wine you keep stashed while we wait for her to get back?"

"Yeah, dude, let her go take care of business, and in the meantime we can get to know Nathan." Tommy hooked a thumb over his shoulder.

Nathan stood rigid, his toothpick threatening to poke right through his cheek. "Maybe this wasn't such a good idea. If ya'll don't mind, I believe I'll be takin' my leave."

"Oh, don't mind them," Tommy said, turning to Nathan. "Dude, they're always nipping at each other's butts." Tommy placed a hand alongside one cheek and leaned in. "Between you and me—"

"I'll give you between you and me, hippie. Just never you mind."

Nathan didn't relax his stance at all. This could be a bit like getting between a couple of hogs in the pen fighting over dinner scraps. "It really isn't that all-fired important. I can find ya'll when things calm down a might. You know, when she's not pre-occupied."

"Oh, relax. Have a seat." Mike gestured to the couch. "Come on, Marvin will break open a bottle of wine, won't you, Brody."

Torn between wanting to know more and wanting to run through the glass doors and leap from the balcony, Nathan's gaze moved from watching Marvin open the wine and the path to freedom. To draw attention away from the heel of his boot tapping against the floor, he started a conversation. "Can I ask ya'll a question? I'm about as confused as a rooster in the henhouse. Is it Marvin or Brody?"

Marvin let out a laugh. "Well, you can blame the Brody on Mike. He started that while we were at Harvard. It's shortened from my last name, Broudstein. This schmuck," Marvin said, handing a glass of wine to Tommy, "calls me Marvin. That is when he's not calling me dude."

"Oh, come on, Marvin. That's not fair. I call everyone dude."

"True enough," Marvin said. "As long as we're clearing things up, is it Nathan or Nate?"

"Oh, it doesn't matter, either one." Accepting his glass of wine, Nathan whistled. "Harvard, huh. That's impressive. I didn't get past the ninth grade. My daddy decided he needed me at the coal mines more than I needed school."

"That must've been tough, being pulled out of school." Mike led the group to the living area and sat at one end of the couch. "Make yourself at home, Nathan."

Nathan perched on the edge of his seat at the other end. "Well, not really. I was fortunate to get that far. Most folks didn't even go to school when I was a kid. Those who did, well, sir, they were lucky to make it far enough to learn to read and write."

"Dude, that's harsh," Tommy said, lighting on the arm of the couch next to Mike.

"Not really. It's the way it was done in those days."

Marvin plopped down into the chair opposite them. "Holy mother of Mary! How long have you been dead?"

Figuring it best to stick to the truth where he could,

Nathan gazed up at the ceiling and tried to recount. "Let's see. I was born in eighteen-twenty-seven, and I was thirty when the explosion happened. That's eighteen-fifty-seven."

"That must've been tough on your family. I mean, your kids losing their dad and all."

"I didn't have any kids." Despite the regret, Nathan gave a small shrug. "Life centered around the coal mines. It would've been nice though because I did come from a large family if you include all the relatives."

Mike jabbed an elbow through Tommy's thigh. "Holy crap. You're not the oldest deadhead around here anymore."

"You were around for the Civil War? Dude, that is far out."

"What a thing to say. You know, I'd bet it wasn't all that cool, ya schmuck." Marvin redirected his gaze to Nathan. "Don't mind him. Sometimes he engages his mouth before his pot-addled brain can override it."

"Look who's talking. Who rants over every little thing?" Mike hefted his wine glass at Marvin.

Marvin shrugged, and a sheepish grin crossed his face. "So sue me."

"Nathan, what have you been doing all these years?"

Nathan figured it best to gloss right over Mike's question. "I mostly spend time on a compound in West Virginia. It's nothing special, but I like it. Every once in a while, I wander on out to take a gander at what's new in the world. But, what about ya'll, how did you meet your demise?" He looked from one to the other.

"Nose to nose with a bus," Marvin replied.

"Commuter plane crash, the week after that jet glided smoothly into the Hudson River." Mike drew a hand gliding through the air and shook his head. "I will never understand why our pilot couldn't... Well, anyway."

"What about ya'll?" Nathan asked Tommy.

Tommy's face darkened a bit, not able to hide the scowl that developed. "Got shot trying to keep a couple of guys from robbing the restaurant I worked in."

Marvin laughed. "Worked, as in past tense? He still serves up midnight snacks and Sunday morning breakfasts. Not that I'd ever complain. He puts together the best corned beef and pastrami you'll ever set your teeth to."

Now Nathan understood why he'd seen Tommy and Mike bustling around the deli the other morning. "Where's that? I'll be sure to give it a try before I hustle on back home."

"Epstein's Delicatessen," Mike said, getting off the couch. "Anyone want a top off?"

"I might could use a freshening." Nathan settled himself all the way onto the couch.

Mike returned with the bottle and divvied up what was left among the four glasses. "So, where is it you're from? Originally?"

"Baltimore, Maryland. My granddaddy settled there and started buying up mountain land. As much as he could, thinkin' he'd sell the timber. And he did, right up to the time one of his surveyors told him what was underground was worth a lot more'n anything above."

"Huh?" accompanied Tommy's quizzical expression.

"The coal was worth a lot more'n the trees."

"He must've had a lot of money to do that." Mike said, returning from the kitchen where he'd placed the empty, and sat again.

Since he'd invested his trust fund well before his death, Nathan almost said 'still do.' Instead, he glanced around the hotel suite. "Ya'll live up here, huh?"

"Marvin and Jenna have this one, Mike and I are at the other end of the building, and Colleen and Patrick used to have one kind of in the middle, but it's empty now." Tommy's expression clouded, as if his mind had traveled to a mournful destination.

"Who were they?"

"This really nice old couple. She was sweet as pie. I kind of miss them."

"Did they move?"

"Hm. No, like a lot of older deadheads, they decided they'd had enough."

Nathan understood where they'd gone and nodded. "Went with that Teresa's sect, huh? I've seen my share of folks who did that. Can't say I rightly understand it, though. I like it here a tad too much for that."

"A tad too much for what?" Jenna asked as she came through the door, a bright smile on her face and a hand extended in greeting.

Marvin rose to give her a peck on the cheek. "Oh, we were just discussing Colleen and Patrick."

A soft, almost inaudible sigh escaped from Jenna, and her smile faltered. "I miss that old woman."

Nathan rose from the couch, removed the toothpick from his mouth and stashed it in a pocket of his jeans. His Big Mama would say, 'Put your eyes back in your head, child.' And that's exactly what Nathan tried to do as he held out his hand to Jenna. The radiance of her auburn hair and green eyes stunned him, and a pang of envy poked at his midsection when his eyes darted to Marvin, who stood taller than he had moments before. "Pleased to make your acquaintance, ma'am."

"I'm Jenna. It's nice to meet you…" Jenna dangled the phrase in a question as her hand held onto his.

"Oh, Nathan, ma'am. My name's Nathan."

"It's a pleasure." Jenna withdrew her hand and turned to face Marvin. "Okay, Marv, what was so important that you felt the need to head off on a rant as I left? Don't think I didn't hear you."

Marvin squared off in front of her. "I knew you could hear. You do that to me all the time, I've got something I need to talk about and you have something more important to do."

"And does it kill you to have to wait?"

Tommy giggled. " 'Kill you.' Dude, that's funny."

Marvin poked a finger at Jenna. "Would it kill *you* to wait once in a while?"

Her hand went right through as she swiped at his finger to knock it away. "Don't start with me, Marvin, you know what I do is important."

"Oh, and I'm not, is that it?"

"Knock it off. I'm not having this conversation with you again." Jenna's stature grew, as a scowl broke across her face.

Marvin broke out into a smile, though from Nathan's perspective it didn't register in his eyes. "Oh, go fall—"

"Not this time, Marv. Now, behave yourself."

Nathan's jaw clenched and bit down on the toothpick that wasn't there, and he again eyed possible exits. The woman's countenance reminded him of the three deadheads in the Cincinnati bar. If she and her anger rose, he might be a goner, as some of the old geezers back home liked to say. He set his wine on the coffee table with as much delicacy as he could muster right at the moment. "Perhaps it's best if I go."

"Nonsense," Jenna said, and waved a hand at him without turning.

"Now, now, children." Mike threw an arm across Marvin's shoulders. "Don't fight. You'll get Tommy all upset, and then he's going to want to run around giving everyone hugs."

"You're right, this is no way to conduct ourselves in front of our guest." The tension in the room eased as Jenna's height returned to normal. With a friendly, pleasant smile on her face, she turned and indicated the small table near the kitchen of the suite. "What is it you needed from me, Nathan?"

"Well, ma'am, I sure don't want to be a bother. If you'd think I could might come back when you have less on your mind, it wouldn't be no nevermind to me."

Jenna waved a hand through the air. "I've done what needed to be done. Never mind us. Marvin and I are always jousting. In all honesty," she said with a glance and a wide grin in Marvin's direction, "we kind of enjoy it."

Following her to the table, Nathan pulled and held a chair. "Ma'am." The expression on her face as she nodded and thanked him as she took her seat told him the gesture of southern kindness and manners might be a bit strange to her. But he couldn't help it. His mama would've boxed his ears a good one if he'd done otherwise. Of course, there was no chance of that since she stuck to home in Baltimore along with a bunch of his other relatives 'still haunting folks' as they liked to say, but still… "I guess I need a tiny bit of clarification. I asked the menfolk here." He pointed toward the living area where Tommy, Marvin, and Mike sat. "They suggested you might be the best to explain things."

"Hold the thought." Jenna held up a finger. Turning to the boys, she asked for Nathan's wine to be brought to him. "And could you pour me a glass, Marv?"

Marvin opened a new bottle, refilled Nathan's glass along with pouring one for Jenna. He nodded to the duet of thank you's and returned to his seat, with "Always my pleasure to serve you," under his breath.

Jenna shot a frown in his direction, took a few sips of wine, and then sat spinning the glass by its stem. She smiled, leaned in to Nathan, and rested her chin in one hand. A finger of her other tracing the edge of the goblet replaced the spinning. "Now, what's bothering you, Nathan?"

"Well, ma'am, it's these new rules and all. It's got folks down south pretty riled up. On edge, you might say." He stole a glance at Marvin to find a scowl and deeply knit brow.

The spinning halted. "New rules? New rules about what?"

"Yes, ma'am. Well, about not bein' allowed to slip into folks." Nathan reached for a toothpick to chew on, but wanted to be mindful of manners and picked up his drink instead. To help relieve his anxiety his toes fidgeted in his boots. "Word is it's an actionable offense."

One of Jenna's brows raised. "It sounds as if you're guilty of it. Are you?"

Nathan skirted the question with one which had nagged him since the scuffle in the bar. "Why is it okay for some but not others, that's what I want to know."

"If it's not done maliciously, there's no harm, no foul, right?" Mike said from the couch.

Nathan swiveled in his seat across from Jenna to address the question. "Well, that's not the way it went down. These poor folks were minding their own business and were told that only certain individuals are allowed."

"Where did you hear that, who told them this?" Jenna asked.

"A band of these new so-called Keepers, ma'am. I've seen it happen, seen them swallow folks up for it with nary a pardon me."

"Where, when did this happen?"

Not one to lie, Nathan figured it might be in his best interest to just leave out a few parts. "Well, ma'am, it was about a week ago, now. I was in the stockroom of a bar when they came busting in, accusing this group of breaking the rules and said it just isn't tolerable. The most awful skirmish took place, and before I knew it they'd gobbled up every specter in the whole place."

"Wait a minute," Marvin butted in. "Jen, the whole gang of you—"

"And even Jason—" Tommy echoed in.

"Hush." Jenna waved them off.

Nathan glanced around the room. "Is it true? We aren't supposed to do that any longer?"

Mike rose and went into the kitchen for a refill. "Oh, please. It happens all the time."

"Messing with the living is entertainment. Dude, a rule like that could take half the fun out of being a deadhead. Truth be known, ninety percent of us would be goners."

"Well, now, see, that's what I thought and I'm relieved to hear it. But, some kind of massive migration happened. Deadheads scattered in all directions; those who were left, anyway. I sure as heck didn't see many in the time I stayed. Hundreds came this direction right along with me." Nathan's toes ceased their antics, but their tightly-curled position remained. "Cincinnati is a ghost town."

"Not any more, dude."

Nathan issued a nervous chuckle; Marvin and Mike let out raucous laughter.

Jenna studied him, her gaze flickering across his face as if searching. "There's something you're not telling me." She put her glass on the table, still more than half-full, and rose. She pecked Marvin on the cheek. "Stay out of trouble while I'm gone."

Chapter 19

Nathan promised to meet the guys for breakfast at ten the next morning, though it was a good four hours later than he was used to. Except on rare occasion, his routine never changed from the days at the mines. He went into one of the suites for the night; the place didn't impress him. He'd stayed in better, but of course that took being in physical form, and his credit card, facts best not shared with these new friends.

After turning on the heat and taking a hot shower, he dropped onto the bed and spent a fitful night filled with nightmares of being haunted, chased by unknown phantoms who grew and loomed over him as they approached. Ducking and escaping their clutches, they would somehow manage to find him again.

He woke with the sun and stood at the window, looking out over the city. A portion of the Wright-Patterson runway glinted in the distance, and the park with his stashed truck, laid out like a ribbon of strange shades of brown and black plaid. With better than three hours before the agreed-upon breakfast, he decided it might be a good time to go check on his truck.

After a walk through the deserted lobby, it took a minute to get his bearings, and then he headed north to the bridge. The streets were still void of much traffic. A linen truck he'd seen from his window, as it pulled into the hotel parking lot, trundled past and he hitched a ride on the rear bumper. At the intersection with the bridge, he jumped off and headed across the river to the park. The tedium of moving through the world on this plane of existence—unseen and unheard except to other deadheads—made him hope for a quick resolution.

At the edge of the park, a steep embankment led him down and through the trees barren of foliage. In true physical form, the ground, strewn with hues of winter would crunch underfoot and offer up a rich aroma of nutrients. As it stood, he passed as silently as a bird floating on drafts of hushed winds high above the earth. He longed for a more tangible and absolute reality.

Halfway to the parking area, he spotted the hood of the truck. Its pale tan blended fairly well with trunks and branches, and the dormant grass. Moving into an open expanse, his step quickened. Something to the south, right at the edge of the tree line, caught his attention. Three familiar, slightly transparent yet darkly dense individuals stood blocking his view of who they were conversing with. Nathan changed course and headed east again, hoping to pass by unnoticed.

Keeping watch on the group, he wended through the trees, until the sensation of walking through solid mass made him realize he'd bumped the front end of his truck. Calling himself a couple of derogatory names as he moved to the driver's side, he noticed a bright orange sticker plastered to the window declaring the vehicle to be abandoned on public property and subject to towing and impoundment. An identical notice had been stuck to the rear window. "Dammit, I was afraid of this."

He moved around to the passenger side, pushed

through the door, and rummaged around under the seat until his hand grasped the handle of the snow brush. It took more than ninety minutes to peel off both signs with the ice-scraper end, layering the pieces of sticky paper as they shredded away from the glass in tiny, exasperating strips. The pile got folded and stuffed into a pocket. Knowing how underhanded some of the county sheriffs back home could be, he looked for and found markings at the back side of each tire; scratches deep enough into the pavement appeared to have been made with a tire iron. "Ya'll thought you would pull one over on old Nathan, huh? Well, now, I've played in this pigpen too many times."

Nathan peered around the parking lot, pulled the key from his pocket. With no one in sight, he melded his way through the door hoping live folks wouldn't stumble upon the act and freak out to see a truck move without a driver. He'd read about several companies rushing to compete in the self-driving car business, and issued an ironic chuckle at the image of seemingly empty vehicles moving along the roadways. Well, nobody was about to believe it of an old Ford pick-up. He started the engine. Another fast glance in the mirrors, the crunching of tiny bits of gravel meeting his ears, and the truck moved slowly to the other end of the parking lot. To make it obvious the vehicle had moved, he backed into the new spot.

He slipped from the truck, gave a satisfied nod, and snuck along the inside edge of the tree line. Of course, it wouldn't do to be seen by any deadheads either, particularly the arguing group on the other side of the park.

Once on the road, he put a hand to shield the sun

from his eyes. The four figures stood in the same spot and, though no words floated along the air currents, gestures told Nathan they were still lost in discussion. A wave of panic washed over him as the flutter of auburn hair glinted from a sudden chilled gust of wind. He hurried away. It was only when he had the thick wooded area of bare tree limbs between them that his steps slowed to a brisk walk along the western down-slope of the bridge.

Chapter 20

He'd been back in his suite for close to an hour, sipping on coffee, by the time Tommy stuck his head through the door. "Dude, ready for breakfast?"

"Ready." Nathan set his cup on the table, stood, and headed toward the door.

Tommy pointed at the cup. "No, you can't leave that."

Nathan halted in his tracks. "Why? Aren't there maids to clean up?"

"Dude, are you serious?" Tommy moved through the door into the room. "Well, once in a while they come up to dust, but that's about it unless the room gets booked. If that happens and the front desk gets a complaint about a dirty room, the manager makes a fuss. All kinds of accusations and finger pointing goes on. We sure wouldn't want anyone to get fired for—"

From outside the door Marvin's muffled voice said, "What are you doing in there? Come on already. Shake a leg!"

Tommy turned around and stuck his head through to the hallway. "Dude, take a chill pill. We gotta clean up a little first."

"Well, hurry it up, I'm starving to death out here."

"Yeah, we can see you wasting away right in front of our eyes, Brody." Mike pushed through the wall beside the door. "What needs doing?"

"About done here," Nathan said from the sink as he dried out the coffee pot and returned it to its rightful spot under the brewer. "What about the towels I used?"

"Did you hang them back up?" Mike asked.

"Yeah. Ya'll might want to check to make sure I did it right, though."

Tommy headed toward the bedroom. "Got it. Any trash?"

"Nothing other than the coffee grounds here." Nathan plunged an arm into the waste basket next to the sink where he'd just dumped the used coffee filter. He bent over and tied the bag closed with a double knot despite the ability of any deadhead to simply slide fingers through and latch onto the contents. Bright orange, dulled against the translucence of the thin plastic, could still be seen inside. He balled up the entirety and held it tight in his fist.

Sticking his face through the center of the door, Marvin said, "Hurry it up in there."

"Dude, you are a handful this morning, aren't you?" Tommy called on his way out of the bedroom. "The towels look perfect. Ready then?"

"Ready," Nathan replied.

Mike moved toward the door with a hand raised to push Marvin out of the way. "What's the deal, Brody? Jenna being gone for a few hours makes you all anxious. Relax, man, it's not like she's gonna die out there without you to protect her."

"Really, dude, I think she's proven she's capable of handling the situation."

"I'm gonna handle *your* situation, hippie, if you don't get a move on." Marvin backed out, but continued his gripe. "I'm getting tired of her taking off like the rest of us don't matter."

"You mean like you don't matter." Mike shook his head. "You are the biggest baby, you know that?"

Tommy took one last glance around the suite and followed them through the door. "Now, children, don't fight. That's no way to behave in front of our guest."

"What're you, the new Miss Manners, or are you channeling Mrs. McC.? Come on, let's go. Maybe food will take my mind off Jenna's being off to God knows where. You know, it's just getting to be too often." Marvin headed to the elevators and let out a long and exasperated sigh. "I mean, what was the point of that huge wedding if I'm just going to spend my time wandering around with you two schmucks."

"Dude, you could do worse."

"That's for sure," Mike agreed. "I'm thinking Diane could still be in town."

"Or your mother," Tommy said with a laugh.

Marvin slapped him upside the back of the head. "Bite your tongue, hippie."

Nathan, still bringing up the rear, spotted a trash can in the lobby, and shoved the bag deep into the bin. "Where to?"

"The only place worth going," Marvin said. "Epstein's."

Tommy, Mike, and Marvin greeted the usual group of deadhead regulars who sat lingering over coffee and headed to the same booth Nathan spotted them in during his impromptu meal. To any live person, abandoned coffee cups and plates of half-eaten bagels and kugel littered the tables.

"Huh. Isn't that odd," Nathan remarked with a nod at Tina-I'll-be-your-server-today, who sat at a table rolling flatware into napkins. "Most places I've been, why the food would be snatched right out from under you if you weren't on the ball."

Marvin slid over on the bench to make room for Nathan. "Tina used to be a nervous wreck, but last year sometime she caught on and calmed down. She's used to us now. There's been no need to hang onto a cup since then. Well, once any live folks are gone."

"What happened was, she threatened to quit until Moe—he's the owner, and chief cook—'fessed up about Tommy. Once she understood we did things just to mess with her, boy, did she grab an attitude. One night at closing, she pointed a finger and told him straight up, 'Tommy, this place better sparkle when I get back in the morning.' " Mike's recount made even Nathan laugh.

After he grabbed a book of order tickets from the wait station, Tommy returned to stand at the end of the table and laughed. "It used to be fun to mess with her. Now, we help her. So, what's your favorite, Nate? It's on the house."

"Well, let me think a minute. The smell of that bacon's bitin' a deep hole in my stomach. I believe it'd go right nice in an omelet, maybe with a healthy dose of cheddar."

"Got it. Marvin?"

"Just a couple bagels. I want to save room for dinner tonight. And don't forget my *schmear*." Marvin nudged Nathan. "Tommy here puts together the best corned beef and pastrami this side of New York."

"Aww, dude…I owe you a hug for that. Mike?"

Marvin let out a chuckle. "Keep your hug, just bring me the bagels."

"You know, I feel like pancakes today. No, make that French Toast."

Tommy ripped the ticket from the pad, jammed it into and spun the wheel above the counter, and smacked the bell twice. From there he poured four coffees, made his way back to the table, dealt out the cups, and sat down.

Ten minutes later, Moe rang out three dings on the bell interrupting their idle chit-chat about the city, places Nathan should visit, and restaurants they thought he might like. Tina glanced around at the empty tables, delivered a curt, "Well, I hope you don't think I'm going to bring it to you," and went back to her task.

Tommy retrieved the plates and placed them in the proper spots, which impressed Nathan. "Dang, you're right handy moving around with your hands full."

"Lotta practice, dude."

Marvin picked up a bagel and slathered it with the cream cheese Tommy brought with the rest of the orders. "He used to work here."

"Do tell," Nathan asked just before taking a forkful of his omelet. "Oh, my Lord, ya'll." His head tipped back and his eyes closed for a moment. "Talk about hog heaven. That fairly melts in your mouth, the blend of cheese to bacon is downright perfect."

"We'll have to leave an extra tip for the cook." Mike winked at Tommy.

"If this don't beat my Big Mama's breakfast, I d—" Nathan's brow furrowed, and his body straightened and froze. The voice he heard loud and clear, called him by name. His full name, which nobody had ever used, except maybe his mama did like the time he and a couple buddies had gotten into his father's still. The voice sounded a bit familiar, but he couldn't quite place it.

The cup moving toward Mike's mouth halted, and Tommy sat with a slice of toast between his lips, both wore wary expressions.

Voices came to Nathan muffled, as if through a dense fog. Marvin asked, "What?"

Tommy pointed at Nathan. "I've seen that before."

"Oh, holy mother of Mary." Marvin jumped from the booth and moved out of Nathan's vision. "Is it Jason or Nancy?"

"Haven't seen them in a long while. I'd bet neither." Mike put his cup down. "It's Jenna."

Nathan laid his fork on his plate, lifted the napkin from his lap, folded it, and placed it on the table. He didn't quite understand what was happening, but he couldn't do anything but follow instructions telling him—no, commanding him—to go to the park where he'd left his truck. He stood without a word to the others and walked out vaguely aware of the conversation of the guys trailing behind.

"Come on, let's see what's going on," Mike said.

"You really think it's Jenna making him do this?" Marvin let out a sigh. "The woman needs to learn how to delegate."

"It makes sense, doesn't it, Marvin?" Tommy grabbed up their dishes and dumped them into the bus tub. "I mean she left last night right after he told her about what he'd witnessed. I'll bet she wants more information."

The closer to the park and Jenna, the more muffled their conversation sounded in his ears. Nathan prayed that nothing more than Tommy's words would be true.

Chapter 21

On the trek over the bridge and down into the park, Nathan moved like a robot, manipulated by an unseen, unknown source. He dodged a few live folks, but deadheads skirted around him as if he'd caught a deadly, communicable disease. The foursome stood in the same place they'd been when he spotted them earlier. Despite the knot in his stomach roiling like milk in a butter churn, his feet moved him steadily toward them.

He entered the small circle. Without bothering to turn to him, Jenna issued no pleasantries or welcome and got right down to it. "Nathan, are these the three people you saw in the bar?"

More automaton impulse engaged his mouth. "Yes, ma'am."

The leader of the rogue group looked him up and down. "He couldn't have. I've never seen him before, and I'd have remembered him."

"Why would he lie? What would he have to gain?"

"Maybe he does it himself, moves in and takes over people. Maybe he wants you to think—"

Regardless of the truth in the statement, or maybe because of it, Nathan's brain engaged as if it had been set free. "I don't want her to think anything. I'm just lookin' for a bit of clarification. Heck, I'll admit to entering some unsuspecting guy so's I can enjoy a few finer things in life. I'm no saint, never claimed to be."

"See? See there?" The woman's voice broke over the top of his, and carried an accusatory, yet defensive tone. "Our kind has become brazen about this and it must stop."

Jenna's expression turned dark. "Nathan, who was in that bar, what were they doing?"

"Well, ma'am, from my vantage point in the stockroom, as far as live folks go?" Nathan waited for a nod from Jenna. "Besides the bartender, only one guy sat at a table drinking a beer. That one there," Nathan pointed to the male of the group. "He stood towering over and studied him real long and hard. That was after they'd swallowed up the four dead folks. And they hadn't been doing anything, just sittin' there, talking, and enjoying their refreshments. They all finally left when the man reached and took a good solid swig from his beer. But, I thought for sure... Well, ma'am, I'm not sure what I thought. My knees were knocking so bad, if I'd been alive the bottles back there in that stockroom would've rattled the roof right off the barn."

After a moment of silence, Jenna cast her gaze from one rogue member of her sect to the next. "What proof do you have that any of the people you've taken did things maliciously?"

One of the subordinates stated, "We aren't to interfere with the living. Isn't that so?"

Jenna fixed her gaze on her. "And what is it, exactly, our sect does if not interfere?"

"We have permission, how else do we fulfill our responsibility?" The rogue leader became defiant and her physical stature rose to meet Jenna.

"Oh, shit. I wouldn't want to be her right now."

"Hush, Marvin, this doesn't concern you. Why are you even here?" Jenna turned to face him.

Mike stepped in and tugged on Marvin's arm. "Curiosity is all. We were with him," Mike jutted his chin toward Nathan, "at Epstein's when he dropped his fork and walked out."

"Keep quiet, or leave," Jenna said, and turned her attention to the matter at hand. She rose up, her visage towering over the others. "Where do you think your authority and power comes from?"

Her opponent's body shrunk down to normal height. She cast her eyes to the ground and turned away.

Jenna moved so quickly Nathan didn't even see a blur. She appeared in front of the witness, huge and glowering. "I gave no permission for you to leave." The woman froze as still as a lizard. "These people you've taken, did they kill anyone? Maim them? Frighten them so much they ended up in a mental hospital? The purpose of this sect, my sect, is to protect the living from the living. You have no reason, nor authority, to police the dead. Who brought you into this service?"

The man of the group shifted his weight, his small eyes darting around the park. He reached up to smooth his hair. "Her name was Diane. She told us to keep the living safe."

"Oh, Jesus H., doesn't it figure."

"Marvin, go home," Jenna warned. When he'd turned to leave, she added, "Tommy, Mike, you too. And take Nathan with you. It appears I've got some things to attend to."

Nathan breathed a quiet sigh as he joined them.

"See? That's what I'm talking about," Marvin said,

his face scrunched in a pout, hooking a thumb over his shoulder. "What's the point of being married? She's never around. She's always busy with this crap. I mean, why did—"

"Dude, she's got responsibilities now."

"I got her responsibility right here, hippie."

"I heard that, Marvin," Jenna said as she turned to watch them leave. "And if you don't like being married, I'm sure there's a remedy. Now, do as I say, and go home."

Nathan's shoulders tensed into knots big enough to tether a horse to a hitching post. "Please, don't make her angry."

Chapter 22

Jenna turned her countenance on her wayward members. "How many innocents have you taken?"

"None!" Arrogance returned to her underling's voice.

"Well, we'll see, won't we." They tried to shrink away from Jenna. She increased that fear with a malevolent grin as her form surrounded the three. Not unlike those she'd observed in Jason, a member of the North American Council of Keepers and equal partner in the World Council, who'd tested her so many months before, Jenna heard the pleading voices, the woe of wrongful capture and imprisonment. Cautioning herself against being tricked, she listened with keen insight to the sadness, the despair of the accused, and the denials of the behavior which caused them to be entombed. She sensed no malevolence, no intent of misdeed.

Jenna backed away from the three wayward members of her sect, yet held them frozen in place without effort. Lifting her face to the rising moon, ignoring the whisper of fallen leaves as they tumbled around in a whirling wind, she called out to her mentor. "Jason, I need your help."

Out of nowhere Jason appeared at her side, and Nancy, the protégé who would soon take his place, appeared next to him. The two looked from Jenna to the three who stood frozen in fear. "These are yours?"

Nancy asked, stepping forward.

"Yes. From the accounts I've heard, they've gone beyond the scope and caused quite a commotion."

"Before we empowered your sect, I asked how we might regulate this police force of yours, and now we get down to it, don't we?" Jason asked.

"I'm sorry. I don't know how this—" Jenna attempted to explain.

He raised his hand. "No. There will be no excuses. You were told. If there isn't the strength to tend the sect, it shall be dissolved."

"The issue is not strength," Jenna responded. "I assure you, these three have earned the ultimate punishment, and it shall be meted out. In fact, you're free to take them yourself and be done with it."

Nancy placed a hand on Jason's arm and his expression softened. "Then why the urgent call?"

Jenna jutted her chin toward her charges. "How can the innocent they've taken be freed?"

Jason and Nancy, Keepers of the worst of the worst, moved to envelop the three. With her shared power, Jenna listened as they questioned, prodded, and dug for the truth of the deadheads begging to be released.

Jenna placed a steady and comforting grip to their shoulders as deadheads tumbled out of Jason and Nancy by twos and threes into the clearing, their hands held out as if to stave off further pain. Dusk had fallen more than twice before the final captive stepped free from the imprisonment of the wayward Watchers, and the three offenders vanished from view.

Her mouth gaped open at the sheer number of them and a chorus of appreciation reached Jenna's ears. She turned to Jason and Nancy. "Thank you. New guardians will be found to keep watch over their city."

"You could've done this yourself," Nancy told her. "You need to have more confidence in your ability, your judgement."

"I'm still new at this," Jenna responded. "I needed to be sure."

A funnel of bright light streamed down from the sky as if the Milky Way itself moved to embed into the earth, and Teresa's form shimmered into view, like heat from an asphalt highway. A strong sense of serenity emanated from her as she bowed in turn to Jason, then Jenna, her equals on the World Council. "My old friend," she said to Jason, "it's a new way of dealing with our plane of existence. Remember when we began? Mistakes will be made, but Jenna will find her way."

A long sigh escaped from Jason, but a gentle smile appeared on his face as he gazed at all the deadheads gathered around them. "Millennia of doing this work have taken their toll. I'm tired, so very tired." He turned to face Nancy. "I'm afraid it's very close to my time."

Teresa touched the sleeve of his coat and studied him for a while. Sadness overcame her expression, though the smile never faded, and she nodded. "There is a bit more you need to do, yet. I cannot say more than that. But, I won't leave it to any emissary. My arms will welcome you as I embrace all who seek peace. Yet, for you, there will be special grace."

They all heard the unspoken offer of sanctuary from Teresa. The same offer that came to the very young and very old who passed from the plane known as life. A mass of deadheads moved toward her. The aura of light around the woman grew, and then she bowed to the three Keepers. By the time her form dissipated completely, the crowd had dwindled significantly.

From the shadows created by the moonlight a timid-sounding voice asked, "Are we free, then?"

"Yes," came Jason's reply.

Those who had been freed and who decided to stay on the earthly plane wandered off. Within minutes Jason, Nancy, and Jenna stood alone.

"I really do apologize," Jenna said.

"Well, I suppose, as Teresa said, mistakes will happen."

"Not again. Not if I can help it. You two have your hands full enough without having to come to my rescue."

"Call your Council members to you. Tell them this is what happens to those who misuse their station and power over others weaker than they."

"I will, Jason. Thank you."

"And, perhaps, you'll learn a bit more about the problems you face," Nancy added.

Jenna returned the bow the two offered as they disappeared from her view. She turned to head home when Diane called out. "Jenna, there's a problem."

"Ugh. Now what?" Jenna stopped short and turned.

"Hey, don't take it out on me!"

"Sorry, I've just spent who knows how long dealing with... Never mind... Look, I need a bit of a break, can't you handle this?"

"I wish. There's a woman who keeps managing to escape our clutches, and we need to find her before she kills again."

Chapter 23

Nathan waited for the verdict in Marvin and Jenna's hotel suite. That night, he even opted to bunk at Tommy and Mike's in the extra room rather than stay by himself. When they woke, they grabbed Marvin and went to the deli for breakfast. As the hours wore on, Nathan's anxiety increased; he chewed up numerous toothpicks, tapped rhythms with a foot, and swayed his legs in syncopation.

Tommy placed his cup down on the table and stared for a minute. "Dude, what's got your panties in a bunch?"

"She's been gone a long time. It's been almost two full days since she let me walk away. But I still don't have any answers."

"You're starting to sound like him," Mike said, hefting his cup in Marvin's direction.

"Hey, watch it there, buddy. I think I've calmed down a lot since Jen's taken this stuff on."

"That you have, Brody. I'm just sayin'—"

"Yeah, well, don't."

"Truth is, Nate, time moves different for Jenna when she's dealing with these things. We just have to let it be. She'll be back when she's taken care of those rogue...agents, or whatever you want to call them." Mike sniffed the air and glanced at Tommy. "I think I need some of that bacon that just came off the grill.

127

Would you mind?"

None of their answers did anything to calm Nathan. His nerves hummed like an electrified fence. Tired of fiddling with his flatware, he gulped down the rest of his coffee and stood. "Well, I surely appreciate the hospitality. But, I can't just sit around like this. I'm as keyed up as a penned bull. I'm gonna go do some of that sight-seeing ya'll recommended the other day and check back in later."

He gave a wave, and "Thank you," to Tommy as he walked from the deli. As soon as he rounded the corner and knew they could no longer see him, he broke into a run. He stopped at the top of the bridge where he had a good view of the park. Jenna remained in the same spot, the "rogue keepers" could barely be seen, but it looked to Nathan as if they had company. A man in old baggy clothes and a well-dressed woman had joined the pow-wow, but they towered over Jenna.

Nathan left to check on his truck. Once satisfied it hadn't been messed with, he skirted through the trees to watch. His tormentors stood motionless, then they faded into a blackness as the visages moved to surround them. Moments later, it was as if they never existed. Many hours later—it felt like at least a day had passed—the clearing in the park was filled with deadheads. He stood, mouth agape, as Teresa's shape took form. A lightness, a sense of pure serenity emanated from her, and Nathan summoned the courage to move forward to join the crowd.

He understood the decision of those deadheads who moved to Teresa, but his penchant for life remained steadfast. At Jason's declaration that the rest were free to go, Nathan relaxed.

Word traveled through the plane of the dead a tad slower than gossip traversed the hollers of West Virginia, but with the head of the sect married to Marvin, Nathan figured there would be no sense in returning to the hotel to let them know what transpired. They'd know soon enough. Since the National Museum of the United States Air Force stood pretty much across the street he headed over.

Not only did he scope out the exhibits, but he kept an eye peeled for possible candidates. Strangely, the crowd contained a lot of families. As much as he envied those men, Nathan couldn't even consider separating a father from his young children. He'd seen how the survivors of those killed in the mine explosion grieved, and it just wouldn't do to take a family man. No, it had to be a single guy.

He went from building to building, exhibit to exhibit, and outside grounds area to outside grounds area. Several contenders piqued his interest, but after a bit of study each one fell short; too young (he'd learned his lesson on that score), prematurely balding (as a hat removal proved out), surly attitude (no excuse for that as his daddy once told him), constant ogling of men (his experience with Chris brought a no-vote). The list could stretch on longer than a vein in a coal mine.

Late in the afternoon, as Nathan stood in an exhibit hall admiring the Boeing F-15 Strike Eagle, a young Air Force Captain walked up with an expression of pure awe and desire written on his face. Nathan wished he could talk to the guy.

He took a few steps away and studied the man. The light brown hair contained waves, the green eyes held a sparkle of intelligence, his stance said confidence with a well-toned physique apparent in the tailored blue uniform. He appeared to be fairly equal in height, which Nathan always found easier to slide into. He took a furtive glance around the immediate vicinity and, while the Captain appeared to be preoccupied, slid in. A tiny shiver ran through his torso.

Nathan dug around for the needed information. Captain James Morris happened to be age twenty-eight, single, and lived in General Officers Quarters of base housing. Nathan slipped out and shadowed his prospective host; even hitched a ride home with him in the man's little Honda Accord.

The small, garden-type townhouse could only be described as old architecture with a utilitarian interior. The sparseness of furniture—couch, television, and sound system in the living room, and a double bed, dresser and one nightstand in the bedroom—left Nathan to believe this guy traveled light.

A picture on the dresser of the young captain in an embrace with a woman eased Nathan's mind on the attraction quotient.

"Well, James, I promise you a much more elegant lifestyle. For some of the year, anyway." He gave the captain a once over as the man stripped down to shower and then change into civilian clothing. "And from all physical appearances, you'll handle life at the compound, and do quite well with the ladies."

James pulled on a coat, strode out the front door, and Nathan settled in to wait.

At midnight, with the young officer emitting short, slight puffs of breath, Nathan made his move. As he'd done before, he dressed leaving all identification on a kitchen counter. Figuring to keep warm and save a bit of time, he grabbed the key to the Honda and drove to the park. He locked the door, then withdrew his arm from James and pushed his hand through the window to toss the key onto the driver's seat. Then he walked the length of the lot to his truck, and drove off.

Marvin, Tommy, and Mike seemed like nice folks, and some of the sightseeing they suggested, and the one steakhouse they mentioned, gave him fodder for thought. Yet, at the same time, consideration to hang around Dayton caused a queasiness to churn in his gut. He needed to chew on it a bit.

He stuck a fresh toothpick in his mouth, and headed north on the 675 freeway. He passed an overhead sign that read I-70 East, Columbus 59 mi, Cleveland 200 mi. An idea popped into his head. He'd always wanted to check out the Rock and Roll Hall of Fame. He could be in Cleveland before his stomach started gnawing at him for breakfast. The sourness in his gut eased when he pressed down on the gas pedal and signaled to change lanes.

"Well, now, I guess that answers that."

The going went fine despite the numerous lines of orange construction barrels narrowing the number of travel lanes. Even the truckers seemed to move at a pretty good clip. About 2:30 a.m., Nathan looked up at the clouded night sky and expected there might be a light dusting of snow before dawn. Somewhere between Columbus and Cleveland, now along I-71, for the second time on the trip, the need to empty his bladder found him slowing to ease the way between barrels, and he pulled off to the side of the freeway. After slamming the truck door closed, he stretched to ease his muscles, and took a glance along the path he'd come. With no headlights in the distance, he sauntered over to the concrete barrier. It took several minutes of abdominal pushing to get started, which was strange considering the pressure he felt. Again, an odd burning sensation accompanied the weakest stream Nathan had ever experienced.

Climbing back into the warmth of the truck, instead of looking for places he might visit and things he might like to do when he arrived at his destination, he sat and pondered. Could he have chosen a guy who'd been indiscreet in his dalliances with the ladies? It was possible, but no images he brought forth conjured anything but wholesome women. No mental film clip contained more than a chaste kiss goodnight. Nathan couldn't even find evidence of a quick tryst in the Accord in a back alley.

Might it be something more? He replaced a chewed-up toothpick and dug deep for information. A medical history had to be buried in memory. With his limited knowledge of medicine, he didn't find anything more than the typical childhood illnesses, a bout of flu last season, and an allergy to Cottonwood trees, which would cause some heavy problems come Spring. Well, most folks suffered from an allergy of some sort. So long as this body wasn't averse to a good side of beef, or rasher of bacon. That thought made Nathan's head jerk up. Though he didn't recall him saying so, he was pretty sure Marvin was Jewish, and he had a whole plate full of bacon, didn't he? What if Morris is Jewish? The surname, the circumcision... It would be intolerable to suddenly have the nose curl up at something Nathan loved.

An internet search might be of use. He woke his

cell phone, launched the search engine, and entered the symptoms. STD topped the list, but Nathan was about as sure as a creek ran downstream it wasn't that. One thing struck him, though delving through the guy's brain hadn't recalled anything of the sort. Nathan got out of the truck, opened his pants, and groped at the testicles. "I'll be damned." Fake. Was there a family history? No.

Now, why would a man bury that so deep as to be irretrievable in the memory bank? Could be mental trauma; a lot of men felt less manly missing parts like those. But wouldn't that require some kind of hormone replacement? Unless those harmless dates with the ladies indicated an inability to—Well, that right there would be a solid deal breaker. It still didn't explain the symptoms.

Scrolling down the list he found and opened a link. Could be... According to the Cancer.org article on his cell phone the important fact remained that men who'd survived were at a higher risk for other cancers; bladder included.

Well, sir, that wouldn't do. It just wouldn't do. He put the goods away, crawled into the driver's seat, and headed off. What now? didn't become an argument. At the very next exit, he got off the highway, turned left, made another left and got right back on.

He pushed the speed limit as much as he allowed might not get him stopped by the highway patrol. After pulling into the lot at the park, he took care to lock up the truck. He slipped an arm out of James, reached into the Honda and grabbed the keys.

There was nothing left for it but to take the man home, and begin a new search. Yet, on the drive to base housing, his mama's voice nagged at him, "Nathaniel Ray, you do the right thing, now. You get that boy to a doctor." Returning the salute of the guard at the main entrance of the installation, Nathan made his decision.

After pocketing the wallet with all the proper identification, he strode back out and drove directly to the base hospital. Regular office hours hadn't begun, so he approached a Staff Sergeant sitting behind a desk of the small emergency room and feigned severe pain in his abdomen and groin. "No, sir, no recent injuries," he responded. "But it hurts like hell."

"Fill this out. I'll get you back to see the doc as soon as I can."

"Thanks, Sarge. I sure do appreciate it," Nathan said through gritted teeth.

Fifteen minutes later, when Captain James Morris sat spread eagle on the edge of the exam table and a Major poked around at the privates, asking if he'd "been out" recently, Nathan slipped free.

"No, sir," James replied, and his cheeks flushed crimson. "Nothing like that, sir. I swear."

Nathan chuckled at the response. Then an expression of confusion creased the captain's brow and he gawked around at the curtained area. "I'm not at all sure what's going on."

"Well, I don't see any indication of STDs," the doctor consulted the chart and scribbled on it. "And the symptoms you describe don't jive with prostate infection. Bladder infection, maybe, but this would be a mighty severe one to cause this much trouble. Just to be safe, let's ship you off to Radiology for a scan and we might find out." James made a move to get off the table. "You stay right here, Captain. An orderly will be in, in a minute, to take you down. In the meantime," he added, taking a specimen cup from a nearby drawer, "I need a urine sample."

"Yes, sir."

Nathan followed the Major out into the hallway, then looked up at the bulky, black-framed clock on the wall: 0510. "Well, I believe I've done all I could. I might as well find something to eat."

He couldn't think of any place better than Epstein's. Not that he had much familiarity with the city. Plus, by his account, anyway, it seemed he was in the clear with the Keepers. By the time he arrived, his stomach mewled at him like the runt of a litter, but the place hadn't opened. He walked through the door, and started a pot of coffee.

Tina gave a suspicious glance at the brewer as she turned to relock the door until opening. Making her way through the diner she offered, "You're here early," to the empty room, and disappeared into the back.

Nathan helped himself to a cup, and sat down to wait for Mike and Tommy. This minor hiccup didn't alter the overall plan. He'd have breakfast with his new friends, find a suitable replacement to free him from this prison of dulled senses, and head out to enjoy the rest of his winter excursion.

Chapter 24

Nathan watched Tina go through her morning routine. The line of customers stretched around the corner of the building, a few deadheads pushed through the storefront and nodded at him. He nodded in return. "Mornin'."

"I wouldn't sit there if I were you. When she opens that door," the woman nodded at Tina, "you'll have someone sitting in your lap in seconds."

"Thank you, ma'am. It did appear a might busy the other day. I'll keep a watch."

Like the phantoms they were, they lined up and drained the pot. Nathan imagined what that would look like to the live folks who peered through the windows: The carafe flickering out of sight, reappearing on the warmer a bit emptier, disappearing again—longer that time—to show up with barely a hint of amber liquid in the bottom.

"That pot better fill back up as quick as it emptied," Tina warned from her spot in the middle of the small diner. She pointed at the coffee machine as her hand, filled with napkins and silverware, poised over a table.

Tommy laughed as he burst through the wall greeting the deadheads who had made the place their regular haunt. "My, she sure is feisty today. Morning, Betty. Hey, how are you today, Dixon."

A chorus of greetings came back to him, Nathan's among them. "Mornin', Tommy. I could might lend you a hand if you need it. Compared to feeding a bunch of hungry, grimy miners back in the day, this would be a pony ride at the county fair. All's you have to do is tell me what you need and point."

"Oh, hey, dude. I didn't see you over there. Nah, you sit and relax. Mike will be here in a few minutes. Though, you might want to take care when Tina opens up. The customers sure move in fast."

"So she said." Nathan hoisted his cup in the direction of Betty. "Where's Marvin? Isn't he coming along?"

Tommy scurried from table to table, dipping into the pocket of the apron he'd put on to fill the jelly trays and pack holders with sweeteners. "He's what's holding up Mike this morning. But, I'm sure they'll be here. As soon as Marvin finishes the rant he's on." Tommy shook his head. "That dude really needs to get a grip."

"What seems to be troubling him?"

"Oh, he hasn't seen Jenna in days. He went to the park this morning before the sun even spit to check on her. She wasn't there, and hasn't been home. Freaks him out, you know?"

"Well, now, when I left yesterday morning, she'd been hailed off somewhere by a woman in a might bit of a panic."

"Oh, man, that's going to burn his bagels." Tommy finished his duties as Tina headed over and unlocked the doors. "Here come the hoards. Dude, I don't mean to be rude, but we'll have to save the chit-chat for later."

"There's nothin' rude about being straight-forward.

Ya'll get on with your day. I'll try to stop on by later, then." Nathan passed his cup into Tommy's outstretched hand, and gave a tip of his non-existent hat. He opted to go through the wall of windows rather than put up with the vibrations of walking through the unruly crowd of the living pushing and shoving like they'd half-starve to death having to wait one more second. The sight of it reminded him of a trip to Las Vegas. People jostled for position along the buffet lines, elbows poking and jabbing. "They're worse than hungry workers at the mines reacting to the dinner bell."

Out on the sidewalk, he nodded to loitering deadheads who waited for a chance to pop into the restaurant to pilfer something for breakfast, and his mind turned to where he might look for a new prospect. Yesterday's candidates hadn't been all bad. There's bound to be a different lot up for bid today, as his daddy used to say when heading out to buy more property.

He ambled along, and made a stop in the park to check on his truck again. There would be no time spent peeling orange stickers from windows again. That had been one tedious task. He arrived at the Air Force Museum before it opened. A fair group of people stood near the front entrance, but he saw no men who looked to be without family. He didn't want a man with a family. What he wanted was...

It flashed into his mind there'd be a lot of time to kill if he wanted to use his typical method of waiting to take over until his chosen new self drifted off to sleep that night. "Well, sir, patience is a man's best friend."

"What's that?"

Nathan turned to his left and saw a young woman sort of leaning against a bollard. He wanted to laugh. The way she half-sat on it gave the appearance of the thing being rammed up her backside. Instead, he gave her his brightest smile. "Oh, I was just musing to myself is all."

"With these ear pieces for cell phones, I can never tell if someone's talking to me, having a private conversation with themselves, or talking to a friend."

"Yeah, at first it seemed like a bunch of crazy people, right?" Nathan laughed. "But, then again, how many of those 'crazy people' happen to be folks like you?"

"Good point," she said. "Makes it less conspicuous for us now."

Nathan wondered again how it was that some live folks were clearly able to see and hear those on his side of existence. And, it dawned on him the woman might be a jumper like himself. The chance to find out stood right in front of him. What could it hurt to ask? "How do you do it? What makes you able?"

The girl shrugged. "Don't know, really. I've been able to for as long as I can remember."

They both heard the locks tumbling in the entrance doors. A man in military garb pulled on the door and issued a brief "Good morning, folks."

"Looks like they're about to open. Maybe I'll see you later."

Nathan fished a toothpick from his shirt pocket and followed her through the doors. The lights flickered on as he passed by her standing in line for a ticket. "Ya'll have a good day," he said, and headed for the back end of the building to check out exhibits that might be in storage. He found an old Lockheed P-34 medium-sized bomber to be interesting, and nosed around the cockpit and bomb bay a bit. The most interesting thing was an Aeronca L-3. The top-wing, single prop plane had large windows which surrounded the flight cabin. A precursor to the spy planes of the 60s and 70s, this was an unarmed observation aircraft according to the metal tag riveted to the fuselage. Beyond that, it was shelves of items and dust-covered crates.

All morning, right through the hot dog he snatched off the grill and the bag of Nachos he pilfered from the rack for lunch, and on into the afternoon his search came up empty. Out on the tarmac, admiring a fighter jet, with his last possibility a bust, Nathan shrugged and went through the building to leave.

The same young man who unlocked that morning stood just inside the exit doors with a smile plastered on his face. "Thank you for visiting. Have a nice evening. Come back and visit us again."

Nathan halted and studied the guy he'd passed by earlier without a thought. He came across as pleasant if not sincere. Light blond hair—almost white, really—green eyes, no wedding ring or evidence of one having been there. At least not recently. He carried a little extra weight around the midsection, as evidenced by the bulge around the waistline of his Air Force blues, but some gym time—if not doing chores at the compound—would be a quick cure. The height worked.

Nathan peered over at the name tag. "Yes, sir, Sergeant Larssen. You might could be a right nice fit."

The ride to the barracks took less than ten minutes. Nathan followed him in to his room, and shook his head in pity at the sight. "It might be better than the cabin, but not by much."

Plain metal lockers stood against one wall and fake pine furnishings made up the rest of the sparse accommodations. A sink and medicine cabinet were separated from the room proper by a small metal divider like one might see between urinals in a men's restroom. The sergeant stripped, throwing his clothes onto the single metal-framed bed, grabbed a towel from inside a locker, and wrapped it around his waist. He pulled a bag of toiletries from the locker shelf, and walked out the door.

Nathan sure didn't want to deal with illness again. First order of business: check the medicine cabinet for any medical issues; nothing but aspirin, nasal spray, toothpaste and brush, hair brush and spray, razor and shaving cream. He nosed through the dresser and nightstand, and found a stash of girlie magazines. He took the wallet from the rear pocket. "Erick. Staff Sergeant Erick Larssen. Allrighty, then. It appears we have a winner."

Erick came back from the shower, his hair in towel-dried disarray, returned the small bag to the locker, and spread his towel on the bunk. Then he reached over and pulled a magazine from a stash in the drawer under the locker, and stretched out on the bed.

Nathan let out a laugh. "Well, I think this is a performance I can skip. You have yourself a good time, Sarge. I'll be back." Nathan scanned the room. "And then, we're going to up your quality of life some."

Chapter 25

Jenna followed Diane to the small city of Ravenna a bit northeast of Akron, a place where homes sit on half-acres and wooded areas abound. The two stood on an otherwise deserted street corner of what might be considered the center of town, the buildings a strange mixture of old houses and large brick buildings. Flakes of snow drifted through the haloed glow of streetlights. "Who are we looking for?"

A perplexed expression ran across Diane's face. "I can't catch her name."

"Tell me again what she's done. Take me through it."

"Well, I can't say I blame her, but—"

"Wait a minute. You rushed down to bring me here and you don't blame her? Was it an accident?"

Diane, the only one of Jenna's council members able to get away with it, changed her stance to meet the challenge. "If you'll let me finish, your highness. You know, Marvin might be right. You're getting mighty big for your britches. I'm here to help. We're all here to help. You might keep that in mind."

Dropping her chin, Jenna released a weary sigh. "Sorry. Really. That man makes me want to crush things so I don't—Never mind, I married him, I'll have to deal with it. Tell me. I'll keep my mouth shut."

"This woman is fast. I mean, real fast. I've never

witnessed anyone on this side disappear like she does. She intervened in a tussle between a man trying to force a screaming little girl into a van. While the girl hollered, 'Help. He's not my daddy!' this woman melded into the guy like her body was made of jelly. I watched her run him down the block, around a corner, and beat his head into the side of a brick building. When he slumped to the ground, his forehead in a bloody, mangled mess, out she popped, and off she went. I called out to her, but..." Diane shrugged. "Either she didn't hear me, or she's able to ignore our commands."

"I'm confused. What was this panicked 'before she kills again'?"

"The guy died there in the street." Diane pointed past Jenna's shoulder. "She didn't even bother to check on him. Not that a scum like him deserved help. Put him in jail and he wouldn't last a week unless they separated him from the main population."

"What about the girl? Did you go back to check on her?"

"Well, that's the thing. She was gone."

Jenna turned away from her second-in-command. A deadhead able to withstand a direct command had never crossed her mind. She'd witnessed Jason and Nancy order even the worst offenders to stop. Well, except for the young man Jenna had killed, and he actually charged Nancy instead of trying to flee. But this. This was a problem far worse than the issue Nathan brought to her door, far worse than Nathan himself. She knew what he did. It deserved further investigation, and certainly a warning. But she doubted them to be actionable offenses to the same standard or degree to which Jason might hold them, if he discovered them. In fact, it surprised her that Jason didn't act when he had Nathan in Eastwood Park.

Diane's voice broke through and interrupted her train of thought. "… or the girl must have gone home. What do you want to do? Should we call in some help from other cities and hunt for this woman?"

Jenna shook her head to clear Nathan out of her mind for the time being. "Let's scout around. There's bound to be a scumbag around for her to go after." Jenna sighed. Abusers would always be around.

Agreeing, Diane offered, "I'll take the east part of the county, you take the west. Does that work?"

"I guess. Meet back here by six tomorrow night."

Jenna considered Diane's words for a moment as the woman headed off. Did Marvin really believe that? Had she begun to think too highly of herself, to think of her job as more important? What she did was important, but was it more important than Marvin?

After twenty-four hours, only traces of the brief snowfall remained in tufts of grass beyond the parking lot of the Beverage Drive-Thru across from them, the streets again void of the living or dead. Neither she nor Diane found a trace of the woman who'd saved a little girl but killed a man in the process. Jenna peered up through sporadic, swift-moving clouds at the stars, and shook her head. "I have to get back to Dayton, then I need to find new recruits for Cincinnati—stable ones this time."

"Ouch. But, as Marvin would say, so sue me. How was I supposed to know they'd start making up their own rules?" Diane held up a hand to halt any response. "I know, I should have made the rules clearer. What do

I do if I find this woman?"

"Bring her to me. Maybe we can turn her around, use her to our advantage. But we've got to find her before Jason does. If we don't, she won't get the same considerations I did when Nancy intervened on my behalf."

Chapter 26

Nathan returned around midnight to light, regular breathing. The magazine Erick had used to entertain himself lay open on the small rug next to the bed. "Okay, buddy, let's get you up and moving."

He laid himself on top of Erick and eased into the midst of a dream that took a sudden switch from lying on a tropical beach to being in a car stuck in a snow bank on a deserted road. A shoulder pushed against the door to no avail, and his eyes fluttered open.

Nathan rose, and switched on the overhead light. A quick inspection determined the need for a shower. The hair resembled a pile of hay in the barn. He grabbed the towel from the bed, slung it around his neck, and went out into the dimness of the central hall.

"Larssen," the quiet voice echoed along the tiled hallway from behind. "You feel okay?"

"Yeah, why?"

"Holy crap. Man, I've never seen you walk the halls like that before. Aren't you afraid someone might see your dick flopping around?" Laughter accompanied the remark. "Or are you finally loosening up?"

"It's late. I didn't think anyone else would be awake." Nathan picked up his pace down the hall to the middle of the building where he found the latrine earlier in the evening.

"Really? At shift change? Or, maybe you're a

closet exhibitionist." Another chuckle and a door closed.

Nathan made quick work of rinsing down. He soaked the hair he decided needed to grow out some, and went back to the room. In the locker, he found a pair of jeans that fit a might snug, which definitely called for a short-term gym membership. Rifling through a row of shirts, all he found were knits that clung to the body and accentuated the pudginess at the waistline, and added a shopping trip to the top of his agenda. He pinched at the love handles. "Erick, Erick, Erick. Ya'll should've been taking much better care of yourself. Now, how in the world can we justify the kind of meal we've been wanting when we're faced with this?"

He combed the hair and gave it a little spritz of spray. He transferred his cell phone to an inner pocket of the leather flight jacket he slipped on, and went down the corridor and out the side door. He was already at the sergeant's old Malibu when he stuck hands into empty pockets and looked for keys. Damn. He discovered the barracks side door needed a key. Then he found the front doors locked as well. Thankfully, a sign told him to ring the bell after hours.

A face popped into the window and studied him. "Larssen?"

Nathan nodded.

"What the fuck?"

"Sorry, forgot my keys."

"You look like shit. What the hell are you doing up so late, anyway?"

Nathan struggled a bit for an answer. As he pushed past the guy on guard duty, he let loose with a terse,

"Couldn't sleep. Decided to go for a drive, that okay with you?"

"No, really, Erick. You look weird. Are you okay, man?"

Nathan kept walking. "I'm fine."

He heard the door get shoved closed as the man responded, "Whatever."

It surely was not Nathan's nature to be curt, but people who knew Erick might spot slight but specific differences if he lingered. He thought it best to keep moving.

A sigh of relief escaped from him at finding the room unlocked. It would've been a bit risky this early in the game leaving Erick in the hallway in order to retrieve the car keys. Once ensconced in the driver's seat, Nathan pulled out his phone.

"Okay, Google." He waited for the tone he'd heard when others used the app he still hadn't tried. "Five star hotels in Dayton, Ohio."

The results were underwhelming, certainly nothing he aspired to. Maybe it was a sign he should follow the instinct of the other night with the captain and head off to Cleveland. He again pulled in next to his truck at the park, and locked the sedan, leaving the keys on the floor. He didn't want anyone seeing them and stealing the good sergeant's car.

"All right," he said, after a check of the time, and patting the dashboard of the pick-up. "Let's see if we can get to Cleveland in time for breakfast."

He gassed up the truck before getting on the freeway, and made only one stop at the Mile Marker 128 rest area on I-71, north of Columbus. Unlike the previous self, this one had no difficulty in draining the radiator, thank the lord. He took a short walk around the building to stretch his legs, and headed out.

Following the signs for the Rock and Roll Hall of Fame, he exited the freeway, and pulled into a convenience store parking lot. Another search of the internet came up with a list of hotels. After studying them, The Ritz-Carlton looked to be nearby and came closest to fitting the level of luxury and amenities he wanted. An indoor pool would be nice but maybe a local gym, which this new self truly needed, would fulfill the wish.

According to the website, all kinds of entertainment could be had within walking distance: Plenty of bars and restaurants, the Cleveland Playhouse, art museums and galleries. Gosh, he could even take in a Cavaliers game if he was so inclined.

Though the hotel offered valet, the old F-150 would give the wrong impression. He used the Tower City parking garage around the corner and hoofed through the shopping center to the hotel.

"I'd like a suite, please. Not the studio type, an actual suite."

The clerk woke the computer. "And how long would you be staying with us, sir?"

"Indefinite."

"On business or pleasure?" he asked as he clicked through screens.

"Pleasure, actually," Nathan responded when the clerk finally looked up.

"I have a city view or a lake view."

"Hm. Lake, I think. Is that what ya'll might recommend?"

"It's quieter, if that makes a difference. Name?"

"Nathaniel Ray Crockett."

A smile crossed the clerk's face a second before the keystrokes began. "Any relation to Davy?" never failed to be asked at least once each winter, and Nathan braced for it. Instead the man continued the gathering of information. "Address? You know, it'd be faster with your driver's license. I'll need it anyway."

Nathan tried to put on an innocent expression as he reached for his wallet. He hadn't spent any time at all in testing out Erick's ability to fib. "Now, I surely do apologize, but I lost that somewheres along the way up here. Here's my credit—"

A stricken expression landed on the young man's face, and his fingers hovered over the keyboard even as he looked down at the credit card he recognized as having no limit. "Oh, I'm sorry, sir. I can't finish a registration without one."

Why did he go and leave all of Larsson's identification behind? He might've used it. But, that may have caused a stable full of trouble, too, when the Air Force began the hunt for their AWOL soldier. "I surely wish ya'll could make an exception this one time. I'll have a new one in a jiffy, I can promise you that. In fact I could have it mailed right here."

"It's strictly against policy, Mr. Crockett."

Nathan peered around the lobby. "Is there a manager I could talk to?"

"Certainly. One moment." Dale Corbel, according to his name tag, picked up a house phone. "Yes, there's a Mr. Crockett here wanting to check in without proper I.D. He'd like to speak with a manager." He replaced the receiver in its cradle. "She'll be right with us."

"I thank you kindly." Nathan turned his back to the

150

desk and leaned against it.

A moment later he heard low mumbling behind him and turned to face them with the friendliest smile he could conjure. A woman in her mid-fifties stood peering around a corner, his Black American Express credit card in hand. Distaste flickered across her face. She shook her head in denial, handed the card to her employee, and left.

Dale returned to his station. "I do apologize for the inconvenience, Mr. Crockett. But, she's declined to accommodate the request."

"With so much fraud going on in these times, I surely understand her reluctance. I thank you for trying, Mr. Corbel, it was right kind of you."

"Perhaps you can return when you have your license?"

"Oh, you can count on it." Nathan left through the doors to the mall in hopes of finding somewhere to bunk down until he could remedy the license situation.

Chapter 27

"Don't that beat all," Nathan said as he walked the shopping center in search of a beige wall to use as a background. He now rued abandoning the clothes he purchased before the regrettable date with Vicky and skipping out of Cincinnati in such a hurried manner. Not that they would've fit properly, but having that jacket on may have provided a bit of a leg up into the saddle with the Ritz-Carlton manager. It reminded him how folks in the South were much less suspicious, more inclined to help than hinder. Heck, even Big Bill, the deputy he'd led to the kid's body, hadn't asked to see identification, and that situation could've been murder for all Bill knew.

Nathan stopped near the food court that bustled with workers and the smells of breakfast foods tantalized him, though no vendors had opened for business yet. He took a self-portrait with his cell phone, one he hoped to be a good facsimile of what the motor vehicle department would get. Wandering past each with a slow gait, he read through the menus the fast food joints offered and then sat at a table to wait.

"Well, I might as well get the still to percolating." He launched the email application and composed a message.

"*Zachariah:*

Lost my license, need a new one. Photo attached.

Stats: Blond hair, green eyes. Now, I'm guessing on the rest of this. I should've snatched the info from him before I left but, then again, I should've done a lot of things of late that I didn't. Height, let's say, 5'11. Weight, 155. That last will be accurate soon enough. Leave the birth date the same. It'll be close enough. I'll tell you where to send it as soon as I can. Thanks, buddy. I surely do appreciate it. Nate

Oh, BTW, I hope everything's okay down there. Tell Sarah and everyone else I said "hey."—N"

He pushed Send, waited for confirmation, and then searched for a cheap hotel. One where he paid with cash, and they wouldn't give a hoot in his holler about identification.

A gate rose on Dunkin' Donuts, and brighter lights came on. He took a large coffee and an egg sandwich back to his table. It needed salt but otherwise it served to fill the hole, and he went back to his search. Before he found anything, the phone dinged and popped its Battery Low warning. "Well, this day ain't starting out none too good, is it?"

He turned off the phone and approached the counter again. The same acne-inflicted kid who took his order stood poised to grab another sandwich. "Do ya'll know of a cheap motel around here where I might get a room?"

"There's one over on Euclid Avenue." He thrust a thumb over his shoulder.

"Is it far?"

The kid scratched at a scraggly sideburn. "Nah. You could probably walk it in less than fifteen minutes."

With directions scribbled on a napkin, Nathan

stopped by the truck to retrieve the charger for his phone and headed out the northeast exit of the garage. In an effort to begin the weight loss on this new self, he jogged and made it, winded, in five. Walking into the lobby, he had doubts he'd get any further here in securing a roof over his head. Still, he had to try.

"A week. I'm happy to pay in advance," Nathan said, sliding the credit card across the desk.

"Yes, sir. No problem. I just need your driver's license."

Nathan repeated his plea, and offered a cash incentive. He had a key within minutes and walked across the small lobby to head up to the room on the second floor. He stopped and turned to the registration desk. "What's the zip code here?"

"Four, four, one, one, four," came the reply from a still smiling face looking down at the crisp one-hundred dollar bill.

In the standard hotel room, with everything glued or bolted down to surfaces—probably to prevent stealing of items, though Nathan couldn't imagine why anyone would want to steal such things—he settled into the chair next to the window. He plugged in the phone to begin the charge, turned it on, and launched the email. He took a slow gander at his surroundings.

—*Zach: Send license FedEx, SAME DAY EXPRESS. 669 Euclid Ave, Cleveland, OH 44114 ~N*—

He went to leave the phone on the table and slapped his forehead. He launched the app for a second message, well, third actually, he reminded himself. "Shit, Nathaniel, pull your head out from that mule's ass."

"You'll find a wad of cash in an old shoebox under

the cold-water sink. Use what you need."

That task out of the way, all he could do was hope that today would be a day Zach pulled the solar and satellite equipment out to the clearing into the winter sun. "Or this might could be a long wait," he said, repeating the gaze around the room.

He needed a plan. First some decent clothes to fit the lifestyle, not only at the Ritz but for any nightlife he chose to indulge in. The opening time for the shops in the Tower Center left him with a few hours to kill. He thought about getting an exercise routine started but a sudden exhaustion overcame him.

He spent a good twenty minutes standing under the spray of hot water, then toweled dry and plopped down on the bed. Despite a mattress he found much too soft, with marked indentations that felt like a chasm, he fell into a deep sleep.

He stood in the woods not far from the family home in Baltimore, hunting for dead wood to cut for use in the kitchen stoves. It being the most strenuous chore anyone would allow him since surviving the mine explosion almost a year before. Movement among a clutch of saplings caught the corner of his vision. He shrugged it off as a squirrel dashing off to safety. A moment later, a man appeared. At first Nathan thought he might be a runaway slave, with his threadbare and unkempt clothes, and unruly hair. But the man didn't look to be someone on the run, he stood stock still and stared with an eerie intelligence reflected in the brightest eyes Nathan had ever seen. And the strangest of all, he appeared a bit hazy, transparent; Nathan could see the saplings behind him without leaning to peer around.

"Can I help you?"

"Sumpin' ain't right 'bout you. Don't lookit me that way. You knows what I'm sayin'. It ain't right. What you doin' ain't right."

Nathan shuddered awake. Sweat poured from his body. The dream again. It cropped up every so often, and always the same, the old black man accusing him of doing an awful thing. This time, the visage seemed familiar but he couldn't quite place him.

Picking up his phone Nathan checked the time. He'd slept for more than six hours. Grabbing the case off the extra pillow, he wiped his face and underarms dry. He rubbed at the goose bumps that invaded his arms and legs. His skin still clammy, he showered again under steaming hot spray until the skin turned red.

In the small bathroom, hunger rolled through his stomach. "I hear you," he said to the image in the mirror. He grabbed at the love handles around his waist and slapped the soft belly. "But, Erick, my man, we have got to get you into shape."

The Ritz had an exercise room but he needed to find something in the interim. It could be a week or better before his new license arrived. "'Course," he mused as he dressed, "good luck finding a gym that will let you in without proper identification."

Strolling through the shopping center, he bought more fast food just to fill the pit in his stomach. Lord! how he longed for a good meal. Then he made his way from store to store buying what he needed, and he needed everything from toiletries to underwear; top to bottom, as his mama used to say. The diversity of merchants, with direct access to the hotel made the Ritz the perfect choice. Even his bank had a branch if he needed personal service.

Loaded down with bags, he walked back to the motel, using the stairs for good measure, and put everything away. Dress shirts and pants hung in order on the rack of the small closet cubby, skivvies and casual things went into the dresser. Personal items sat on the small counter space in the bathroom. He placed the soap, shampoo, and shaving needs in a row onto the ledge of the tub.

To plan ahead for dinner, his mind wandered to the places he'd passed in the mall. Should he hit Morton's Steakhouse, which in reality was nothing more than a chain restaurant, or check out what might be available in the Horseshoe Casino? A chime from his cell phone brought the decision-making to a halt.

Though it couldn't be anyone else, he looked skyward and muttered, "Please be a response from Zach."

—*I hate to break it you, buddy, but tomorrow is Thanksgiving. You'll have to sit tight until next week. ~Zach*—

"Well, don't that beat ever'thing. Shit."

Chapter 28

Jenna sat next to Marvin in their usual booth at Epstein's while Tommy and Mike ran through the place dropping plates of food on tables. She offered again. "Come on, let us help. It's silly for us to be sitting here like this."

"Dude, no. This was our idea, and our pleasure," Tommy said, as he slid a plate across a nearby table to a ghostly diner.

Glen, Tommy's assistant on days the diner was closed but hosting a full house of deadheads, stood behind the counter. A row of turkey carcasses lined the space next to him. "I could use some help back here, scooping potatoes and stuffing."

"I'm on it," Mike hollered over his shoulder.

In a rare moment of inactivity, Tommy gazed out the window. "I wonder where Nathan is? I thought for sure he'd be here today."

"Anyone who would not take advantage of this is crazy. And, if you ask me, he seems a bit off," Marvin said.

"Oh, I don't know… I kind of like him."

"That figures, hippie."

Jenna turned her face up at Tommy. "I don't know, but I'd sure like to see him."

"For what?"

"Never you mind, Marv." She waved him off. "It's

nothing you need to know about."

"Oh, here we go. You seem to have an awful lot of secrets lately. Why is it that you—"

"Dude! Zip it. Don't you dare spoil my feast," Tommy interjected with an unlikely glare.

"Yeah, Brody," Mike said over the din of conversation. "You can go off on a rant later."

"Don't encourage him. He rants and pouts enough already." Jenna elbowed Marvin. "I haven't heard Nathan since the park incident."

Tommy stopped midstride on his way to retrieve a pot of coffee and whirled around. "What does that mean?"

Her ability to sense the dead may not have been as acute as Jason's, or Nancy's, but once she had come face to face with someone she could pinpoint their location within a fair radius. Jenna knew Nathan watched from the periphery of the crowd the day Teresa stood in the park with them to accept those who desired the peace she offered; an option he didn't take. Jenna still had her concerns despite Jason's blanket statement of freedom to the crowd. To cover for her own slip of the tongue, she cleared her throat. "Nothing, really. I meant no one seems to have seen him, or heard from him. I need to...I need replacements in Cincinnati. I thought maybe he could help me."

"What about me?"

A long, exasperated sigh escaped Jenna. "What about you, Marv?"

"Why can't I help? Why don't you ever ask me?"

"Done." Loaded down with four plates, Mike placed them on the table, and slid over next to the window. "Come on, Tommy. Stop fussing and sit."

"Fussing?" Tommy grabbed at his chest. "You wound me."

"And, yet, you don't bleed." Mike pointed to the empty spot on the bench. "Sit. Eat."

Marvin laughed along with the rest of the deadhead crowd. "Laurence Olivier, you're not," he said, directing the comment to Tommy. Then he twisted in his seat. "Seriously, Jen, I can help if you'd let me."

"You," Jenna asked. "What in the world do you think you could do?"

Marvin's shoulders slumped. "Nothing, I guess. Never mind." He pushed his plate of untouched food to the center of the table, stood, and backed through the bench. "I need some air."

Jenna heaved a sigh as she watched him leave the diner. "I don't know what to do with him. I told him. I told him a hundred times, I have a lot on my mind and my position has to take precedence. He insisted on getting married, I went along with it, and look what it's gotten me." She pushed her plate away. "I'm sorry, guys, I'm not in the mood anymore."

"Jenna, wait," Tommy grabbed at the sleeve of her jacket. "It's simple."

"What I do is far from simple."

"No, that's not what I mean. You're off doing your thing, he gets left sitting around moping. Mike and I do this," Tommy said as he swept a hand over their dinners. "Even though we always include him when we head to a movie, most of the time he's not interested in them."

Mike nudged him. "Get to the point."

"Dudes, he's bored."

"I'm sorry, do I keep him from doing what he

wants to do?" Jenna tossed her napkin over her plate.

"He did nothing except pine over you until you kicked it and joined us over here. He's no different than anyone who crossed over so young. There we were being useful, doing something we enjoyed—well, most of us enjoyed what we did in life—and wham!" Tommy grasped one of Jenna's hands. "He wants to be around you, but most of all he wants to feel needed, like he's doing something useful, something worthwhile."

"Whoa. Listen to you, all serious," Mike interjected.

"Scoff if you want. But, I am dead serious about this."

"No one's scoffing. It's just not...you. You're usually the optimist in this group."

Jenna gazed out the window, and saw no trace of Marvin, but she sensed him a few streets away. Well, she'd deal with it when she saw him at home. On one hand, what Tommy said made sense. He did love his work at the ad agency. His daily rush out the door made it evident, and death left him no options on that front. On the other hand, it seemed ridiculous to her to have to worry about him. Married bliss? Evidently, not in this lifetime.

"Well, I'll think about it. Though I have no idea what he could do to assist me."

"You never know. He's a bright guy, Jenna. He never mentions it, but he graduated Harvard near the top of the class. He's a great idea man. You find yourself in a pickle of some kind, he just might have a solution for you." Mike put his empty plate under Jenna's. "Tommy, my man, that meal was superb." He leaned around Tommy, and hollered out, "Glen, good job. Thank you." A chorus of thanks from around the small diner echoed his.

Glen stood at a table nearest the kitchen. "You're welcome. There's plenty here, folks. Help yourselves to seconds."

"And thirds," Tommy chimed in. "Moe won't like finding a bunch of turkeys in here when he opens up Monday."

"Hey, speak for yourself," someone uttered from the middle of the room to rolling laughter.

"That's it, Dixon. You got KP!"

The room burst with laughter, and broke into a flurry of activity. When Tommy and Mike finished an inspection an hour later, they announced the place resembled a perfectly set and arranged restaurant. Tina wouldn't need to fill even a single salt shaker.

As they walked through the locked doors Tommy hugged Jenna. "Happy Thanksgiving. Think about what I said."

After returning Tommy's hug and greeting, and after she made the same exchange of wishes with Mike, Jenna left for home. Thinking about Marvin, Nathan, and her responsibilities as the head of a new sect of Keepers, was all she'd been doing. What more did anyone want from her?

Chapter 29

A bitter gale off Lake Erie made it too miserable for most, but Nathan figured he could use the time on Thanksgiving Day to explore the vicinity. He walked the mostly deserted streets of downtown Cleveland past shops and stopped in at a bar or two, also pretty much empty. When hunger struck, he found a small café. He tried to savor each bite, but culinary wasn't a word he would use to describe the gray slab of pork on his plate. Even smothered in "our own special homemade BBQ sauce" didn't improve the experience. He washed it down with a bottle of lukewarm beer, and shuddered at the thought that some folks might actually consider this good.

None of it dampened his anticipation of being able to get back to life once he acquired proper identification. The city beckoned him with promises of a fine winter. LeBron had returned to the Cavaliers, the Lake Erie Monsters, the new American League hockey team might be fun, he could browse through several art museums, and Playhouse Square's immediate offer of *Irving Berlin's White Christmas* might ease the nostalgia for home and family. Heck, he might even stay long enough into the Spring to see *Kinky Boots*, the new show promising to set the theatre world on fire.

Black Friday sales held no interest; he had what he needed for the time being. Besides, the pushing and shoving, being jostled around, and the chances of a deadhead running smack into him, well, no thank you. He ventured out for breakfast, lunch, and dinner at the coffee shop of the casino. He could get in there without dealing with the throngs of shoppers in the mall. On Saturday morning after grabbing a fast food breakfast sandwich and coffee, he wandered down to the Tower Cinema. *Wild*, *Into the Woods*, and *The Theory of Everything* looked interesting, but none opened until later in the month.

Saturday bade no better. Sitting around and waiting about bored a body to death. Maybe he should've stayed in Dayton for the holiday weekend. Tommy probably cooked up a real feast. Nathan sighed. His daddy would tell him, "Well, I s'pose you should've thought about that before you jumped on that lame horse."

After a light breakfast of yogurt and coffee and a brisk walk through the mall, he walked to the lakefront. Pushing his nose skyward to a thin cover of clouds, he breathed in the crisp air, and watched the gulls. Life on this side smelled sweet, tasted sweet—well, for the most part—and he wanted to wallow in it. He stood close. So close. His frame of mind soured at the thought. Not even the long circle-route back to the hotel where he planned to change for lunch lifted his mood. He launched himself into the lobby and headed for the stairs.

"Excuse me, Mr. Crockett."

His mood soared. He turned and expected to find the clerk holding out a package, and even walked toward the desk. The man pointed to an alcove in the lobby. "There's a gentleman here to see you."

Zach rose from the chair and headed across the lobby. "Nathan. How you doin', buddy?"

Nathan grabbed him in a hug, and clapped him on the back. "Like a baby itching to get out of the womb. Am I ever glad to see you. You brought my license?"

"I did." Zach reached into an inner jacket pocket and pulled out an envelope. "I figured there ain't nothing to do, what with a blanket of snow keeping the hills warm. I might as well deliver this in person."

"Thank the Lord. I's about to start gnawing at my arm to get out of here." Nathan turned to the clerk. "No offense."

The clerk smiled. "I get it."

"Oh, you'll be needing a copy of this." Nathan pulled the new license, and walked it over to the clerk.

"I suppose this means you'll be checking out?"

"Most likely. But, leave it be for now." Nathan waited. As he accepted his license he slid another crisp bill into the clerk's hand. "For bein' so kind to a stranger." With business taken care of, he turned to Zach. "Are you hungry?"

"Well, now, I might be able to cram something in on top of the bag of peanuts from the plane ride, long as I can grab a smoke on the way."

Nathan returned his attention to the clerk. "What's the best place you can recommend for a meal?"

The clerk posed in thought. "Depends on what you want, I guess. The Blue Seale Grille, over on St. Clair, specializes in seafood, but I hear they do a mean steak."

"I believe that'll do. What do you think, Zach?"

"Is it far?" Zach tossed out.

After a shrug, "Not really. About a twenty-minute walk. But you'll need a reservation."

"I think I can handle that. Thank you." Nathan woke his cell phone, perused the website, then highlighted the phone number and hit Dial. "Yes, ma'am. I'd like to make a reservation. ... Yes, ma'am, in the Board Room, please, if it's available. ... For two people, yes ma'am. ... Would half an hour work?" He nodded. "Thank you, I appreciate it."

A low whistle came from behind him. "Must be some occasion you're celebrating."

Nathan turned and winked. "It most surely is. In fact, I might could declare this my birthday."

Out on the street, away from misunderstanding ears, Zach drew an oval in the air in front of Nathan's face. "I like it by the way. It suits you."

Despite the quick walk to the restaurant, Zach managed to suck down two cigarettes, and was on his third when they stood at the front door. "Trying to make up for the trip here."

"Well, either put it out, or smoke faster. I am dying for a decent meal."

"Hold your horses." Zach took another long drag, then tossed the smoldering butt to the gutter.

Nathan placed a hand against Zach's shoulder and nodded toward the street. "No, sir. Pick that up and put it out properly. Just because we ain't in West Virginia, and there's concrete instead of trees to worry about, doesn't mean you can toss that to the ground."

"Sorry." Zach stomped on the ember, picked up the butt, and shoved it into the watch pocket of his jeans. Nathan held the door open, and followed him in.

At the reception desk, the woman curled her nose. "Can I help you?"

Nathan recognized her voice, and didn't appreciate

the dour expression or the haughty attitude. It put his hackles in a tizzy. "Yes, ma'am, I believe we have a reservation."

"You're the man who called? I'm sorry," she said, "but the room isn't available. I made a mistake."

Nathan looked past her to a sprinkling of patrons in an otherwise empty dining room. He pulled his credit card and new license from his wallet, and handed them to her. "I don't believe you did. And, if you insist, let's call a manager over. Maybe he'll change your mind."

"We have a dress code here, Mr..." She glanced down at her list. "Mr. Crockett."

"If you'll pardon me, ma'am, that's precisely why I asked for the private room."

"You and your friend might want to go…clean up a bit first, and come back. Then maybe—"

Trying to stay pleasant, despite the rising blood pressure, Nathan said, "Let's call the manager over, shall we?"

Zach tugged on his sleeve. "Nate, forget it. Let's go."

"Absolutely not. I don't take kindly to folks thinkin' they're better than others based on how they happened to be dressed at the moment." He turned again to the hostess. "Now, you'll lead us to what I reserved, or we'll seat ourselves right here in the main room. And," he wrapped a hand lightly around her wrist, and looked her square in the eye, "should you not, I think I'll arrange to buy the entire company, just so's I can fire you."

The woman pulled away, and returned his card and license. "Wait here a moment. I'll make sure the room is ready for you."

"Sir," Nathan corrected.

"Jonathan," the woman called out, and waited.

"Nate, come on, we can eat somewhere else."

The latest affront sealed the deal. "No. No, we can't. We'll eat right here." He considered his hankering for a good meal may have made him more insistent, but backing down from this fight now wasn't an option.

A man in a tuxedo came through a swinging door. "What is it, Sidnee?"

"I believe your hostess here has a problem." Nathan waved the credit card toward her.

Jonathan walked over. "I apologize. I'm sure she didn't mean anything by it; she's just looking out for the interests of the establishment. I'm the maître 'd, is there something I can help with?"

"You can show us to the Board Room and make good on our reservation," Nathan said holding the card out. "And, then, I believe, Sidnee is in serious need of an attitude adjustment."

The maître 'd took the card, and scowled at the woman. "Right this way, sir."

"Now, ya'll see how difficult that was?" Nathan asked sweetly as he lifted his palms.

"No. Yes. Sorry." Sidnee's face flushed red.

"Excuse me, ma'am. I don't believe I caught that quite right."

"Sorry, sir."

Nathan nodded, gave a beckoning wave of the hand to Zach, and they followed Jonathan to their table.

The walls of the room were oak clad to the halfway mark and capped with an oak chair rail. Capable of seating fourteen, it had been set for two at the end closest to the door. Jonathan handed Nathan his credit card, held their chairs to seat them, placed napkins in their laps, and then handed them each a menu. "I apologize again, sir. Allow me to offer you a bottle of wine for the trouble. I have a beautiful Argentinian Cabernet."

"That'd be most kind."

Jonathan opened a door on a side cabinet to reveal a wine cooler, pulled a bottle, and put a splash of rich, deep red wine into Nathan's goblet. He swirled the glass until small bubbles appeared at the sides, lifted it, gathering more air as he sipped, and allowed the liquid to wash over his tongue. He swallowed, waited a moment, and nodded.

Setting the bottle in front of Nathan after he filled their glasses, Jonathan stepped back. "I'll give you a few moments to look over the menu," he said, and left the room.

After the door closed, Zach let out a whistle. "Hoo, boy. I've never seen you put on airs like that."

"That ain't airs, Zachariah. That's expecting to be treated properly, commanding a bit of respect for—"

An argument ensued, albeit muffled by the doors. Finally, "That man could probably buy this place ten times over. Don't ever—ever—make that mistake again. If corporate hears about this, you'll be lucky if you don't find your ass out on the street tomorrow morning."

Zach and Nathan both burst into quiet laughter. Nathan raised his glass. "Ah, just desserts, properly served."

The menu, hand-selected by Nathan, brought expressions of surprise to Zach.

"An order each of King Crab to start. Follow that with Caesar salad. We'll each have the Commodore. No, change that. Let's go with the Jumbo Cold Water Lobster accompanied by the New York Strip, the steak barely red in the center, baked potato instead of mashed with plenty of butter and sour cream." He paused to consult Zach, "Chives?" Then, "No chives. And open another bottle of this here wine."

"Yes, sir." The waiter backed out of the room, never once having put pen or pencil to paper.

"Holy shit, Nate. Do you eat like this all winter long?"

"As much as I can. It kinda makes up for all the hog slop we eat at the compound." Nathan smiled and pointed a finger at him. "If you ever repeat that to Sarah, I'll drown every body you come home with in the creek."

He planned it as much as a compatibility test with this new self as anything else. If anything went odd, why, he'd just have to take Erick right back to where he found him. So, when each course found its way to the table, Nathan focused on the meal and let Zachariah talk. If he tossed in a question, Nathan fielded it as if each word cost him a wad of cash for the privilege. He closed his eyes and held each sweet morsel on his palate, as if the Eucharist itself melted there. The lobster, dipped in clarified butter, tasted every bit as fresh as the trout they reeled in each year; the romaine so crisp it snapped in his mouth like it'd just been picked from a garden. Then the steak…rich flavor burst through in the juices flooding his mouth, and melted like a savory caramel.

Between courses, he told Zach about the newscast

that focused on Chris wandering around like an amnesia patient, and hoped the man regained himself and found his way home. Then answered the inevitable question: "What brought on such an early switching of selves?"

Zach only smiled and said, "Took a bit of a walk on the wild side, did you?" and winked. "But, what the hell, Nate, that's why we do this, right? To experience life?"

Nathan nodded. "But, you know how we mostly keep to ourselves out there is important. There could be trouble brewing if we ain't careful."

The door opened and the waiter offered them dessert menus. Nathan declined for himself, and hoisted his wine glass toward Zach. "But, ya'll go ahead if there's something there appealing to you."

"I'm stuffed. Honest. I don't think I could sneak a single peanut into my stomach, even if the airline had given me extra to take with me."

"Then I reckon we'll just go walk this off," Nathan replied, handing the credit card to the waiter. When the check came, surprised to find it lower than expected, he added a hefty tip to compensate for taking up a table meant for fourteen, drank the last of the wine in one gulp, and stood.

"Thank you, Nathan. That was epic."

"Well, sir, you deserved it for your effort. Now, if we can make it to the mall before closing, I plumb forgot to get myself a suitcase. Can't go hauling my clothes around in bags, and I intend to move into better quarters tomorrow."

"I've got nothing better to do." Zach held the door open, and swept an arm into a deep bow. "Lead on."

They half-ran the couple city blocks and dashed

through the mall. Nathan picked out a Filson duffle bag for the casual stuff, and a garment bag for dressier things. Then he sought out the clerk. "I'm still in need of something small for personal things, like my razor. Ya'll know what I mean? Can you recommend something that might fit in this duffle?"

Not finding anything properly lined in case of spills, he settled on a bike bag. Then he insisted on buying Zach "at least a change of skivvies and a clean shirt to return home in tomorrow. It's the least I can do."

By the time they headed out for the hotel, a light snow drifted in large flakes. The wind had died and their pace slowed, giving Zach plenty of time to enjoy the smoke he hadn't gotten during or after the meal. Not that he hadn't tried, running was not very conducive to sucking down a cigarette. During the meal, he attempted to sneak out between courses; it happened the waiter popped in with uncanny timing.

Nathan approached the desk and punched the bell a couple times. A clerk rounded the doorway with a smile. "What can we do for you, Mr. Crockett?"

"My friend here needs a room for the night. Ya'll can add it to my bill."

Her expression clouded. "Oh, I'm terribly sorry, sir. We don't have any vacancies at all. Would you like me to call another hotel and see if they can arrange something?"

"You know, Nate, I can just take a cab to the airport and go home."

"What flight do you think you're gonna find headed to Roanoke at this hour. No, sir. You'll stay the night. Well, now, the plan is to move to the Ritz-

Carlton tomorrow. Let's see if they have anything."

They leaned against the counter and waited for her. Her tightly woven braids swung as she shook her head. "Not until tomorrow. Most people check out on Sunday. I'm really sorry, Mr. Crockett."

"Guess you'll just have to make do bunking down with me. That is, if you don't mind." He addressed the clerk, "That's all right, isn't it?"

"If you don't tell, I won't. How's that?"

Chapter 30

A street light still cast a shadow through the gauze of the sheers drawn over the windows when something shook Nathan awake. His body dripped with sweat. He sat up and ran his hands across the top of his head. The damp hair clung to his scalp as if he'd recently dunked it in the creek.

Zach's voice came at him. "Are you okay? You were thrashing around a bit."

He turned to look at Zach, then gazed around the room before the realization hit. He'd never had the dream repeat so soon, but this time it played out a bit different. This time the old man was at the compound. "Sorry. Just the strangest dream, is all. What time is it?"

"Not quite six."

Nathan swung his feet over the side of the bed, sat there and ran his hands over his face. "I swear I've seen that old man. I just can't place it. Feels like I'm trying to wrestle a hunk of coal from the side of the mineshaft."

Zach shifted on the bed. "What old man?"

"What?"

"You said something about an old man wrestling a hunk of coal."

"This old black guy, dressed all disheveled and such. He stares at me and shakes his head."

"Doesn't he say anything?"

No sense in going that far into it. It wouldn't do to throw a scare into Zach or any of the others at the compound if he spilled the beans when he went back. "Not a word. He just shakes his head real sad-like, and walks off."

Not exactly true. The heater kicked on, and despite the rush of warm air a shudder ran down Nathan's torso. He rose and went into the bathroom to stand in the shower under the spray of hot water.

Zach's voice came to him from the darkness. "Is it okay if I put the light on?"

"I expect so." Might as well get a start on the day. Maybe the gym in the mall would be open by the time he'd dressed and hunted down some coffee and breakfast. Nathan showered and shaved, then called out to Zach and swapped places. "Use what you need."

Nathan had already dressed and sat in the single casual chair when Zach stood pulling his new clothing from the bag and asked, "What do I do with the dirty?"

"Throw 'em away."

Zach halted in buttoning his pants. "The shirt, too?"

"Don't see what else you can do, 'less you want to carry around a smelly bag. You hungry?"

"A bit. Mostly, I want coffee."

With the mall locked, they walked around the outside to gain access to the casino. In the coffee shop, over a breakfast better than what Nathan expected, Zach insisted with his questions about the dream.

Weary of the avoidance game, Nathan spit out, "Nothing to tell, Zachariah. It's just some old geezer shows up and tsk-tsks, then walks off shakin' his head."

"Live guy, or deadhead?"

"Deadhead." Dropping his fork to the table, Nathan added, "What difference does it make? It's a dream, nothing more."

"Well, I'm just trying to help you figure it out, analyze it a bit."

"And, I appreciate that. I do," Nathan said. "But, what good does it do? My Big Mama always told me, 'Nathaniel Ray, don't chase after the fox once he's got a hen in his mouth. All it does is tire you out.' "

"I don't get the analogy, there."

"It means, conjecturing on the meaning of my dream certainly won't solve any waking issues. You done?" Nathan stood and plucked the check from the table.

Zach drained his coffee, and made a point of checking the time. "I guess I best get a move on. I figured I'd be back by now. You think I could hail a cab from the hotel?"

Truth was, a spark of recognition about the old man had snapped in Nathan's brain. If it got some air maybe, just maybe, the ember would flare. But something in his gut told him he didn't want to remember. "I think we can do a might better than a taxi."

"You aren't thinking of chauffeuring me out to the airport, are you? There's no need for you to cut time out of your holiday," Zach offered on the way to the cashier.

"Don't you worry about that none. I have plenty of time. Besides, it'd be my pleasure. Ya'll have gone above and beyond for me and it's about time I do something nice in return."

"Now, you do plenty for us. It's your land we live

on, scot free I might add. And you get us things when we go on our supply runs."

"Oh, hush, now," Nathan demurred, stuffing his change into his wallet. It always did embarrass him to have folks fuss over a kindness. "All that saves me from livin' like some kind of hermit. I do appreciate what all of you do, let me show it once in a while."

Nathan led the way to the Ritz lobby and, handing over his credit card and ID, reserved his room, long term. Signing the paperwork, he gave the desk clerk a smile. "Now, then, I know it'll be a bit before I can go up. Do ya'll think you could rustle up a limousine? I need to hustle my friend here off to the airport."

"Absolutely, Mr. Crockett. Please have a seat near the front door, and he'll pull around for you. Is there anything we might do for you, or get for you, while you wait?"

"No, thank you. But, it's kind of you to ask."

Once they were ensconced in the car and on the way, and Nathan had raised the window between the passengers and driver's cab, they considered it safe to talk.

"I imagine you've had quite the adventure so far."

"Cincinnati was the worst. Some new sect, call themselves the Watchers or some such thing, turned the place into a real ghost town. I mean, you know how there's usually plenty of dead folks wanderin' around any city. Well, sir, they were being swallowed up like they'd stepped into a bog and drowned."

"How do you think you made it out?" Zach opened a window and reached for his pack of smokes.

"Sorry, buddy," Nathan shook his head. "Not allowed in here. You know, that part's a bit on the foggy side. I mean, I drove out, obviously, but how I escaped detection, I'm not entirely sure. But, then, you remember hearing about that big wedding?" Zach nodded. "Well, the bride, she's the one who heads up the Watchers. I met her when I stopped for a bit in Dayton."

In response to Zach's expression, Nathan recounted the meeting. As he was about to go into the details of the park, he stopped short. The tightest knot he'd ever experienced formed in his stomach.

Zach grabbed his forearm. "Nathan, what's wrong?"

"Nothing. Winter chill. Maybe this new self has caught himself a cold." Nathan coughed for good measure.

The ember blazed.

Chapter 31

Nathan dropped Zachariah at Departures for his flight out of Cleveland Hopkins back to Roanoke. On the trip to retrieve his luggage from the hotel, and heading to the Ritz to check in, he fought against the panic. A cold sweat made his skin clammy. A shiver ran through him and he fired up the heat in the passenger cabin of the limo. The man who invaded his dreams, this Jason, he'd been right there in the park. Stood not thirty feet from him.

The idea of instructing the chauffeur to turn around and take him to the terminal where he could hop a flight to any remote place on earth, maybe Fiji or the like, struck Nathan as a possibility. Part of him wanted to do just that. At the same time, he couldn't leave Zachariah and the rest to fend for themselves. Not that they weren't capable, but it would take a mighty bit of paperwork and what-not to give Zach the legal authority to handle the compound's affairs. Plus, they'd become the family he couldn't have, and he surely would miss them. Every one of them.

The old man had to have known Nathan stood there as mesmerized as the rest of the deadheads in that park. Yet, he never turned those eyes on him. So, if he'd been that close, that able to nab him with a simple command, why didn't he? It didn't make sense.

Maybe Nathan and his clan weren't such awful

179

criminals after all. Tommy had said lots of folks took over the living for a jaunt. Maybe they could lower their guard a bit. Nathan's gut refused to listen on that score. But, he might make a stop in Dayton on his way back to the compound in the Spring. Talk to Jenna. Plain as the dust covering a miner, he would come right on out and ask her.

The idea loosened the granny knots in his shoulders. Yet, when he arrived in the room, after a hefty tip to the porter for toting his luggage, he shed his clothes and stood under a hot shower, and tried to push the whole affair out of his head. This was his winter vacation, a time for fun, a time for the finer things in life. It wouldn't do to have it interrupted by some nightmarish phantom. He simply wouldn't allow it.

As his head hit the pillow, he smiled at the luxuriousness of it, and drifted off. When the nightmare invaded, half-awake, he pushed it away. Nathan burrowed around in Erick's brain to find something pleasant to dream about.

The sun poured through a hole in the clouds and drilled into Nathan's sleep. He rolled over to check the time. "Ten A.M. Holy… I slept all the way through."

With arms above his head, he pointed his toes, and held the stretch for a long moment. He picked up the phone, ordered breakfast along with a pot of strong, black coffee, and went into the bathroom. As he stepped out of the shower, a deep voice called out "Room Service," and a tingle ran through him.

"Just a second." Nathan pulled on the thick terry robe provided by the hotel. When he opened the door to his suite, he peered at the man, looking for any trace of Jason. What was to stop him from stealing a body himself to confront and snag Nathan? But, opening the door, he found nothing except, perhaps, his own guilty conscience. He chuckled as he signed the bill and showed the guy out.

He ate at the small dining table leisurely savoring each morsel of the Eggs Benedict. Then he opened the drapes, and kicked back with his coffee. The corner suite offered him a grand view of both Lake Erie and the river it helped feed. Freighters cut the surface of the lake between the diamonds of light sparkling off the tips of waves. Following the wake of a smaller one, he found the mouth of the Cuyahoga River, where fleets of boats scurried up and down a flowing body of water.

Returning his gaze to the lake, Nathan watched the birds. Their bodies held aloft on invisible waves, they floated and turned in long, wide arcs in search of food, and he allowed them to mesmerize him into a deep slumber.

The canopy of silver maple and dogwood spread their new leaves providing thicker cover over the cabins that ringed the glen at the compound. A group of children played a game of tag in the less-used portion running through the white blanket of Queen Anne's Lace. A corner of his mind found that odd. There were no kids living there. With Zach, Sarah, and another woman at his side, Nathan watched them, and laughed until he caught sight of the old man standing at the head of a worn path leading to the holler where the creek wended its way through the vast holdings of land. Nathan froze. Fear crept up quivering legs and filled the pit of his stomach.

"We gon' meet agin. You jes wait and see if I ain't right."

"Go on about your own business, old man. Go away." His words didn't interrupt the delighted screams of the kids or the obvious enjoyment of the adults following their antics.

Jason turned his sights onto one particular giggling toddler, who sat in the middle of the hubbub, and nodded at him.

Anger boiled, causing Nathan's hands to ball into fists, as he ran toward the child, and scooped him to the safety of his arms. "You leave him alone!"

An old finger pointed at Nathan. "Maybe one day you ain't gon' have on no coat of protection."

Nathan trembled and mumbled in his sleep.

Chapter 32

Jenna and Marvin sat in their usual booth the Sunday morning after the new year, while Tommy and Mike scurried about the diner. Not a single seat was empty. Gazing around Epstein's, Jenna sighed. "Gosh, I miss Colleen. That old woman was such a life raft."

Marvin slathered a *schmear* onto his bagel. "I'm glad she was around to help you."

"Oh, yeah. Right. Like you wanted me to get over your death and move on in life," Jenna joked.

"Hey, I eventually came around."

As Tommy moved past to set plates in front of a group of deadheads he tossed a comment Marvin's way. "Dude, you came around all right. Right after Jason put the fear of eternal hell into you."

"Can it, hippie. Nobody asked you." Marvin parried his knife loaded with cream cheese in the air.

"My, aren't we snappy this morning," Mike said sidling between tables to deliver plates of food. "You've been cranky all week again. What happened, Jenna, didn't you get him anything for Christmas?"

"I gave him something. A swift kick in the rear end." Jenna poked an elbow into Marvin's side.

"Oh, do you need a hug from your Uncle Tommy, is that what you need?"

Marvin grinned. "I need a hug from you like I need to jump off a cliff."

"Well, look at it this way, Marvin. Jumping off a cliff won't kill you." Tommy laughed and ran to serve the last guests.

Jenna pushed her empty plate to the middle of the table. "Speaking of missing people, I sure thought Nathan would've been around for the holidays. Have you seen him?"

Mike set two plates of food down on the table and called over the din of phantom voices. "Come on, Tommy. Sit. Eat." He scooted into the booth. "Haven't seen him in a long while now."

"Seen who?" Tommy asked and took his place across from Jenna.

Marvin lifted his coffee cup in Jenna's direction. "She was asking about Nathan."

"Oh. He was in a while back. It was the week before Thanksgiving. He was here one morning before we even opened, but left when Tina unlocked the doors. I'm sure he's around somewhere."

Jenna turned to gaze out the window. "I still can't seem to find him, and I need to talk to him."

"He said he wanted to check out some of the sights and things we suggested. He's probably off running some unsuspecting person around the city," Tommy offered with a shrug. "You know, I still think he was in that guy that morning. Remember, the one who was here for breakfast that day, and then stumbled out of the park in a stupor?"

"And, that," Jenna pointed a finger at Tommy, "is precisely why I want to talk to him."

"He's not in any trouble, is he?" Mike chomped his way along a strip of bacon until it disappeared.

"He really shouldn't keep doing that."

"Why? We all slide in once in a while. What's wrong with having a little harmless fun."

"A little harmless fun would be fine, Marvin. If that's all he did," Jenna pointed out.

Tommy's forkful of Eggs Benedict halted halfway to his mouth, and then went back to the plate. "So, okay, I don't get it. You didn't say a word when I did it. You and your entire group do it. I mean, we all know everything is a bit diminished for us. What's so terrible about him sliding into someone to experience something more intensely?"

"Wait a minute," Mike said. "A month ago you thought anyone who did that should be held accountable."

"I'm only asking for clarification, Mike. That's all. I mean, Nathan seems like a nice guy. I don't want to see him go where...well, you know."

Jenna leaned back in her chair and studied the three men who'd been such a large part of her life since she'd crossed over. Tommy, ordinarily a goofball, rarely put forth such serious discussions. "Well, it's tough to answer. My group does it strictly to help the living, you know that. What you did, Tommy, was commendable because not only did you help Moe when he needed someone to run the place, but the homeless man you took over got a lot in return. There's a good reason to believe that Nathan—and others like him—reside in the living for lifetimes. For what? To satisfy their own wants and needs and desires, and nothing else. If they did some honest good, maybe Jason and Nancy would allow them to get away with it."

Mike swallowed a sip of coffee. "But, that's not really what the Watchers do, right? I mean, Jason's

Keepers manage those of us on this plane, Teresa's sect accepts those ready to move on, and yours protects the living from the living. So, how does this Nathan guy figure in with you?"

Jenna gave him a gentle smile. "We have a situation brewing. If I'm right, if my hunch plays out, Nathan might be able to help us. That is—"

"Wait a minute. This schmuck can help but I can't?" Marvin interrupted with a bite of bagel held in the side of his mouth.

"Marvin, look, let me get this figured out. Then we can talk."

"It's always later with you, isn't it? Later on the wedding, later on—"

Jenna stuck a finger at him. "Don't start with me."

"I'll start anything, anytime I please."

Marvin's "Ow!" prior to Tommy's, "Dude, would you let her finish, please?" indicated an unseen kick somewhere.

Marvin scowled and turned away. "Fine."

"And stop talking with your mouth full. I know your mother taught you better than that." Jenna jabbed an elbow into Marvin. "So, what I need to do is get to him before Jason does. Remember when Nathan spied on us in Eastwood Park? I think the only reason Jason didn't grab him was because he's too tired. He told Nancy he's very close to needing to disburse his burden."

Marvin put his coffee on the table. "I'm not surprised. The things he maintains…"

Jenna's brow creased at the sight of a close-to-violent shudder that ran through Marvin's body. She'd forgotten about his experience within Jason. The reminder kicked some wheels into gear in her mind. Maybe Marvin could help. Maybe he could talk to Nathan and get him to understand what horrors awaited if he didn't stop. But, her focus shifted to the more important, more immediate issue. "Well, before I worry about Nathan, I need to find this young woman Diane has been trying to chase down. I need to get to her, too, before Jason does."

Tommy put a generous dose of salt and pepper on his hash browns. "What did she do?"

"Killed a man who had been attempting to abduct a little girl."

"You killed a guy, and Jason let you go," Mike said.

"Not without a lot of convincing, and I think it was only because Nancy intervened."

Marvin chimed in, "She wasn't the only one who helped, you know."

Jenna let loose an exasperated sigh. "I didn't say she was. Dammit, Marvin, stop already."

He shrugged. "I'm just making the point."

Jenna's brow furled. "Point noted, okay? Can we move on now?" She shook her head in disgust. "Now—"

Diane burst through the front doors of the diner. "Jenna, I think we found her. But, I sure could use some help in cornering her."

Jenna rose from her seat. "Okay, Marvin. You wanted to help? Let's go."

Chapter 33

Through Christmas Nathan managed to push the nightmares down deep to the recesses of his mind. It became a little bit easier as time passed, and the holidays breezed by without a single occurrence. Not that he could recall, anyway. The blues of the season never found him like they typically did; missing family. Not that he could've visited them in Maryland while facing the need to deal with a new body. More rested, peace of mind settled into his brain.

After exercising in the hotel gym the morning of New Year's Eve, he stepped from the shower of his suite and tried to pinch at the love handles that had melted off in little more than a month. He smiled at the image, and slapped at the now-flat belly. "Diet and exercise; diet and exercise. As my grandpappy used to say, ya'll can't lay around like a sow and expect to look like a racehorse."

Late that evening, with the nightmares having been tamped down, he smiled broadly at the driver as he climbed into the back seat of the limo. "Dean, see if you can steer me to the hottest nightclub around."

"Yes, sir. I think we can accomplish that."

Nathan lowered the privacy window between the driver and passenger portions of the car, turned on the radio and, though they ordinarily bugged him, he hummed along to a carol that should've been put away now that Christmas was over. Large cities intrigued him and he found himself peering up at the buildings. He shook his head in disbelief at the sight of century-old classic architecture with modern glass and steel behemoths dropped in like odd nails deliberately driven into the landscape. City structures here were as different as the people who inhabited them; people who always hurried to go somewhere, or do something. They lived their lives as if in constant emergency.

Country folk, his people, took things at a slower pace. Sure, certain times called for quick thinking, and quick action. Like the explosion which took his first life. But, what was life for if not to enjoy, to chew on it for a spell; to soak up and savor every minute?

Thirty minutes later, the car slowed and drove past a block-long line of people. "My, they sure do get all gussied up around these parts, don't they?"

Dean laughed. "Yes, sir, I guess they do. Especially on a night for partying." With the car idling curbside of the entrance, he jumped out, ran around and held the door. "Shall I wait, Mr. Crockett?"

"Well, it would save me the wait, and you the drive, later on. Ya'll could even park and then join me if you want. But, whatever you decide is fine."

"It's doubtful I'd have any better luck getting in than she is." Dean pointed to a woman in a just-below-the-knees sapphire blue dress, being held back by a man at the stanchions.

"Are you kidding? You're letting my friends in but not me?" The woman heaved a sigh, and Nathan chuckled when she flipped rather short brown hair with a shake of her head. "You know what? That's bullshit."

The group she'd evidently been with strode

through the doors as one called over her shoulder, "Calm down. Come find us when he decides to let you in."

She raised her voice, and wrapped her arms around herself against a sudden chilled breeze. "You know what? You guys suck."

Nathan gestured for Dean to hold in place and approached the doorman. "She's right you know. It's bullshit." He placed a hand on the girl's forearm as he held a hand out toward the guy blocking the way into the club. "Ya'll think you might have any private booths left open in there?"

The bouncer glanced from Nathan to the car and back again, nodded, and unclipped the rope while he slipped the money into a side pocket.

"And," Nathan continued, upping his volume for Dean to hear, "you need to let my man in after he parks the car."

"No problem."

"What's your name, darlin'?" Brown eyes too big for the face stared up at Nathan. "I swear on my mama's grave, I don't bite."

A grin broke over her face. "Shelly, Shelly Platt."

"Well, Shelly Platt, I'm pleased to meet you. My name's Nathan—Nate, if you like. Now that we've been properly introduced, how about we go in? Then, I want you to do me a favor."

Shelly pulled her arm from him, a crease formed above the bridge of her nose.

"When we go past your friends, the ones who allowed you to stand out here alone, I want you to conjure the biggest smile you can muster and give 'em a nice little wave. Can ya do that for me?"

To his delight, a rather mischievous smile returned to her. "I'm sure I can handle that."

Inside the club, music blaring, Nathan leaned in close to the next man to greet them and pointed. "Up there, behind the speakers. I'd like to spare these ears for old age."

A grin and a nod acknowledged the request, and he led the way. True to her word, Shelly smiled and waved to the group she now abandoned, and Nathan nodded and tipped his non-existent hat with a middle finger. Not exactly gentlemanly, but it felt good to see the reaction of gape-mouthed disbelief cross those faces.

"Now," Nathan said. "What would you like to drink? Would champagne be all right?"

"I've never had that, but sure. Live to experience."

"I like that thought." He returned his attention to the waiter. "Let's start with two bottles. Oh, and my driver will be coming in to join us, so we'll need three glasses."

He returned his attention to Shelly, who wasn't his standard taste in women. "My, but you're a bitty little thing. It's a wonder you don't get blown like a bird's feather right into Lake Erie."

Shelly laughed, her front teeth slightly protruded. "I'm not that skinny."

"Well, still, I'll ask you to remind me to keep a tight grip on you when we head back outside later on."

Long past the hour of countdown and obligatory toast, and her friends having stopped to say they were leaving, to which Shelly only replied, "Whatever," she and Nathan sat in conversation. The longer he spent talking with her, the more his attraction to her mounted. Simple statements of her life came from her in easy conversation. They hadn't made a single excursion to the dance floor, not that it bothered Nathan. With what seemed a parade of new selves of late, dancing was about as frivolous a thing as all get-out. Heck, maneuvering without noticeable stuttering took enough concentration.

Shelly didn't make a single request, anyway. He liked that she appeared content to sit and talk. The quantity of drinking over the course of the night didn't have the slightest effect; no slurred speech, and no weaving or wobbling the few times she excused herself to the ladies' room. He liked that, too.

A little after 4:00am Nathan noticed the club had quieted considerably. The flashes of dance floor lighting ceased. Background music oozed from overhead speakers, and only a smattering of distant conversations accompanied quick bursts of laughter. He stood and held out a hand. "Well, I expect we should let these fine people close up and go home."

They found Dean on a stool at the bar, his head resting on his arms, sound asleep. "Have a seat, Shelly. It might be best to let him wake up a tad before he attempts to take us anywhere." Nathan called to the bartender, "Can we get some coffees?"

As Dean sucked down his coffee, Nathan studied Shelly, drawn to her. It didn't have much to do with physical allure. She was pretty in a way though, and he sensed the tiniest twinge of temptation in that direction. No, it had more to do with her confidence; the way she held her head, the way she laughed, the way she never avoided eye contact. A genuine sparkle radiated from her even in her inquisitiveness about his life. Regardless of any financial status, it's what he had wanted in his original incarnation, longed for when he lived.

The mine explosion had taken that away, though his kinfolk badgered that new self to no end about marrying and keeping the family thriving. Well, he kept the name alive, anyway. That was something, wasn't it? It's not like he could explain anything at the time. And even though he knew they suspected something odd about him, Nathan hadn't even dared after his mama and daddy crossed over and kept phantom-like residence in the family home.

Dean tipped his head back to gulp down the last of his coffee, and Nathan took the chance to shake off the thoughts invading his brain. "If ya'll have pushed the yarn out of your head, we should probably get our girl here to home. What do you say, Dean?"

Sliding the cup to the back of the bar, Dean stood and dug in his pockets for the car keys. "Ready."

Nathan held a crooked arm out to Shelly, and they followed Dean to the entrance where they waited for him to retrieve the limousine. A shiver ran through Shelly. "The car will be warm by the time he pulls around." Nathan would've given her his jacket, had he worn one. Instead he wrapped a cooler than normal arm around her shoulders in hopes it would help some.

Once Dean had them settled in, he headed out toward the west side suburbs. Nathan raised the privacy panel between the compartments. "I surely have enjoyed the evening."

Shelly smiled. "Me, too. I bet my dad's frantic right now, though."

"Oh?" Something Nathan hadn't considered.

"Don't get me wrong. He doesn't hover. But, I

haven't been out this late since right after I finished graduate school in June."

"Are you working already?"

A shake of her head. "No. Not that I haven't been applying for positions with every major college."

"What is it you want to teach?" Nathan's interest in her shot up another notch.

"Education."

And another. He shook his head to rid the fantasy beginning to build. "That's a right nice goal." As soon as the words exited his mouth, he mentally slapped himself. What kind of impression did that make? Then again, maybe it was better. A might silly of him to think about such things, anyway.

The intercom beeped. "We're here, ma'am." Dean jumped from the car to hold the door open.

Shelly laid a hand on his forearm. "I really have had a very nice time. Thank you, Nathan."

Nathan leaned in and planted a soft kiss on her mouth. "I'm pleased. Maybe we could go out to dinner sometime?"

Shelly cocked her head the slightest bit. "I'd like that. Good night, Nathan." With Dean's help, she exited the car.

His mama's voice rang in his head. "Nathaniel Ray, where are your manners?" he mumbled, scooted across the seat, and escorted her to the door. "Lights are on inside. I hope I haven't caused you too much trouble."

Shelly uttered a quiet laugh. "He'll get over it." She stood on her toes, gave him a peck on the lips. "Good night, Nathan." Then inside before the door closed behind her, "Morning, Dad!"

Halfway back to the hotel, Nathan again lowered the privacy window. "Dean, do you think you could find the house again?"

In the rearview mirror, a smile appeared across the man's lips. "Yes, sir. I'm sure I could."

"Is tomorrow too soon, do you think?"

Dean laughed. "Mr. Crockett, it's not what I think that matters."

"Would late afternoon be all right?"

"You want my honest response?"

"I do."

"I think sleep is going to be highly overrated for that young lady."

With thought and emotion warring, Nathan nodded and watched the scenery go by.

Chapter 34

Even with drawing the draperies closed as much as possible to avoid the sun creeping around the edges, sleep evaded Nathan. He tossed, rearranged the massive pile of pillows, and tossed some more. He pulled the covers over his head, and moments later threw them to the bottom of the bed. He yawned, he stretched, he nuzzled into the mattress.

Hours later he issued a loud exhausted moan which echoed through the room. "It's not like she's going anywhere. You've got more than two months before you head back. And that's all you can do. You know that. Now, stop this nonsense. If you think you can pull a fast one over on her, let alone escape the goblins and gremlins, and Lord knows what else might be determined to stop this life..." Despite the attempt at levity, the first thought of Jason in weeks caused a violent shiver to snake through him. Regardless of the lecture, spending time with Shelly continued to haunt his mental images. But, real time. He wanted to be with her Spring and on into Summer. And Fall. Come Winter they'd head off to any destination she pleased, and do whatever she wanted, any time she wanted.

At noon, he rose, opened the curtains, stared out over the landscape and found nothing to distract him. Nothing moved out on the water, no cars had ventured to take to the roads—not within his view, anyway. He grabbed the phone from the nightstand, ordered milk and toast to neutralize the sourness churning in his stomach. In the bathroom, he wished the steam that billowed from the shower would fill his head with "a might bit of common sense."

After he finished dressing, and while he consumed the meager breakfast, the phone was in his hand before he could stop.

Mirth colored the response on the other end. "It sure took you long enough, Mr. Crockett."

"Well, now, I wanted to give you recuperation time. How long will it take you to be out front?"

Dean let out a small laugh. "Would now be fast enough?"

As he stepped from the elevator, Nathan greeted Dean. "I sure do appreciate ya'll doing this."

"Any time, Mr. Crockett."

On the drive, Nathan mused, "Where the heck is everyone today?"

"Watching football, of course."

Nathan snorted. "Never could wrap my brain around that one. I didn't take you away from anything, did I?"

"There's been a big party raging in my living room for the past three hours already. All the wives and girlfriends got together and made this huge spread for breakfast, we've got kegs of beer…"

Stealing a glance, Nathan saw the smirk. "You know what, Dean? I think I like you."

"That's good to know, Mr. Crockett. That's good to know." The car slowed and pulled to the curb in front of a modest Victorian that hadn't been fully visible in the early morning. "Here we are."

Nathan opened his own door before Dean even unlatched his seatbelt. "Thank you."

"You want me to wait?"

"That'd be right nice, if you wouldn't mind. Just long enough that I can determine the lay of the land, as it were."

Nathan walked up the steps to a porch that spanned the entire front of the house and pushed the button of the doorbell. Muffled Westminster chimes rang out in perfect tones. The door opened a moment later to a rather burly, tousle-haired, middle-aged man in sweatpants and t-shirt. He appeared to assess Nathan, as well as the car at the curb, for a moment. Then he turned away. "Shell!"

Her bellowed response echoed through the oak entry. "Yeah?"

"Visitor!" The man swiveled to Nathan. "Well, don't just stand there. I'm not paying to heat the outdoors."

"Yes, sir. I sure do apologize." Nathan crossed the threshold and closed the door with a tiny click. The hand he extended in greeting found a retreating backside.

The man's bare feet padded without sound. "Game's on."

Shelly's face popped around the corner, then a generous smile spread. Shaking her head, she walked toward Nathan dressed in gray sweatpants and a dingy-white cable-knit sweater that hung to her knees, and her feet as naked as her father's. "I am surprised."

"I do apologize. I should've called first, but I plumb forgot to get your number. If it's inconvenient—"

The bridge of her nose scrunched, and she pursed her lips in response. "Come on in."

"Are you sure? He's watching his football, I shouldn't disturb him."

The laugh fell out as easily and as brightly as Nathan remembered from the night before. "He's already disturbed," she said, and drew a mocking circle around her temple with a forefinger. She led him to the living room where her father sat on the couch, his feet up on a coffee table. "Dad, I'd like you to meet Nathan. Nathan, this is my father, Phillip."

Nathan extended a hand in greeting. "Pleased to—"

Phillip jumped out of his seat, a fist pumping the air. "Go! Run, you stupid fuck! Go, go go!"

Startled, Nathan pulled back, and turned his attention to the television. The camera followed a player as he ran down the field barely ahead of a pack from the opposing team. The roar of the stadium crowd blared from speakers placed in all four corners of the room and grew louder as the man crossed the goal line.

"Now, that's what I'm talkin' about!" Phillip put a hand out. "Nathan." After a one-pump handshake, he nodded at a chair and his attention returned to the television. "Have a seat. You like football?"

"Well, sir, I'm more a basketball kind of guy."

"Shell, get your guy a drink. How about a beer? Plenty of beer."

Shelly shook her head, but a wide grin remained on her face. "Don't mind him, Nathan. His brain will engage again once the game is over. Would you like something to drink?"

"I thought we might go to dinner somewhere. Unless, of course, you'd like to stay and watch the game. I could tell Dean to come back later." Nathan gestured toward the front of the house.

"Don't you drive?"

Phillip's question struck Nathan as odd, coming out of nowhere as it did. "Yes, sir. I just find it easier to hire a car in unfamiliar surroundings. Gets me places faster that way."

"There's this thing called GPS. You might want to think about getting one. Oh, what the—get your head out of your ass so somebody can shove that flag up it!"

Nathan laughed. Despite manners he ordinarily found rude, he liked this man. There was something straight-forward, honest in his behavior. "I'll take it under advisement."

"Dad, we're gonna go get something to eat," Shelly said, and got a quick wave of her father's hand in response. "Let me go get changed."

"Oh, there's really no need. We don't have to go anyplace fancy."

"Are you sure? It would only take a minute."

Nathan took her in from the feet up and settled on her eyes. "Positive. You're stunning just the way you are."

A giggle escaped her. "Pardon my language, but that's bullshit. It's nice bullshit, but it's still bullshit."

"Seriously: Put on a pair of shoes and you're ready."

"Let's go then. They're in the rack next to the door. Later, Dad."

She moved up again in Nathan's estimation. Imagine, a female these days willing to head out in sweat pants, baggy sweater, and no make-up. "It was a pleasure to meet you, sir."

Phillip's gaze never faltered from the game. "You can stop with the 'sir' crap, Nathan. Have a nice time."

They sat across from one another at a pizzeria. Amid lively conversation about her college days, wherein Nathan managed to fend off questions about himself with, "Now, that there's a pretty dull story. There's a trust fund that lets me do pretty much whatever I fancy," he watched her consume half of the large meat-laden pie. How she managed to stay so rail thin if she ate as heartily all the time only served to engage him that much more.

Shelly leaned back in her booth, and let out a gush of air as she groaned. "Oh, my God, I'm full."

"I'd say you've got a right nice appetite. It's a pleasure to see someone eat like they enjoy it. Food should be savored."

"Well, I'd say I savored more than I should have," Shelly said with a laugh. "I think I need to move a bit, if I can get up from this bench."

Nathan slid money under the check the waiter had left at the edge of the table, then held out a hand and helped her to stand. He paused for a moment at Dean's side on the way to the door. "We're going to go for a bit of a walk."

Dean put his fork down and wiped his mouth. "You want me to follow with the car?"

"No, no. Relax; finish your dinner. We'll be back."

Thirty minutes later, as Dean thanked him a second time for the meal and closed the door of the limo, he asked, "To the lady's house?"

Nathan gave a questioning look to Shelly, who snuggled in close and looped an arm through his. "Wherever you'd like to go."

"To my hotel?"

Shelly nodded. "I'd like that."

There was minimal conversation during the twenty-minute ride. Up in his suite, without a word about the accommodations, she tossed her coat onto the back of one of the dining chairs. Of course, what with the limousine and the private booth at the nightclub, it was possible she expected it. But the woman was highly educated, with a bright personality, as comfortable in luxury as eating pizza in a hole-in-the-wall dive, and his estimation of her rose another notch. She turned to Nathan, wrapped her arms around him, lifted onto her toes, and kissed him.

He embraced her and returned the kiss.

"I'm not fragile, Nathan. I won't break."

Her response made him smile. The deftness of undressing him as she pushed him toward the bedroom brought his body temperature up—almost to a living person's normal. The time Stacey had done the same drifted against his brain for only an instant. Then he lost himself in a part of life he longed for, a part that made him anticipate each winter.

As she lay sleeping in the early evening, Nathan's brain strayed into the fantasy of spending life, a real life, with her. Walking together through the wildflowers of the glen at the compound, wandering through the woods as she gazed in wonder at the colors of fall— while he gazed at the wonder of her. Sharing everything, dreaming together. But would she understand if she ever learned the truth? Or would she run?

She stirred, and an arm snaked its way across his chest. "You're cold." She pulled the blanket up, snuggled under it, and her hand moved to fondle him.

"Well, that's sure to raise my temperature." He placed a hand over hers to still it. "Tell, me something, where is your favorite place? If you could be anywhere in the world, where would it be? Mountains, beach..."

Shelly laughed. "I love the mountains. There's nothing more beautiful to me than standing in a mountain glen of wildflowers. But, the sound of waves can lull me to sleep and make me feel...I don't know...safe. Isn't that weird?"

"No, darlin', not at all. I'd love to show you my mountains someday. But the accommodations are what ya'll might call rustic."

"Rustic, as in?"

"Cabins, outhouses, and no cell service at all."

She shrugged against his side and tried to snuggle in closer. "I've been camping before with nothing but a tent and a sleeping bag. Having a cabin, and some privacy, could be fun." Her hand moved underneath his.

An hour later they showered together, and dressed. Nathan was surprised to have Dean again answer when he pushed the button marked Limousine Service on the hotel phone and chuckled. "Do you even have a home to go to?"

"I do. But, I also knew you'd need me again today. Are you ready?"

"We are."

"I'll be waiting at the curb," Dean said, and hung up.

At the Platt house, Nathan walked Shelly to the door despite her protestations that he should stay in the car and keep warm. "Blame it on my Southern upbringing. If I didn't walk you up my mama would never let me hear the end of it. 'Nathaniel Ray,' she'd say 'I surely taught you better manners than that. Now, you get off your backside and do what's right.' "

Shelly let out a laugh and shook her head. "Well, we wouldn't want your mother chastising you for the next month. She sounds like my kind of person. I'd love to meet her some day."

"Well, I wish that could happen, but it could be a might tough. Both of my folks are dead. I just meant I'd hear her voice ringing in my brain."

The expression of delight on her face faded into dismay. "Oh, I'm so sorry."

"It was a long time ago already, but thank you," Nathan said, though he kept the exact number of years to himself. "Can I see you again? Would tomorrow night be too soon?"

"I'd like that. And maybe the games tomorrow won't interest my dad to the point he'll have his face buried in the television."

The kiss lingered longer than Nathan expected. He stood mesmerized for several minutes after she went in, called out, "Dad, I'm home," and the door closed behind her. He shook his brain back to life and walked to the car. A block down the street, he sat up ramrod straight. "Nathan, you are a pinhead if there ever was one." He lowered the privacy panel. "Dean, go back. I forgot to get her phone number, again."

Dean made a u-turn at the next intersection.

Nathan jumped from the car before it came to a complete stop, ran to the door, and rang the bell.

Phillip opened the door, said "Hey, Nathan," turned into the house and walked toward the living room. "Shell! Visitor!"

Remembering the earlier admonishment, Nathan stepped into the foyer and closed the door. As Shelly came into view on the staircase from the upper floor, he grinned. "I'm as dumb as pack mule. I plumb forgot to get your phone number."

She let loose with the same sparkling laugh he'd heard on New Year's Eve. "216-555-SHELL."

Nathan plugged it into his cell phone. "Got it. Thank you, ma'am." He gave her a tip of his non-existent hat, and turned to open the door.

She grabbed the back of his jacket, spun him around, stood on tiptoes and kissed him. "Goodnight, Nathan."

"Goodnight. I'll call." Nathan walked back to the car, where a smiling Dean held the door, and crawled in without a word. He maintained his silence for the trip back to the hotel, despite noticing a smirking Dean checking him through the rearview mirror.

Dean walked with Nathan to the hotel and held the door for him. "Will you be needing me tomorrow, Mr. Crockett?"

"It's possible. But, you really should take a day off. You've been running me around for almost forty-eight hours; ya'll have got to be plum tuckered out."

"It's been my pleasure, sir." Dean pulled a card from his inside jacket pocket and handed it to Nathan. "If you need a ride, you call me."

"Thank you, I will. Now, you go get yourself some sleep."

In his room, Nathan shed his clothes and dropped onto the bed. The smell of her still clung to the pillow, and he put it to his nose and inhaled: clean with a tiny trace of perfume. An unbidden smile came to his lips as he rolled and wrapped himself around the pillow. Thoughts of how sweet she was, how good it would be to share the days and nights, the weeks, months and the years into old age, permeated his brain as he drifted off.

He again stood taking in the beauty of the silver maple and dogwood ringing the glen at the compound. A group of children played, running through the white blanket of Queen Anne's Lace, the occasional wild yellow daffodil poking a head out to be noticed. Squeals of laughter rode the light breeze to his ears as he stood at the edge of the clearing in the afternoon sun with Zach, and Sarah. A smiling Shelly stood at his side, an arm around his waist. Movement at the head of a worn path leading to the holler where the creek snaked its way through the property caught his attention. Nathan froze at the sight of Jason. The old man leaned against an old, thick-trunked tree and his eyes bored into Nathan's. Like a bank of thick, dark clouds had formed, his world dropped into shadow. Fear churned in the pit of his stomach, and he trembled in his sleep.

Chapter 35

Date after date, filled with conversation, their connection deepened. Taking her father with them to dinner one evening proved a good move, too. The conversation had been lively. The guy was funny and didn't seem even slightly suspicious of Nathan's attention to his only daughter. Nathan found himself praying Shelly felt the same about him.

Through one-sided conversations, he convinced himself the probable chances of success with her stood somewhere right around ninety percent; if he dared to believe in a dream, in a future with family, a real family to call his own. That was if he remembered the words from the nightmare; if it were true that Jason couldn't touch him so long as he stayed in Erick. Though, he'd have to be very careful. Because Nathan wanted to seal the deal with Shelly. Turn it into more than "let's go out to dinner, or meet for drinks, or spend the night in bed."

Walking through the mall with his mind pre-occupied, he didn't pay much attention to anything but the floor ahead of him; a habit he'd acquired in his youth when deep in thought over solving a problem at the mine.

A sudden jolt rattled him. He sat up, shook his head, and realized he was tangled up in another person. A woman had run headlong into him, and tossed them both to the ground like old feed sacks dumped on the floor of the barn. Deadheads in the near vicinity stood to watch the commotion. Some laughed even as others gazed at Nathan as if in awe, or confusion.

The woman pulled herself into a sitting position and faced him, then brushed her hands along her very short blonde hair. "Sorry."

"Sorry?" Nathan mimicked. "Ya'll knocked me for a real loop, and all you can say is 'sorry'?"

She shrugged her athletic shoulders. "I didn't see you."

"Well, obviously." Nathan stood. "Are you okay?"

Blue eyes gazed up at him. "I'm fine." A curious expression crossed her face, then she glanced around at the people streaming along in that weird dance they do to dodge oncoming foot traffic in crowded places. "We should've breezed right through one another. Where did you come from?"

His stomach dropped, and Nathan looked around in a panic only to discover his new self walking steadily along. If Jason was anywhere in the vicinity, Nathan was a true goner.

This could not happen. Even if he survived, he could not go through finding another new body this soon. Zach would kill him if he had to deal with the machinations of creating yet another new identification within weeks. Worse, it would mean Shelly slipping through his fingers. An odd ache stabbed his heart.

Nathan did his best to grab control of his emotions without letting this woman in on his secret. Even as he moved a couple of steps in the direction his errant body had gone, and craned his neck to peer above passing people in search of Erick, he asked, "What's your name?"

"Heidi." She stood and pushed a hand out.

"Name's Nathan. Pleased to meet you, but where in the name of—"

A male voice called out his name, another familiar male voice laughed and said, "How about that? A two-fer!"

Heidi turned to run and halted as if she'd been frozen in mid-stride when a new, booming, ominous voice called out her name. A woman Nathan had never seen before approached Heidi. "Finally. Girl, you are one tough nut to crack, you know that? It feels like we've been chasing you through half the state."

Nearby deadheads took off running in all directions, though a few stopped inside adjacent stores and peered through the display windows to watch while Heidi, moving like Frankenstein's monster, returned to stand next to Nathan.

Nathan's throat went dry, and his body shook. This cannot be happening. Not now. He turned with longing in the direction he'd been headed.

His new body had stopped and gaped at him, as if he saw him. "Nathan, what happened? Are you coming?"

This turn of events confounded Nathan. In all the years of taking over living people, not a one had ever been aware. "Erick?"

"What should I do? You want me to go ahead and pick something out for Shelly, or wait for you?"

Nathan didn't doubt that Erick would be able to communicate. There were plenty of people capable of seeing and hearing the dead. But, this guy seemed especially adept. And, now, Nathan wanted to know why. Even more than when he'd talked to that woman at the museum the day he'd decided on Erick. Could it be a result of having occupied the body for so long? What about all the others he'd shed, the kid left alone on the roadside? Though he'd never noticed any apparitions following him, Nathan scanned the crowd.

"Oh, shit…" Erick's voice trembled. "This is what you've been afraid of. What can I do, Nathan?"

Nathan took a step toward him and opened his mouth to respond, and a hand touched his shoulder. He jumped away, wanted to run.

Jenna's voice boomed in Nathan's ears. "Nathan, you stop right there and turn around."

His feet refused to do anything but obey the command.

"Now that's something I've never witnessed before." Marvin stood smiling. "Hey, someone wants to talk to you."

Jenna moved into view. "I have to admit, Marvin, it was a good idea to have you ahead of us. Now, the two of you are going to come with us. We have a lot to talk about. The question is, will you cooperate, or do we have to take you?"

Heidi found her voice, although it quivered with vibrato. "What do you mean take us? Take us where?"

Nathan knew what Jenna meant, and squeezed his eyes shut. "I've seen it, and ya'll don't want that to happen. It's best we do what they ask."

The smirk on the face of the woman with Jenna made her words redundant. "Like you have a choice."

"Before we do anything, I think you need to talk to that guy over there." Marvin indicated Erick, who waited in place. "It's either that, or figure out a way to get him to go along."

Nathan turned his head. "You leave him alone. He hasn't done nothing."

Heidi glared at him. "Is this what got us in all this trouble? I'm stuck because of you?"

"I don't know about that," Marvin stated. "They've been looking for you for a long time and, personally, I'm tired of her," Marvin hooked a thumb over his shoulder toward Jenna, "being gone all the time."

"Marvin, shut up. You're breaking my concentration."

"What're you talking about? I'm not doing a thing but hel—"

"I said, shut—"

Heidi broke away, running through the throngs of shoppers.

"Dammit! Now look what you did."

In the commotion, Marvin took off to chase after Heidi as Jenna's form turned into a storm-cloud of swirling dark matter. A tornado-wind of chill air spun around the mall's path. People wrapped their arms around themselves, grumbling about air conditioning being tested in the middle of winter. A great voice roared out of Jenna. "Marvin, get away from her."

Erick made a beeline toward Nathan. With his stomach lurching into his throat, Nathan ran right at him. "Hurry, Erick."

"Oh, no you don't!" The blonde stranger jumped in front of Nathan. As she struck into Erick's right side Nathan pushed into the left.

Erick's muffled voice burrowed into Nathan's head. "Oh, my God, it's like I'm in a freezer. Nathan, do something. Get her out, it's too cold." Then another, female voice commanded, "Get out. Now."

"Erick, I'm sorry." What would happen to the clan if he didn't return? What would happen to the compound, to the land holding itself? He never made any arrangements on that score. A deep sadness rained down on him. Defeat descended over him like a heavy cloak.

"I'll go wherever Nathan wants." Erick moved next to Nathan, but his voice sounded odd, as if a basso was attempting to sing tenor.

Wearing an expression that revealed mistrust, Jenna, returned to the spot with Heidi in tow. "You," she said to Heidi, "stay put, if you know what's good for you. Try getting away again and you'll regret it. I promise you that."

"Fine. Whatever. I don't know what you want, but you people can suck it."

"And shut your mouth. I'll get back to you in a second." Jenna focused on Erick and Nathan. "Diane, move out of him. You're a willing host, is that what you're telling me?"

"Are you kidding?" Erick's laugh sounded nervous. "I've had a better life in the last two months than ever before. I'll admit it was a little strange at first, but once I got used to him being there it was great."

"Well, so maybe we don't need anything more from him."

Jenna didn't bother to turn to say, "Hush, Marvin," she kept Heidi and Nathan locked in a visual grasp. "Did you think I didn't know what you've been doing all these years, Nathan? Though you haven't literally taken lives like she has," Jenna pointed at Heidi, "you've stolen them. Heidi, I don't have to tell you it's unacceptable, because if you thought otherwise you wouldn't have kept running from Diane," Jenna indicated the blonde woman standing with her. "You're both lucky it's me you face right now and not Jason."

"Isn't that the truth? That guy is a hard-ass from way back," Marvin said.

"Careful," Jenna warned. "He's still part of the World Council and the most powerful Keeper there is. I'd maintain a respectful tongue in my head if I were you."

The mention of Jason sent a shiver down Nathan's spine, followed by a buzz and severe tingle in his left side. Erick was attempting to push himself over, to deliberately envelope Nathan. Movement on his right caught his attention, a blur of motion as Heidi turned to dash away.

Jenna scowled, her face a thickening cloud of darkness. She pointed and shouted, "Heidi, you come over here now." Heidi froze, then swiveled, then moved to stand in front of Jenna. "Dammit, Marvin! Now, I told you to stop pulling my focus. Shut up and let me do what I came here for."

"Well, pardon me, your highness—"

"Oh, no you don't." Before Erick completed the move, Diane grabbed onto Nathan's wrist. "Don't worry, I've got hold of this one. But, damn, she's strong, isn't she," Diane said, pointing at Heidi. "No wonder she kept getting away from me."

"Another try like that, and I'm done with the both of you," Jenna shook her head.

"Then let me go, bitch."

Diane snickered. "Oh, believe me. You don't want her to be done with you. That's an end you don't want to meet."

Heidi crossed her arms. "Fine. Then stop with the bullshit, and tell us what the fuck you want, already."

After a bit of throat-clearing, Nathan found his voice. "So, now what?"

"We're going to get some things straight, or the next time you step out of him—or get knocked out of him—it'll be your last." Jenna fixed him with a solid stare. "If I don't turn you over to Jason."

Chapter 36

Jenna couldn't restrain the small grin that spread across her lips. Heidi reminded her of herself, determined to help those who couldn't help themselves. The woman paced around the hotel suite.

"Quit being impertinent." Jenna's gaze followed each step her captive made. "You killed someone."

"So what? One less scumbag in the world to prey on children." Heidi indicated the street below.

"I'm not arguing that. But, the one absolute on this plane of life cannot be broken. Jason, or any member of his sect, would've taken you without hesitation. You don't realize how incredibly lucky you are to be here right now." Jenna paused. "My question is, why didn't you help that little girl to safety?"

Heidi snorted. "Yeah, how?"

"How did you take the scumbag around the corner and beat his head against the brick building? The same way he does." Diane pointed at Nathan, who sat in a dining chair as stiff and quiet as a mannequin. "You slide yourself in."

"And where do you propose I should've taken a kid? Have you ever seen the inside of a shelter for children? Do you have any idea what the foster care system does to someone?"

Jenna laughed. She'd been passed through more foster homes than she cared to remember. It hadn't been great, but not all of them had been houses of horror. "I suggest you don't underestimate what any of us lived through. Barring taking a child home to their parents, where they belong, there are shelters that can help."

Heidi stopped her pacing and jabbed a finger at Jenna. "Then you haven't seen the shitholes they pass off as shelters around here. They suck. Kids aren't allowed to be kids."

"I don't recommend that attitude," Diane said.

"Fuck you, bitch. Who are you to tell me how to act? I've got news for you—"

Jenna whirled around to face Heidi. "Stop! This doesn't solve anything, and I'll tell you what I told her," Jenna waved a hand in Diane's direction, "you best keep a civil tongue in your head. Because I can call Jason and that would not be good."

"What do you suggest I do? I can't get into them like I do to people who are trying to molest or abuse them, they're too small. And I can't exactly grab them by the hand, now can I? I'm not going to stop. And you know what? You can kiss. My. Ass. So, you call this Jason, or whoever the fuck you want. I'll tell them the same thing." Heidi crossed her arms, a defiant expression on her face.

"She really needs an attitude adjustment."

Jenna smiled at Diane's comment. "In fact, I think I like her for it. She's got a fire that I find admirable."

"Spunk," Marvin tossed in. "I wonder who she sounds like?"

"Hush, Marvin."

"Don't tell me to hush. You know it's true."

"Stop. Now." Jenna's volume rose as she turned and saw Marvin sitting, one leg tossed over an arm of the chair he occupied. "True or not, you need to stop interrupting."

"Fine. Don't let me help." Marvin stomped toward the door but stopped when the lock disengaged.

The door swung open and Erick walked in carrying a small package. "I hope this will do, Nathan."

"That will have to wait," Jenna said. "We may not have any power over you Erick, but take my advice: go over there," she pointed to the small sofa, "and sit. You, too, Marvin."

Nathan cleared his throat. "I may have a suggestion that might could help ya'll...."

Jenna returned her attention to the purpose of hunting down these two. Nathan's situation could wait, Heidi had to take first priority. "Which would be?"

"Well, ma'am, she said the kids were too small. Now, granted, most of the folks I've slid into over the years were like puttin' on a pair of comfortable old overalls for slopping the hogs. But, if they aren't going to be safe at home, which is awful because a person's mama and daddy should be a refuge, the thing I find helps is to wait until they're sleeping. It gives you the time to adjust yourself, you take over kind of gradual-like."

"And exactly what do you suggest I do with them? I won't take them to a shelter. They don't need any more abuse. If there's no one in institutions to show them love, they at least deserve to be somewhere with people who will care. And protect them from the assholes that prey on them. I don't see any—"

Marvin butted in. "I don't know about you but, from the looks of this suite, I'd say Nathan is pretty flush with funds."

Diane shuffled over. "What are you suggesting, Marvin?"

"I'm suggesting he part with some. What about it, Nathan? Can you think of a way to help out? Maybe make a sizable donation to—"

Heidi erupted in laughter. "If you think giving anything to the money-grubbers around here would actually help the kids, you might want to get your head out of your ass."

"They aren't all like that," Jenna argued. "My life in the system may not have been princess dresses and tiaras, but it wasn't terrible. I had food, clothes, and a clean place to sleep."

"Yeah, well, what about young boys and men? I don't see shelters taking them in. Most get turned away. I've even seen shelters turn women away if they have a teenage son. I'm telling you they don't provide for everyone who needs it. So, let me ask again—you know, just in case you didn't hear me the first fucking time. Or maybe I need to talk slower. What would you suggest I do?"

"Stop being bitchy." Jenna's tone ended the argument. "Because it's not going to get you anywhere. Believe me, I can be damn stubborn."

"I'll vouch for that," Marvin said.

Jenna ignored him. "Okay, I grant you, shelters are crowded. It proves there's a lot of work to be done. But, if they don't accept boys over a certain age, laws demand they find safety for them somewhere."

Heidi let out a snort. "Laws. Laws work for those who follow them."

Diane laughed. "Oh, that is rich. True, but rich."

Everyone in the room turned toward Erick when he

piped up. "Nathan, what about the compound?" In the ensuing silence, Erick shrugged. "What?"

Marvin whistled disbelief. "You have a compound?"

"Well, now, it's nothing fancy. Just a bunch of small cabins up in some woods my granddaddy left me."

Diane asked the obvious. "But it's habitable?"

"Mmm…you might could say that. In a pinch."

The room remained still while Jenna mulled her options with this new consideration. Finally, she addressed Nathan. "Do you think your property could provide a safe haven?"

"With some improvements, yes, ma'am, I expect so."

"What the hell? You're letting him off the hook? This is bullshit." Heidi stalked toward the door.

Jenna whirled on Heidi and held her in place. "I'm not done with you, yet. Now, turn around and face me. He may have borrowed…"

"That's putting it nicely," Diane muttered.

"…but you killed a man," Jenna continued. "Now, we can settle this if you stop with the attitude."

"And if I don't?"

Tired of the game, Jenna glowered and her stature increased to tower over Heidi. "I don't have to play nice."

"Holy mother of Mary!" Marvin scrambled out of his chair. "Don't do that, it always freaks me out."

Jenna directed her countenance onto Marvin. "You stay quiet or leave." He cowered and slunk to the couch.

Heidi stood defiant, her blue eyes glaring. "Are

you going to stop harassing me if I agree to some bullshit suggestion?"

"I'll do better than that," Jenna replied.

"How?"

Diane stepped between Jenna and Heidi. "Do you know anything about us, our sect here on this plane of existence? What we do, how we operate?"

"Yeah, you bully people like me."

"Oh, you have no idea what we can do." Diane's height grew to match Jenna's. "But, bullying is the least of your worries if you don't stop mouthing off."

"You know what? That's it. I'm done." Jenna's countenance grew huge and dark, and enveloped Heidi, removing her from everyone's sight. She listened to the woman's laughter turn to utter silence at what Jenna revealed, whimpering increased to an all-out cry for help. Jenna released her and waited. The dim light in the room showed her how much time had passed, and she gawked around to find Marvin, Diane, and Nathan sitting at the small dining table, the remains of room service cluttering the top. Leaning to peer into the master bedroom, she found Erick huddled under blankets, fast asleep.

Several moments later the visible quivering ceased, and Heidi found her voice, though it came out in a contrite whisper. "What do I have to do?"

Chapter 37

Nathan sat near the window of the suite's bedroom. Early morning light sent shivering glints on the waves of the lake, and gulls left their rocky perches to take to the air in search of breakfast. This conversing with a guy he'd slipped into and lived life for gave a whole new meaning to talking to oneself. This was all strange but in a good sort of way. Nathan turned back to the chore of packing the clothes he'd purchased. "Could you grab the suit out of the closet for me? No sense in leaving this stuff behind this time."

"You mean you usually do?"

"Yes. Usually with a note to donate them to a homeless shelter."

"Oh. That's cool." Erick pulled the hanger from the rod. "Is there a garment bag for this?"

Nathan's hands dropped to his side, two pairs of rolled-up briefs in one. "Damn. Well, put it back in there. Can't go making any side trips to buy one." Nathan heaved a long, loud sigh. "What would I need a suit for anyway? This surely is not how I planned for this to go. I can hear my daddy laughing at me. 'Boy, you done put your cart right in front of that horse, now, didn't you?' "

"It's a shame. Not that I won't miss the luxury after the dreary barracks room." Erick shrugged, and dropped the hanger onto the rod. "I guess I believed the

221

Air Force ads…you know, 'you'll touch the sky' and all that. Adventure intrigued me. Where did I go? Working day in and day out at the museum. But, this sounds like one heck of a ride to me. Tell me about the compound."

"Well, to start, it's a far piece from this. If you thought the barracks was lean, well sir, wait 'til you get a gander at the place you're about to call home." Nathan shoved shirts into the bag. "For starters, it's one room, no heat except what the wood stove manages to put out without generating a plume of smoke, only cold water… You know, I need you in order to get the truck back. Once we get there, if you want me to—"

"I know what you're going to say. Nope. If you do this kind of thing every winter, I'm more than happy to keep the arrangement." Erick handed him the small case with all the toiletries.

Nathan zipped up the bag and dropped it onto the bed. "I'd have to say, you're a better man than I am."

"Don't say that, Nathan. It's…I don't know…weird in a sense. I mean, I did have my own thoughts, though yours took the lead somehow. But it didn't bother me, you know? I liked the things we were doing." A wide grin exposed even teeth. "Especially with Shelly. I'm going to miss that."

That didn't surprise Nathan considering the performance at the barracks he'd skipped out on. For Nathan to say he'd miss the woman would be like saying he missed living. The stolen lives of the past were empty, hollow compared to this, and the difference hit him like jumping into a snowmelt-cold creek to bathe. In the short time he'd been with her, Shelly had burrowed into him so completely, so thoroughly that she may as well have taken over his entire being. He didn't understand it, but leaving her ripped something inside and created an ache he couldn't touch. "Where's her gift?"

"On the desk in there," Erick pointed to the living room.

Nathan sat at the desk, with the box wrapped in plain gold paper with a silver ribbon and bow taunting him. He pulled a sheet of hotel stationery from the desk drawer and composed a note of apology. After holding the pen poised in the air for a moment, he finished with, "I'll be back. That's a promise. Love always, Nathan."

He never wrote that before, except maybe on a card or gift to family. But it was true. Folding the note, he slipped it into an envelope and sealed it. Then he grabbed the house phone to dial the concierge. "Yes, ma'am, when Dean comes in, would you be so kind as to have him come up to my room? Yes, ten would be fine. There's an errand I need to run. Thank you, ya'll have been more than kind."

With that decided, he looked out on the lake. "Erick, it's best we get some sleep before we head out." After an affirmative response, he waited. Once Erick's soft snoring drifted from the other room, Nathan went in to join him on the bed. In slow, deliberate moves, he pushed his way into a willing host and drifted off to join him in sleep.

Repeated pounding on the door, alternated with the insistent chimes of the doorbell, woke him. He rose, pulled on a robe, and discovered Dean holding a tray of pastries and coffee.

"Good morning, sir. I hope you don't mind, I took the liberty." Dean lifted the tray a bit. "Figured you might want a little something to tide you over."

Nathan followed him to the dining table, still cluttered from the previous meal of his phantom guests. "Let me stack some of this to make room. You surely have gone over the extra mile. I appreciate that."

"It's my pleasure. Anything you need, you just ask. That's what I'm here for."

Nathan poured two cups of coffee and pushed one across to Dean. "Here, have a seat. I was wondering if you might could do me a favor."

"Anything. Well, anything that won't get me arrested." Dean grinned.

"I have to leave today on some urgency, and need a letter and gift delivered to Shelly. Would you do that for me?"

Though he nodded, an expression of disappointment painted itself across Dean's face.

Retrieving the box and letter, Nathan set them on the table. "I'll be back as soon as I'm able. But, it wouldn't sit right at all leaving without some explanation. I sure would appreciate it and I'll make it worth your while."

"Mr. Crockett, there's no need for that. I'm happy to do it for you." Dean emptied his cup, and stood. "I hope you'll call on me when you return."

"You can count on it. And, please, tell Shelly the same for me, would you? It might pain my mama to hear this," he said with a grin he couldn't repress, "but Shelly's the finest woman I've ever met in my life."

He showered and dressed, stopped at the lobby desk to check out. He left a generous tip for the people in the concierge office who'd catered to his every whim over the past few weeks. After a quick walk to the bank, a separate envelope, addressed to Dean, contained a personal note of thanks and a hefty amount in one-hundred dollar bills. Then he made his way to the old F-150 parked in the garage of the mall.

Through it all questions pierced his mind like a million lengths of straw poking from a bale of hay. The forced early return to the compound complicated things. How the others would handle this, he couldn't figure. Everyone had worked hard to keep the place off the radar of the truly living world. Who would stay and who would leave when he told them what was about to transpire?

Chapter 38

Nathan tried to make the best of the long ride to West Virginia with tedious attempts to start conversations with a passenger no living person—no, make that no typical living person—might detect in the seat next to him. As he neared the turn-off to the long road on his property, the need to make sure her mouthy attitude wouldn't cause trouble popped to the forefront of his thoughts. "You've been as feisty as a badger trapped in a den. These are good folks here. See if you can conduct yourself with a bit of decorum and they might go along for the ride. It's not like your life has been upended, you'll get to keep doing what you set out to do."

Heidi continued to focus out the front window. "How about if you quit bitching. It seems to me you've got nothing to complain about considering how many lives you've lived. Try getting cut down by a train in your mid-thirties—"

Nathan's raucous laugh cut her short. "Now, that there's mighty rich. You don't know a thing about us, what-all happened to us, or at what age."

He braked and made the turn, the truck quickly devoured by leafless bramble and ever-larger trees. After more than forty-five minutes of jostling over ruts and tree roots, running down into gullies and back up the other side, Heidi let out an exasperated cry. "Where the hell is this place?"

"Not much farther, if you don't count the mile hike after we park." Nathan pointed to a small clearing ahead where a half-dozen snow-covered vehicles sat. "There."

"You're kidding, right? You couldn't build a little closer to civilization?"

"Seems to me you should be happy. If you don't think folks won't be looking for missing kids, you're dumber than a plow mule. This is well away from prying eyes. You'll need that more than we do."

Nathan pulled alongside Zachariah's Jeep Cherokee and cut the engine. At the bed of the pick-up he slung the duffle bag over a shoulder, then gestured to a small suitcase. "Would ya'll mind?"

A woodpecker tapped somewhere among the trees. The snow crunched under their feet. Those were the only things to break the silence as he led the way along the path. Heidi's silence suited him just fine. For all the enjoyment of luxuriating each winter with fine food and such, walking this path should bring him peace; this was home. The people here were family. Chosen family. He didn't want to lose them. Moreover, if this was to succeed, he needed them. Despite the beauty surrounding him, dread built in his body, his muscles tightened with every step. He hadn't been able to conjure up a single explanation for the circumstances of this early return. At least none which didn't sound lame in his own head. Repercussions could be fierce. The change would be about as welcome as...well, suffering a blast at the mines.

Nathan whistled low as they approached the footbridge; Zachariah hadn't been idle. Newly hewn upright studs stood out from weather-worn gray, and new lengths of ship's rope spanned both sides for handrails. "Right nice work, Zach." He twisted at the waist. "Careful, it tends to be a might slippery, could be ice under the snow."

Heidi laughed. "It's not like I'd get hurt if I fell."

"No, but I don't cotton to having to scramble down there to retrieve a busted-up suitcase come Spring." Nathan forged on.

Twilight sparkled on the snow as they broke from the cover of the woods. The glen of the compound opened up before them. A sight he would never tire of, even in winter. Faint wisps of smoke rose from the chimney of every cabin, their little square windows shed rectangles of light on small snowdrifts.

Nathan pointed to a newly occupied structure. "Looks like we picked up a new member."

"Who's he?" Heidi's forefinger indicated a guy standing on the porch of the largest structure, Nathan's 'summer home,' as he liked to call it. A cigarette dangled from the man's lips as he wrestled to close the buttons of his fly.

"That there would be Zachariah." Nathan lifted an arm in greeting. "Hey, Zach!"

"Hey, Nate. What're ya'll doing back? Too much rich food and high living chase you out of the city?"

"I wish," Nathan called back, and headed across the meadow. "Sorry, but it looks like I'll be needing my bunk."

Zach jumped down from the porch and headed toward Nathan. "Who's the lady?"

"Well, now, bless her heart," Nathan responded blandly. "She's the reason I'm here."

"Don't blame it on me. I'm not the one stealing lives," Heidi retorted.

"Oh, I beg your pardon, ma'am," Nathan responded drolly. "I stand corrected, you just kill people."

The outstretched hand dropped to his side and Zachariah halted. "And you brought her here?"

"Oh, simmer down, Zachariah. It's not like I had a choice." Nathan made a dismissive hand gesture toward Heidi. "Besides," he said in her direction, "if it wasn't for you slamming into me, neither one of us would be in this predicament."

"Oh, cram it. You whine worse than a kid who didn't get his pony on Christmas."

"And you're all sugar and spice yourself." After she flipped him off, he made the introduction. "Zach, this here's Heidi."

"Hey," was all either of them bothered to say.

Nathan shivered, stamping his feet. "Let's go in. Tromping through the snow after the heat in the truck, I'm about to freeze my nuggets off. I hope you have coffee sitting over the embers. And a few shots of whiskey."

"You'll have to do with the whiskey 'til I get a pot going," Zach said, heading for Nathan's cabin.

"I think I might could handle that. Then, we need to gather the clan. I have some news I'm afraid not everyone is going to take very kindly."

Zach took a glance at Heidi and a scowl creased his forehead. "Do tell."

"I will, once we have everyone here," Nathan said as he pushed the door open. Inside he headed straight for the wood stove. "Ah, that feels good."

"I'll go round everyone up," Zach said.

Nathan stopped him from shutting the door. Chilled air pushed across the floorboards. "Who's the new person? We have a single or double? Trust me," he added before Zach could ask the question. "It's going to matter; soon, I'm afraid."

"Young kid. Name's Marcus. He's a wise-ass. You'll like him." Zach grinned and strode off.

Nathan closed the door and turned to see Heidi in the middle of the room.

She held out the suitcase she'd been tasked with. "Where do you want this?"

"Just drop it in the corner, at the foot of the bed." A thud issued as the bag hit the floor. She was a pain in the ass, this one. About as cooperative as a mule pulling loaded carts from the mines. "Grab a chair from the stack against the wall and make yourself at home. We're as casual as the surroundings." Nathan opened the single cupboard above the sink and reached for a cup. "You want a shot?"

"I'm good, thanks."

"Suit yourself." Nathan poured a double shot of whiskey, tossed it back, and let out a sigh as the heat snaked its way down into his stomach. After another one spread warmth into his limbs, he set about starting the coffee. He pulled the ancient dining table he'd made with his own hands to the middle of the room, opened it and put the extensions in. He placed a stack of small glasses and the bottle of whiskey in the center. Why couldn't this be summer? Why couldn't it be two glasses instead of a stack? Why couldn't a smiling Shelly be about to sit across from him instead of the frightened faces he expected?

Chapter 39

The humidity of late May hung like a shroud. Gnats swarmed through the shade of the canopied tree limbs surrounding the small plot they'd cleared the previous week. Their buzzing louder than the honeybees in the meadow, and provided a backdrop to the sounds of hammers from across the meadow Nathan swiped a forearm at the sweat dripping from his face, launched a two-by-four onto a growing pile, and gawked around. "Marcus?" No response. "Where'd he go?"

"That way." Zachariah thrust a hammer to his right, and then pounded another nail to secure the last piece of subfloor for the new cabin.

Nathan peered at the tree line and called out, "Marcus, slap that dick down and get back to work. Good Lord, Zach, I thought I was a horny cuss at his age. That boy is forever sneaking off into the trees. Why doesn't he do that in his bunk at night like a normal kid?"

"Come on, Nathan. Give him a break. With the other cabins already filled and having to share my place, he's probably too embarrassed. And, if he's thinking like a normal kid, he believes we don't know what he's up to out there." Zach joined in on Nathan's laughter. "Now don't let this offend you, but it would appear he takes off like that right after he's a spent a good spell gawking at the two of us."

"Really? You think he's," Nathan removed a hand from the saw he held poised over a piece of lumber and wobbled it in the air. "you know."

"Ha! It's not like you haven't gone there yourself. You admitted as much."

"I'm not saying anything, I'm just asking. To each his own."

"Just yanking your chain." Zach tilted his head in thought, and a grin spread over his face. "'Course, I have seen him trying to hide a log of wood when the girls are working in those shorts and thin blouses they bought on the last trip into town. So, who knows, maybe he's just a normal, horny seventeen-year old kid."

"I suppose. We need to get this bunkhouse done, though. You never know when Heidi is going to show up with another one." More than double the size of the other cabins on the compound—except his own which was about this same size and held communal meals during inclement weather—this one would house three bunkbeds, a chair and side table for each of the six inhabitants. It would have a cold-water sink, as soon as the pipe from the spring could be extended. Nathan shrugged and bent to his work, putting a tape measure to another length of board. "This is all happening at a much faster pace than I ever imagined."

With the eight existing cabins already full, it forced the original inhabitants to double up. Heidi had brought six kids; four girls and two boys. The youngest, a little dark-skinned girl of six with the curliest hair Nathan had ever seen, the oldest a fourteen-year old boy as thin as a cornstalk; all battered in one way or another;

verbally, mentally, physically, or all three at once. How many more did they expect him to provide for? Yet, each new arrival broke his heart and getting one decent gander at them made it impossible to send them somewhere else. To see these children flinch and shy away, to have them hide like rabbits in a hole...he couldn't imagine what things they'd been forced to endure.

Heidi brought them—how he didn't know and, furthermore, didn't want to—and stepped clear of them. Cooing reassurances they were safe, Sarah and the other women surrounded the kids before they could shake themselves awake. Nathan sure did bless those women for having the gentleness and patience of a mama sheep. Lord, almighty, a couple of the youngsters had to be coaxed out just to use the outhouse.

The exterior walls lay on the floor, framed and ready to stand. Nathan, Zach, and Marcus finished securing the first in place when Sarah showed up with a pitcher of cold water. "Straight out of the spring."

Nathan wished, not for the first time since returning and embarking on the chores around the compound, that Shelly was the one standing with the sun glistening off her hair, offering her smile and encouragement. Nights were the worst, as he lay on his bed imagining her body curled around his, listening to her even breathing as it moved into a shared tempo with the songs of crickets and nightingales, and the occasional hoot of an owl.

After wiping hands on jeans, the men accepted filled glasses with a trio of "thank you." Nathan took several swigs before noticing Marcus chugging his and nudged him with an elbow. "Slow down there, or you'll be retching it all back up."

Zach sat on the newly constructed porch and wiped sweat from his body with his shirt. "This one's finally beginning to take shape. How're Steve and the guys coming along on the other building?"

"Well, not to encourage competition," Sarah paused and grinned at the sound of hammers pounding filtering across the distance, "but, they're about to start putting trusses on for the roof. Look for yourself." She pointed to a framed-out structure to the south of Nathan's cabin. "It's gonna be a real nice place to gather for meals and such. I expect you'll be happy to have your place back to yourself, huh, Nathan?"

"I haven't minded, really." That wasn't the exact honest truth, but like his Mama told him once, 'white lies spare feelings. That goes twice for girls. You remember that when you get hitched and you'll have a good marriage.' He nodded toward the other building. "I wonder if they'd be willing to come over here and help us catch up."

"Lunch'll be ready soon. You could take a look at how far they've come and judge for yourself," Sarah suggested. When Zach excused himself, and headed to the brush, she refilled their glasses and placed the pitcher on the porch. "I better get back. Bring that with you, if you would. Glasses too, if you expect to be able to drink anything with your meal."

"Are you telling me we need to get more kitchen things?"

Sarah stopped her trek across the meadow. "Might be a good idea, Nate. I can go into Roanoke this afternoon, and take a couple of the girls with me to help."

Making his way back out of the bushes, Zach returned to the conversation. "Do you think that's a good idea? What if they're recognized? You know, from posters or something? You never know how far and wide these Amber Alerts reach."

"Now, I didn't think of that. You could be right." Sarah inhaled and held it for a moment. "Well, I guess it'll have to wait, then."

"I think we'll be in need of the next batch of building supplies by mid-morning tomorrow, anyway. If you make us a list, it's just as easy to grab that while we're there."

"I can do that." Sarah resumed her trek to Nathan's cabin.

Marcus piped up for the first time in more than an hour. "How's come ya'll keep making these trips? Why don't we get all we need to finish this at one time instead of back and forth?"

Nathan scowled at him, but chuckled. "And have the building supply store call the county? Before you could crack a whip on a pony, the authorities would be swarming this place like ants on a sack of sugar in the root cellar. Inspectors crawling up our butts? Them asking all kinds of questions? No thanks."

"Kid," Zachariah said, "if you think multiple trips is bad, you should've been here for building the other places. At least we have an ATV and trailer to haul supplies along the route through the trees you developed using that Google Earth thing. We used to have to drag everything almost a mile from the parking area." His expression changed and he burst into laughter. "One time we were hauling a big load across the footbridge and Nate, here, slipped and tumbled halfway down the gully. Took a full two hours to get him and all the supplies up. Then he barked out an 'ouch' with every step the rest of the way up here. I swear to you, I spent three hours of my evening with a pair of tweezers pulling bramble stickers out of his ass."

"I'm glad ya'll are getting so tickled over my discomfort," Nathan said, through a laugh as full-throated as Marcus'. "But, you know, Zachariah, you stretch that yarn more every time you tell it."

"It's all true, Marcus, every word of it," Zach said with a wink at Nathan.

Nathan glanced skyward. "Well, come on now. We best get back to work. Looks like a right-big storm could be brewin'. It'd be good to have the wall frames up before we head over for lunch."

An hour later, as they wrestled with the first roofing truss, Sarah's voice reached them, "Nate, Zach, Marcus, lunch!"

Zach stood spread-legged across a corner on top of the joists. "Let 'er down, Marcus. We'll get it later. Maybe this wind will die down a bit. If those clouds don't dump buckets, we might even get the roof on by sundown." He jumped down from his perch, and grabbed his shirt off the floor. "I suppose if we don't dress, there'll be hell to pay."

A scrunched-up expression hit Marcus across the face. "I'm hot and sweaty, and I have to be dressed for lunch?"

"Well," Nathan paused, pulling a t-shirt over his head. "My Big Mama would slap me up the backside of my head, grab an ear, and send me off howling. 'You wasn't born in the barn Nathaniel Ray. You know better'n to come to my table like that.' We've got a gaggle of kids here now. We need to teach them some manners."

Zach punched Marcus on the shoulder, and moved upwind of him as they headed to the main cabin. "Whew. Boy, you're lucky he doesn't make you go take a bath first."

Marcus flipped him a middle finger, then indicated the mouth of the path. "Looks like we got us another one."

A young boy, about twelve-years old, stood gaping around the meadow. A woman old enough to be his mother had a hand on his shoulder. Sunlight glared off a cast on the boy's left arm. A voice called out, and the two moved toward the group already gathering around the tables set up under the shade of the largest cottonwood tree.

Nathan's chin dropped to his chest and he sighed. When would there be time to enjoy life, that's what he wanted to know. After all, isn't that what this jumping into bodies was supposed to be all about? Lord, how he wanted to go back to Cleveland and Shelly. Each time the solar and satellite systems got set out, he wished he'd asked for Shelly's email if she had one. Every trip to a neighboring town, he reached to turn on his phone to call or text, but some issue cropped up to distract him. By the time he managed to retrieve his brain for his own purposes, they'd be out of range of any cell towers.

Days were stretched to the limit with chasing after one or another of the children, scolding, instructing, or fixing something. Sarah and the other women worked non-stop in daily chores. Some adult-sized help needed to show up or they'd all be frazzled to their wits' end.

He peered over to watch the new woman make her way. She moved with an obvious limp in her gait. But, maybe, if she wasn't in too bad of shape, she might could chip in.

No sooner had the women of the clan surrounded the newcomers than Jenna and Heidi stepped clear.

Chapter 40

Nathan watched Jenna turn a full three-sixty and take in the structures that ringed the glen. She nodded. "It looks as if you're holding up your end of the bargain."

"We can't keep up with all the kids." Nathan faced Heidi. "You have to find somewhere else to take them."

"There is nowhere else, buttface."

Nathan's hands balled into fists. "Do you understand, there's no running water, no electricity, we use wood stoves for heat. These children have a tough enough time, and you expect them to adjust to a place like this? Bathing in a creek, using outhouses? This place was not meant for a village."

"So, what's your problem, jerk-off? Fix it." Heidi moved closer, her stance that of a challenging wrestler.

A small voice from the group asked, "Who's he talking to?"

"I think he's just working something out in his head. He does that sometimes, talks aloud to work through an issue," came Sarah's response.

Jenna moved between them. "Stop. Both of you."

"We've run out of room. The two structures here," Nathan pointed out the framed-out buildings, "are as far as we can go without calling attention to ourselves."

"Would you be willing to show me around?" Jenna headed toward one of the small structures.

Nathan's shoulders drooped. "Sure. Why not?"

They walked along the perimeter of the meadow. Jenna poked her head into each cabin. A might on the rude side and nosy for his taste. But, intimidation held his tongue.

When they stood on the far side, in front of the beginnings of the new bunkhouse he, Marcus, and Zachariah toiled over, Jenna sat. "How much land do you have here?"

"I don't know for sure. Couple thousand acres, I guess."

"And this is the only spot capable of housing?"

"What are you getting at?"

"I'm just thinking out loud, here." She stood and moved toward the foot path. "What if you were to build a real place. Dormitories. All legit?"

"I came here because it provided a refuge for us," Nathan pointed out. "For me, Sarah, Steve, Zachariah, Marcus, and...well, people like us. A place we could live without fear of discovery. Some left because of the trouble I caused. Now, you want me to tell the ones who stayed that they have to give this all up?"

"You knew you were breaking the rules. This was the deal. Besides, how can you deny helping those kids?" Jenna pointed to the picnic tables filled with people in front of Nathan's cabin.

"What you're asking would require architectural plans, permits, contractors, and workers crawling all over my property. This is pristine land. I won't have it ruined."

"I'd take a close look at what she's suggesting, if I were you."

"Marvin, I told you to stay in the car." Jenna's

expression matched that of a a bull about to charge.

Marvin shrugged. "I wanted to see the place. So, sue me."

Nathan ignored him. "Besides, it would cost four or five million."

"More like ten or fifteen. That's a drop in your bucket, and you know it." Marvin poked a finger into Nathan's arm.

It was true Nathan had amassed a solid fortune over the years. Though the mine operations had been sold off years before, the companies leased the land. New contracts every few years upped the income and his equity continued to build. Not only did the investment company manage his trust with expertise, Nathan kept expenditures to a minimum. Yes, he admitted the winter excursions could be indulgent but he never outspent the income.

These Watchers, or whatever they called themselves, stole a blooming relationship away from him. They breached his privacy. Now they wanted a big old chunk of his fortune. They wanted his land. Moreover, they were endangering his people. The very ones who'd put their trust in him to maintain a certain level of privacy up here in the hollers. His jaw locked tight, his hands clenched. The gall of these people incensed him. "And exactly how do you know that?"

"Let's just say I know how to make use of my old boss' computer programs," Marvin said.

"I don't care what you think you know," Nathan continued his denial. "We are not capable of providing for these kids. They need counseling, they need schooling, they need medical attention. We have no teachers, we have no therapists, and we have no doctors or nurses. Like my grandpappy said, 'You cain't get no roast beef out of a sow's belly.' No. We can't do what you're asking."

"What if I told you we know someone who could accomplish what is needed without disrupting one more wild daisy?" Marvin jutted his chin at the flowers dotting the meadow.

"I'd say you were trying to feed me Rocky Mountain Oysters and pass 'em off as Swedish Meatballs."

Jenna swiped a hand through Marvin's arm. "What do you think you're doing? How many times do I have to tell you to stay—"

"Helping you both get what you want." Marvin's tone tinged with anger. "How is arguing and threatening him accomplishing anything? Let me handle this."

Nathan didn't like where this was headed, but he'd seen his folks get into rows and knew better than to infringe. Best to take a step back and let it play out.

"You?" Jenna asked. "You're going to make everything right with the world here?"

"You don't think I can help? You've gotten so full of yourself, you've lost touch with what others might be able to offer. Or is it that you just think I'm lazy—or incompetent?"

A rather rapid train of expressions crossed Jenna's face before she said, "Oh, go step in front of a bus."

Marvin's lips pursed and he shook his head. "Nope. Now it's my turn to tell you that isn't going to work. Not this time. Sorry, kiddo. So, why don't you and Heidi take your pushy, self-important bullshit back to Dayton?"

With a grim smile on her face, Jenna folded her arms. "Hmph. And what are you going to do? Stay here? There's no Hilton nearby, you know." Her head shook in a slow, sad rhythm. "Marvin, this is way out of your league."

"You think I can't live without luxuries? You think I can't help these kids? I got news for you." Marvin turned away and walked toward the gathering.

Jenna let loose with an exasperated sigh.

Nathan put his hands up to ward off any incoming wrath. "Sorry, I don't mean to be the cause of trouble."

"It's not… Never mind. Look, we need a place for these children, and women if the one I brought is any indication."

"She can stay if she can help tend to the little ones," Nathan acquiesced.

"She has to stay. Didn't you get a look at her? Bruises around her neck, a black eye, contusions and lacerations. Nathan, she's as battered as her son. We had to bring them both."

An extended growl emitted from Nathan's midsection. "I best be getting some fuel put into my stomach. There's a lot of work to be done yet before the sun goes down."

He left Jenna standing at the head of the path, and gave a nod as Heidi passed on her way to catch up. He stopped, turned around, and called to her. "Heidi, wait…" He closed the gap between them. "I've been meaning to say thank you. Really, I mean that. What you do…it's…it's a good thing, and I apologize if I've acted like a mule's back end."

"It's okay, Nathan. I get it. I know I come off…well, like an angry bitch sometimes. It just tears me up to see anyone in pain, no matter what the cause." She brushed the back of a hand at the tears forming. "But, what people like these have been put through, especially kids, it hurts me so much that I can't stand by and watch it happen."

Nathan studied her for a moment. "You know, if I'd been paying attention, I might've seen that heart of gold sooner."

He hugged her, then held her gaze for a moment, and walked away. When he reached the outskirts of the group of picnic tables, he hesitated and watched the two women vanish down the path into the woods.

Marvin appeared at his side and murmured, "Go fall down a flight of stairs."

Nathan didn't want to pry, but there was a wistfulness to the statement that touched him, and he thought again about Shelly and wished she was here with him. To put Marvin at ease, and to stop brooding over Shelly, he asked, "So, what did you have in mind?"

Chapter 41

Tufts of cottonwood and dogwood had ceased floating on the breezes that alleviated the heavy humidity. Summer passed into a slow emergence of normalcy. The new bunkhouse and common buildings had been finished and outfitted. Yet the place again stood about two folks past exploding. The boys came around to acceptance faster than the girls as chores were augmented and seasoned. At first, they lamented the lack of electronic gadgets. But as the days wore on they found things to occupy the time. The boys teased with frogs brought up from the stream, or all manner of toads and bugs captured in the woods. The girls fed the fun with screams. Raucous laughter in voices high and low played on into dusk hours chasing fireflies.

Nathan stood on a hilltop more than a mile from the compound, looking out at the tops of timber that already showed signs of the oncoming spattering of blazing colors impossible to recreate from a painter's palette. Any day now, it would happen overnight if the coolness in the air was to be any judge; they would wake to trees dressed in scarlets and oranges and tans. He separated himself from Erick. Something he'd taken to doing every so often despite the looming threat of Jason's appearance, and what the repercussions of doing so meant to each of them. It provided time to talk in a more normal manner.

Erick didn't move, as if mesmerized. "It's so beautiful up here. I don't think I'd ever get tired of this."

Nathan nodded. "This is the best gift I ever got."

"Have you seen it all? Every piece of it?"

"You mean walked it? No. There's something about the thought of it being pure in every sense of the word that always stopped me." Nathan sat on a large granite boulder between two trees.

"I do thank you. Really. This is a tranquility I would've never known." Erick breathed deep.

"I should be thanking you. If you hadn't done what you did in the mall, called out to me like you did, I'd be... well, I don't want to think about it."

Nathan's soft laughter brought Erick to sit next to him. "It's all missing one thing, though."

Despite the quiet sense of dismay that poked Nathan's heart at the loss of her, it was good to hear Erick express his feelings; the same feelings Nathan himself had for the bitty woman who'd touched his heart in such a large way. "Shelly. Oh, how I wish... But, I'm sure she's moved on. Probably forgot all about us, if she hasn't burned us in effigy a hundred times for leaving the way we did."

Erick pitched a small granite stone over his shoulder. "It's not like we didn't have it coming."

"Ya'll think she got as smitten as we did?" Nathan wanted to believe she had.

"That'd be nice, wouldn't it?" Erick pulled the jacket closed. "Well, what say we try to find out when the snow starts?"

"If things have progressed far enough with the new campus, I think I might could get on that buckboard.

The way Marvin jumped right into the challenge impressed me. That Davy guy he brought to us is a might excitable, but I'll admit he sure does get things done."

"I'll say. And the people he managed to rouse is amazing. When we looked over the plans, and I said it looked as if Frank Lloyd Wright had done them…the withering expression and the way he said, 'Imagine that.' stunned me. I mean, think about it. How does he do it?"

"He's got a way about him, that's for sure. He's a bit on the nelly side, as my daddy would call it, but it serves him well 'cause he sure is a likable sort. According to deadheads, he pulled off the most elaborate wedding ever witnessed for Jenna and Marvin. Out in the middle of the Caribbean, no less. If he puts the same level of detail into this job, this will be some shelter."

Erick moved across the small clearing, scattering a cloud of gnats as he walked through the grass. Putting a hand to his brow, he asked, "Where is it from here?"

"You won't be able to see the site. Not even from up here." Nathan joined him and pointed to the northeast. "About three miles that way. Zachariah says it's far enough away to ensure no one interferes with us, close enough to keep an eye on. Though, it's beyond me what we need to watch over. I'm just glad it's out of sight. Still sticks in my craw a might, knowing it's making a mark on the land."

Agreeing to build surprised him as much as it did the folk around these parts. The construction made a splash farther than one would imagine, though the locals had no idea as to the real purpose.

"Did ya'll think ever in your life that the Crockett land would see some high-falutin' huntin' lodge built on it, of all things?" went the wagging of tongues in the four counties the property touched.

"Never," came each and every response Nathan had heard about. "The way I figgered it, that family would hoard it to themselves past the second comin'."

Erick dropped his lookout stance. "If it makes you feel any better, Davy did say it would blend into its surroundings so well you'd need a hawk's eyes to make it out."

"That there remains to be seen."

"And, if it keeps us on our communal path, it's worth it, right?"

Nathan had to agree. Odd at first, this free sharing of information was much better than mining for information, or hearing Erick's thoughts burst forth in his head. That was downright freakish, though it had saved their collective bacon more than once during the drive from Cleveland to home.

"Brake, Nathan, brake," shouted in his head. Nathan's attention returned to find he was about to drive right up the hind end of a tractor-trailer. A foot slammed down on the pedal, while the opening bass drum salvo to "My Hero" thumped and resonated in his chest. The old F-150 squawked and shuddered its way to a halt about eighteen inches from disaster. "What the hell. If you can't stop thinking about Shelly, maybe you should slide on out and let me drive."

"Erick?"

"Don't Erick me. It's one thing to let you use my body, and I can see I'd be just fine on the other side, but I'm not ready to die just yet. Now, pay attention."

"Sorry." Nathan drew a deep breath. Thank goodness Heidi looked to be sleeping or she'd be bitching in his ear. At least Erick faded into the background. When traffic cleared, he pulled around the semi and continued.

The next day, rounding a bend on a backroad, Erick again jumped to the rescue. "Bike! Bike!" The image in his head of Shelly dissolved, and Nathan pulled the wheel to the left and swerved. The kid on the bicycle flipped him the bird and yelled "Asshole." But at least he was able.

The genuine friendship felt good and right. Particularly here on the grounds of the Crockett property. Nathan knew his host cared about the land, loved it as much as he and, should Jason catch them separated, Erick would continue to protect it. With the requisite paperwork completed naming Erick as guardian, or whatever the lawyers had cited as the proper term, he would see that it stayed pristine. And the clan protected.

Nathan placed a hand on Erick's shoulder. "Well, I suppose we should get a move on. Dinner'll be on soon."

Erick sat on the boulder and waited. Nathan slid in and headed back to the compound. He ambled along, taking his time to gawk at trees, listen to birds squawk at his passing, and critters rustle through the underbrush as they scurried away.

Before he broke through the woods at the north end of the meadow, the aroma of roasting apples and pork drifted into his senses. Zachariah had made good on his promise of one more pit-fired barbeque before the weather snapped. The crowded tables played a dissonant symphony of discussion and laughing.

A single voice stood out from the rest. "Who's that?"

Nathan followed the extended finger. And ran.

Chapter 42

Halfway across the glen, all doubt dissipated. The brown hair was a might longer, but the small, slight frame made denial impossible. Her unmistakable voice called out to him, "Nathan!"

He picked up speed. His arms opened wide, spread to sweep her off her feet. She jumped into them instead. When they came up for air after a hundred kisses, he managed to ask, "Oh, my lord, how did you get here, how did you find this place?"

Shelly separated herself from his grasp, and pointed to the carrier on the ground. "Him."

Nathan stared with his mouth agape. "I don't understand."

"I don't either, but he did." Shelly laughed, and picked up the carrier and pulled the blanket away from the baby's face. "Nathan, I'd like you to meet Daniel. Somehow, this little guy told me exactly how to find you. Every road, every turn. The precise place to find the rutted path to your parking area; everything. I'm not sure I believe in telepathy, but I don't know what else to call it."

"He's yours?" Nathan stared down at the most angelic face he'd ever laid eyes upon. Bright blue eyes stared up at him from under light brown hair.

"Ours," Shelly said. "Daniel, this is your daddy." The tiny face broke out in a smile, and a giggle broke forth as Shelly placed him into Nathan's arms. A tiny hand worked its way from under the blanket and reached out.

Nathan had heard folks talk about instant, unconditional love. It never occurred this would happen to him. He'd never have a family, a real family; it couldn't be possible. Yet, here she stood. A woman he cherished. And now a son. My God, a son. If any one of his clan members asked him to describe what he felt right now, his mama would be telling him to shut his trap lest he swallow a dragonfly whole. "Hello, Daniel. Welcome home."

He wouldn't relinquish Daniel, so Shelly grabbed the carrier. Halfway to the crowd gathering for dinner at the picnic tables, Shelly stopped and pulled on his arm.

"Are these all your kids?" More than a tinge of apprehension poked through.

"In a manner of speaking, you might could say that. Yes, ma'am." Nathan gave her a tug. "Come on, you'll understand when I introduce you to everyone."

Zach met them halfway across the field, and he winked. "I suppose this means we have to find room for two more."

"I suspect so, Zach. This is Shelly. Shelly, this here's Zachariah. He's my right-hand man around here, and—dare I say—best friend."

The slightest blush traveled up Zach's face. "Pleased to meet you. Here, let me take the baby's carrier for you."

"Zachariah. What a pretty name."

"Well, I don't know about that," Zach said, hooking an arm around hers as they continued their way to the group, "but it's what my folks stuck me with, so I suppose it'll have to do."

All chatter ceased when Nathan halted their tangential parade at the head of the line of tables. "Everyone, I'd like you to meet Shelly. And, this here little fellow is my son, Daniel."

Cooing and babbling like a bunch of hens in a coop, every woman jumped from her seat and ran to see the baby. Zach nudged Nathan. "Congratulations. Why didn't you say anything? I would've found a way for you to leave."

"Firstly, I had no idea. Secondly, how could I leave? You know what Jenna and them laid on me. It's on me, it's my responsibility."

"Are you gonna tell her?" Zach jutted his chin in Shelly's direction.

Nathan blew out a stream of air. "If I can figure how." Then he raised his voice. "Well, come on, then. Ya'll scoot over and make some room. Sarah, Maryann, get the lady a plate and something to drink, if you would please. She's got to be hungry after such a trip. Steve, Marcus, and Zach, would all ya'll help me get her things up from her car after we've gotten our bellies filled?"

Three heads bobbed assent.

During supper, with Shelly next to him and Daniel in his carrier on the bench to the other side, Nathan couldn't keep from watching his family. "There's a lot to show you here. And a lot to catch up on. A lot to explain."

"Well, sometime real soon, I've got to call my dad. I tried from the road just before I pulled in, and again after I parked. Couldn't get a signal."

"Oh, sorry. There's not a cell tower within miles.

We'll have to take a ride into Roanoke for you to do that. How is your father?"

"Well, that explains why my calls and texts kept saying you were 'Out of range.' As for Dad... Let's put it this way, if he could find you, he's got a shotgun he'd like to introduce to you. To be brutally honest, I was ready to do that myself until Daniel pointed the way here."

"Oh, no. I surely did not intend for that."

A woman from the opposite end of the table asked, "Do I hear a wedding march in your future Mr. Crockett?"

"I expect so," Nathan responded. Then he smiled at Shelly. "I surely hope so."

"Well, I might agree to that. If I can be sure you aren't going to send me a note and gift and go running off on me."

"About that. I surely do apologize. My mama raised me better'n that, and I promise to stick by like a burr; you'll get downright tired of me and probably send me off packing."

"Well, then—"

Davy's excited voice broke out. "Oh, my God! Oh, my God! A wedding? When? No, wait, we have to get this project done first. But, I'm thinking maybe right here in the meadow."

"Think quieter, Davy. You're scaring the wildlife," Marvin said to laughter from those who could hear him.

That night, Nathan couldn't sleep. He slipped on pants and a shirt. After Heidi showed up with the first young girl, the menfolk being naked halted like a gristmill with a boulder stuck in it. Chalk up one more thing to the plus side once the shelter was finished: The freedom to return to the kind of lives they'd led for more than one-hundred years.

He slipped free of Erick, and sat on the edge of the porch. "How can we explain this to her?"

"You're asking me? You're the one who's been at this for almost two centuries."

"She'll take off like a freed badger." Nathan sent a small plume of dirt and grass through the air with a swift kick. "I'm afraid to lose her."

Erick looked down at him. "We love her, right?"

"We do."

"Then we have to trust her. She's bound to find out sooner or later, don't you think?" Erick nudged Nathan's leg with the side of his foot.

"I suppose," was Nathan's desultory response.

"How is it that son of ours told her how to get here? You'd think that alone would've freaked her out."

Nathan stood. Walking into the dew-laden grass, a shiver ran through him. "Did you see him wave at us? And I swear I heard him in my head."

"Nathan?" Shelly popped her head out the door. "Who are you talking to?"

"Myself. I do that sometimes when I need to work something out," Erick sounded like a magpie in the explanation given earlier that summer to one of the children Heidi brought. "You okay?"

"Yeah. Daniel woke. He's hungry. I have a bottle warming on the stove." Wrapped in a blanket, she stifled a yawn as she moved to stand beside him. "I thought you said you were talking to yourself. It's cold out, aren't you cold standing there in the grass like that?"

"Who are you talking about? No one's there."

"I see him. Just like I saw the two guys, Marvin and Davy, at the table tonight. Just like I've seen people on that side all my life. That Davy guy is funny; the way he flapped his hands and blathered on when he heard the mention of a wedding cracked me up."

Another moment of amazement for Nathan. "Shelly…"

"Yeah?"

"How freaky would it be," Nathan began, moved to stand next to Erick, and nudged him.

"If Nathan," Erick continued.

Nathan slipped in, "and I were the same person. Sort of."

"I'd say I've seen it before." Shelly slid an arm around his waist. "If you're trying to tell me that you were in there the whole time in Cleveland…Nathan, I don't care. You're the guy I met and fell in love with. You're Daniel's father."

Nathan pulled her into an embrace. "That is a load off the mule. But, someday, I'd like to talk about it at length."

"I don't have a problem with it, really."

"No, that's not… What I mean is…" Nathan shrugged. "About how you've always been able to see and hear the other side. Someday, I'd like you to explain it to me."

"I'm not really sure I have an answer for that." After a moment, she pulled from his embracing arms. "Tomorrow, would you take me to see the site for the shelter?"

"Yes, ma'am. I'd be pleased."

Shelly tugged on his shirt sleeve. "Come on, then. Come back to bed."

Nathan sat on the bed and watched her pick Daniel from the carrier. A splatter of milk on her wrist prefaced the tilting of the bottle to the ready mouth. Nathan held out his arms. "Can I?"

Chapter 43

Nathan woke early the next morning. He stepped off the porch and waved to Sarah as she headed toward one of the outhouses and he circled around the back of his cabin. This was getting to be tiresome. But normal had marched into history like last year's Hit Parade. Still, the schedule needed to be pushed. The compound had to be returned to the clan members, that's all there was to it.

Personal need satisfied and back inside, Nathan heard Daniel mewl in his carrier. "I'll get him, darlin'. You go back to bed." He pulled the infant into his arms, prepared a bottle and placed it into a pot of water on the wood stove. Too cool. He tossed a small split log in. "We need to get you a crib, little man. I think a major shopping trip is in your future. Let's just hope your mama isn't a complete typical female and has you trying out a hundred beds before buying one."

"I heard that," Shelly said, and rolled in the bed. "When, sir, did I ever give you the idea I was a typical female?"

Nathan grinned at her. "Beggin' your pardon, ma'am. That there was just man talk."

"Man talk already? Are you planning on teaching him to believe such terrible things?" Shelly rose and pulled on her jeans and blouse. "So, tell me, how does this whole commune thing work? Shouldn't I be out there helping get breakfast ready?"

A loud laugh broke from Nathan, and a small gurgle from Daniel. Based on the smile, Nathan swore a laugh issued from the bundle in his arms. "Your mama is going to fit in here right nice," he said to his son. "They might appreciate an extra hand, if you wouldn't mind."

"I'm happy to. It'll give me a chance to get to know them." Shelly shoved her feet into shoes, then pointed at the computer in the corner. "Does that thing work?"

"We might have to gather some power with the solar equipment, but it should. Zach would know better than I would." Nathan pulled the bottle and went to tip it to his son when Shelly stopped him with a short yelp. Following what he'd seen his mama and Big Mama do, he shook a few drops onto his wrist, then set the bottle on the floor.

Shelly retrieved it, gave it a few shakes, and handed it to him. "Can I connect it to the internet, then?"

"Yes, ma'am, you surely can. If we pull the satellite dish out. You need to look for something?"

She stood poised to open the door. "If I can get to my email, I do need to let my dad know we're okay."

"Well, then we'll make it happen."

The chill of the morning forced breakfast to be served in the new building. The sounds of chatter echoed through the room too much. But, it would be rude to take his meal to his cabin. It wouldn't do well for Shelly to abandon the others, either. Folks might get to thinking they were being snooty. No sir, sit still and deal with it.

"When breakfast is done, I'd like to take Shelly to the construction site. Would that be okay with ya'all, Davy?"

"Are you kidding? You're asking me if it's all right to show off my masterpiece?"

"You shouldn't demure so, Davy." Steve's comment brought laughter from the clan members.

They piled into the carts they'd used when building the new cabins, and headed out. The bumpy ride through the underbrush, over tree roots, down into and up out of numerous gullies took a good hour.

Davy parked at the bottom of a particularly deep ravine. Standing at the edge of a bulldozed, dirt lot, he pointed at gaping concrete lined caverns in the side of the hill. "There it is. Every room, even parking for staff will be built right into the side of the ravine. The only visible sign of a structure will be vents, and those will be camouflaged by the trees above."

"Oh, my gosh." Shelly moved forward.

Walking alongside her, Nathan swept a hand along the manmade caves. "Thirty dorm rooms will sleep four each. They'll have beds, study tables and chairs. A full bathroom will be between two rooms. Down there to the right, will be a cafeteria for meals. Full kitchen facilities behind. Meeting rooms for group counseling and school rooms, offices, and such will be over there, off to the left."

"This is amazing. I mean, Nathan, this…what you've done here for these people…"

Nathan shrugged.

Davy piped up. "Don't let him fool you, Shelly. It's more than amazing. You see the hallway there just left of center on the lower level? That leads to a movie theater and a game room." Davy pointed at Nathan. "His idea. All the extras, his brainstorm."

Heat ran up through Nathan's neck, and into his cheeks. "Well, life can't be all chores. Folks have got to have some playtime."

"Speaking of playtime," Marvin said, coming out of the darkness of the building. "Can we build a playground of sorts out here?"

"I expect so. It's not like the place is any secret."

"We'll be careful to keep it covered from aerial snooping. They'll see the access road," Marvin gestured to the graded ribbon of dirt rising up the side of the hill. "But that's about it. Up at the top, there will be electronic, monitored gates."

"What good will that do? We can't hardly wall in the entire property." Nathan swept his arms in a wide arc.

"No, but we don't want this place exactly accessible, either. We want the people who come here to know they're safe. Twenty-foot high steel fencing will be put in around these six acres, painted to blend with the surroundings," Davy explained. "The perimeter will be monitored twenty-four, seven. And a guard will be stationed at the entrance. Don't you worry, it's all under control."

"Nathan, if my dad could see this, he wouldn't wonder why we hadn't heard from you. He'd be clapping you on the back, saying 'good job.' "

"Well, I hope so. But, still, I sure do owe that man an apology of some sort. I'll find some way to make up for the slight."

When they returned from the building site, Shelly sat down and typed her message, then handed a print of it to Nathan.

Daddy,

I told you. Your grandson put a picture in my head and here we are. Daddy, the place is amazing. Nathan is doing great things here. He's housed almost twenty-six victims of domestic violence—mostly children. There's a brand new complex of buildings going up on his land, several miles from the compound I told you about before we left. There will be dorm rooms, classrooms, a fully-equipped medical clinic, offices for counselors, and rooms for group therapy. When it's done, they'll house almost 100. It's nothing short of amazing.

But, what's really phenomenal? He's set up a trust fund for them. Whenever someone is ready to move on, go back to the world, they'll be given $5k to get them started with a new life.

And, guess what? I've got a job. I'm going to run the school for him! He's a good man, Daddy. You're going to love him when you get to know him.

Maybe we can come visit at Christmas. Lots of love, Shelly, Daniel, and Nathan

P.S. Nathan sends apologies and his best regards.

"Christmas, huh?" Nathan lowered the page.

"I know it's a lot to ask...."

The pleading of her voice and the hopeful expression left Nathan helpless. "Now, I can't make any promises, but let's see what we can do."

Chapter 44

A year later, as the staff made final preparations for the shelter complex to be inhabited, Nathan, Shelly, Zach, and Sarah stood watching a game of tag take place in the meadow. The children's laughter rang through the air as they hid in Queen Anne's Lace taller than some. Daniel, now a good-natured toddler sitting right in the midst of the action, giggled at the goings-on.

Movement at the far end of the glen made Nathan's breath catch in his chest. He followed Jason's gaze, then ran to scoop Daniel into his arms. "You leave him alone!"

"You've taken too many liberties. You, and those like you, your time has come to an end."

Marvin appeared as if out of nowhere. "You have no idea what you're talking about."

Jason stood in the middle of the glen and glared at Marvin. "If these people would be trying to do good, it might be a little different. But they take over other's lives for selfish reasons. If they would seek out a Gadaffi, a Hitler, a Saddam, to stop atrocities, it could be forgiven. But the greed here is beyond anything. The world is filled with enough gluttony and avarice. No. This I cannot condone, this I will not allow.

"The arguments you and your friends put forth remind me of another such discussion so many, many years past when I lived on that first continent when the vast land still stood silent and innocent, unscathed and untouched; the virtuous wife on her wedding night."

Jason recounted how he stood on a fertile plain, keeping watch on the stands of verdant trees where bands of marauders hid on the way to a neighboring village, golden reed-thin stalks of tall grass swayed in a gentle breeze, the cobalt blue of the sky lightly painted with thin white clouds, and held his ground against the position of his counterpart, Teresa. "Humans, as we call ourselves, are the worst scourge ever to be dropped on this earth. We are the most vile, vicious, disgusting things. We are a plague that cannot be contained. No matter the foulness I consume and keep enfolded within me, it has already found its way into others. The hatred, the jealousy, the bigotry has already been passed down."

Teresa had smiled in response. "You don't see the good, Jason? What about the mother who nurtures her child, the man who nurses the wounded animal, the innocent child who finds a floundering chick and, with such loving hands, gently places it back in the nest? No, my friend, there is much that is good. And it too shall spread. Wait. Watch. You shall see in time."

"And what of them? How will goodness and kindness perpetuate?"

"Like you, I enfold, but unlike the evil you keep, the kindness and loving I've enveloped is released again, given rebirth."

Jason returned his gaze to the group gathered around him on Nathan's compound. "Now, after all the millennia that have passed, I find little to nothing changed. This clan takes over lives, stealing what belonged to others: life itself. Nathaniel Crockett, how many lives have you stolen over the years?"

"But my son, Jason, if I do as you ask, how will he know his father's touch? I can't leave him. Look at him," Nathan pointed to the child he'd released to the ground, who now smiled up at the vision of the gathered deadheads. "He knows me. Even when I step out of this body. In a short time that would fade from his memory. I would fade. I'm sorry, I can't."

Deep furrows creased along Jason's forehead. "You will be under constant watch. The first time you—"

"Jason, please. I beg you," Nathan dropped to his knees, rivers welled from his eyes. "I promise you, when this self dies…"

"So you can cheat him out of everything you ask to experience?"

Marvin broke into the fray. "But he hasn't. I've seen the man. I've actually talked to the man he embodies. Have you?" Marvin stood defiant, arms crossed. "Erick agreed to this. If you don't believe me, go find Jenna, or call her to you. That's how that works, right? You command and she obeys? But, she'll tell you the same thing. In fact, it was her idea to keep this arrangement."

"To what end?" Jason demanded.

"For the children you see over there," Marvin pointed to the spirited romp. "For the adult men and women she and her sect have saved from living horror. An entire complex has been built at Nathan's willing expense to house them, to hide them from further harm, to protect them, to help them heal."

Jason pointed at Nathan. "This is your last life,

Nathaniel Ray Crockett. Use it wisely. For when it is done, you are as well."

"That would be a big mistake. Trust me," Marvin said with the trace of an ironic laugh. "Someday you're going to need Nathan, and the people he's gathered here."

"You best be careful, Marvin." Jason's eyes narrowed. "I've been too lenient, given more latitude to you and yours than is deserved."

Marvin shrugged. "So, sue me. I'm just telling you from my gut. I don't know how or when, but if you do as you're threatening, you'll regret it."

Jason gazed past the gathered group, nodded, and his visage faded from sight. The group heaved a collective sigh of released tension.

"That was impressive. I'm proud of you, Marvin." Jenna's voice came from behind them.

Everyone turned to find her smiling.

"When did you get here?" Marvin asked.

"A little while ago. I saw Jason come out of the trees and I started to move in, but you stepped in before I could get a word out. I decided to let you handle it."

"I thought you said I wasn't capable."

"Marv, I'm sorry," Jenna said, joining the group. "Maybe I got a little full of myself."

Marvin's eyes grew wide. "Maybe?"

"Come on, Marv…"

"Maybe?" Marvin folded his arms across his chest. "I tried to help and you told me to shut up. All I wanted to do is spend more time with you. Was that too much to ask? And what did you do? You told me you didn't have time for me. And now you tell me 'maybe'?"

"I said I was sorry."

"Now you're sorry. After I've been gone for a year? What changed? Did you find out I'm not useless, after all?"

"No, Marv." Jenna's shoulders slumped and she dropped her gaze to the ground. "I missed you."

"Awww, dude, isn't that the bomb?" Tommy's voice came from the edge of the trees. "How can you resist that?"

"And, we've missed you, too," Mike added. "Besides, another one of your rants isn't exactly going to make her feel better."

The two phantoms rushed to Marvin in a jumble of limbs. Through laughter, Marvin said, "Get out of me you schmucks," though he held on to them both. "How did you find this place?"

Tommy's smile beamed from ear to ear. "We nagged Jenna, how else?"

"I mentioned a few times. He nagged," Mike poked Tommy in the ribs.

"Nathan, dude, that is one far out building you put together. I knew you were a good guy right from the start. Didn't I say that?" Tommy cast an inquisitive expression around the circle.

"We took a bit of a self-guided tour of the shelter," Jenna explained. "You've done well. All of you. And, I owe you a debt of gratitude."

"Well, ma'am, it took a might bit of doing, I won't lie. But, ya'll are welcome. What with Shelly and my little guy...why, I truly understand. I'm right happy I obliged."

"I think these two lugs would like to stay for a visit, if you don't mind." Jenna jutted her chin toward Tommy and Mike. "But, we should let you get back to enjoying your day." With that, Jenna walked toward the canopy of trees ringing the meadow. She stopped, turned to them, and smiled. "Are you coming, Marv?"

"I don't know. There's something about this place. It kind of grew on me."

"Pfft. Something grew on you all right." Jenna winked.

Marvin's expression dropped into a poker face. "Maybe I should stay. Tell me again, what changed?"

"Really? Fine." Jenna placed her fists on her hips. "What's changed? Everything." She dropped her hands to her sides and smiled. "But, I'll tell you what hasn't changed. You can still be an arrogant prick."

Marvin grinned, and he walked to her. "You know, you can be a petulant bitch."

Mike and Tommy burst out into infectious giggles. Nathan and his new family, and the clan members who weren't working to put everything in place at the newly completed shelter watched the two link arms.

As the two faded into the trees their banter continued.

"Oh, go fall down a flight of stairs."

"Go step in front of a bus."

A word about the author...

Paul Atreides turned writing for his own amusement into a career. A former theatre critic and columnist for Nevada's largest daily newspaper, he now reviews for EatMoreArtVegas.com. He's had several short stories published in anthologies and is also a playwright. His two-act comedy-drama, *Phallusies*, premiered in Las Vegas, Nevada, to good reviews, received *Las Vegas City Life's* "Pick of the Week," and has played to sold-out houses. His ten-minute play, *Fusion*, is scheduled to tour the U.S. as part of *The Grief Dialogues*. He is a former Coordinator of the Las Vegas Writers Conference and sits on the University of Nevada—Las Vegas College of Fine Arts Advisory Board.

Connect with Paul at:
Website: http://www.paul-atreides.com
Twitter: https://twitter.com/atreides_paul
Facebook: https://www.facebook.com/paul.atreides.391